PI
TO FETCH A SCOUNDREL

"From tiny terriers to lumbering Rottweilers, man's best friend can also be crime's worst enemy. In *To Catch a Scoundrel,* four pooch-loving mystery writers tell "tails" of savvy canines and their loyal owners solving murders with keen noses and sharp wits."

~Maria Hudgins
Author of the Dotsy Lamb travel Mysteries

"These four tales of intrigue are filled with unexpected twists and delightful dogs who help solve the mysteries and capture the culprits. From the Rottweiler Director of Security, Oliver, to Yorkshires Cagney and Lacey, who prove even tiny terriers can tangle the plans of any evil-doer, you'll love these mysteries."

~Cherie O'Boyle
Author of the *Estela Nogales Mysteries*
and working dog suspense stories

"Dog lovers rejoice! *To Fetch a Scoundrel* is a charming collection of 'tails' by four talented mystery writers."

~Maggie King
Author of the Hazel Rose Book Group Mysteries

"Dogs always save the day in this delightful canine novella anthology."

~Linda Johnson
Author of mysteries and psychological suspense

"Couldn't stop reading this collection of fabulous felonious stories!"

~Marilyn Levinson aka Allison Brook
Author of The Haunted Library series

To Fetch a Scoundrel

Four Fun "Tails" of Scandal and Murder . . .

All characters in this book are fictitious, and any resemblance to actual persons, living or dead, is purely coincidental. Furthermore, all incidents, descriptions, dialogue, and opinions expressed are the products of the author's imagination and are not to be construed as real.

Copyright 2020 by
Heather Weidner, Jayne Ormerod,
Rosemary Shomaker, and Teresa Inge

All rights reserved. No part of this publication may be reproduced, stored in a retrieval system, or transmitted in any form or by any means—electronic, mechanical, photocopy, recording, or any other—except for brief quotations in printed reviews, without the prior written permission of the author.

Cover Design by San Coils at CoverKicks.com

ISBN-13: 978-1-7327907-6-6
ISBN-10: 1-7327907-6-0

Published by
Bay Breeze Publishing
Norfolk, VA

TO FETCH A SCOUNDREL

Four Fun "Tails" of Scandal and Murder . . .

Contributing Authors:
✓Heather Weidner
✓ Jayne Ormerod
Rosemary Shomaker✗
✓Teresa Inge

Foreword by:
Richard and Kathy Verlander

ACKNOWLEDGMENTS

To Fetch a Scoundrel is the second book of novellas in the Mutt Mysteries series. This edition focuses on villains and scoundrels that the pups help bring to justice.

We love our pets, and these stories are a way for us to share the importance of the animals in our lives through our writing. Our dogs, who provide love, companionship, and often story inspirations are Disney and Riley (Heather), Tiller and Scout (Jayne), Current (Rosemary), and Luke and Lena (Teresa).

The authors would like to thank Bay Breeze Publishing for all the work involved in publishing this series. We would also like to thank our cover designer, San Coils of Cover Kicks Designs.

Special thanks to pet lovers, animal welfare advocates, and authors Richard and Kathy Verlander for writing the foreword to this book. A portion of the proceeds from the sale of this book will be donated in support of various animal rescue organizations.

We are so grateful for all the love and support from the mystery writing community. We appreciate all the great ideas, endorsements, and encouragement.

Finally, we appreciate you—our readers—who follow our dogs' adventures. We hope you enjoy the latest Mutt Mysteries collection. For more information on the authors, their dogs, and the stories, please visit http://muttmysteries.com.

~Heather, Jayne, Rosemary, and Teresa

TABLE OF CONTENTS

FOREWORD
By Richard and Kathy Verlander i

THE FAST AND THE FURRIEST
By Heather Weidner 1

PAWSITIVELY SCANDALOUS
By Jayne Ormerod 57

RUFF GOODBYE
By Rosemary Shomaker 125

A DOGGONE SCANDAL
By Teresa Inge 205

FOREWORD
By Richard and Kathy Verlander

For the longest time it seemed to us that there was nothing quite like a sporting event to bring such a diverse group of people together. Having been blessed with two sons who have enjoyed the good fortune to play professional baseball, we have witnessed this bonding effect firsthand. The sight of tens of thousands of fans waving flags for the home team in unison and cheering as one has been an uplifting display of fellowship that we would love to see more of in the world these days. Whether telling our story at speaking events, or through reading to children at an elementary school, it is an experience that we love to share.

Since retiring a few years ago, we have discovered a new passion to devote our time and energy to that is also a great unifier: Animal Rescue. By volunteering as dog walkers at our local shelter and joining an effort to build a new adoption facility, we have found another activity that also seems to bring out the best in people. Don't believe it? Put a bunch of overstressed, short-fused humans in a room and bring in a puppy! In fact, as a result of our volunteering and as the owners of two rescue dogs ourselves, we were suddenly inspired to write a children's book. *The Shelter Gang* and Their Secret Adventure is a tale about kids, dogs, cats, and (you guessed it) baseball.

Since this effort unfolded, a door has unexpectedly opened on a new cause: promoting literacy and reading to children in our area schools. In fact, that's how we met the authors of the wonderful Mutt Mysteries series and others who seem to embrace the notion that our four-legged friends create a space in our lives for happiness and togetherness.

Using animals as characters gives us an opportunity to show kids how even though we are all so very different, just like the dogs in our own story, it is those very differences that make us all a better team when we join together. Children often ask, "Can dogs and cats really play baseball?" We always reply, "In our imagination they can!" And now, as we have now learned from *To Fetch a Scoundrel*, it seems they are also pretty darn good detectives!

So it seems to us that the more good that we are able to do, the more doors open to other opportunities for providing the fulfillment we hope to spend our retirement years enjoying. Inherently, this is something we have always known, but not being authors in the traditional literary sense, we never really tried to articulate. It seems after thinking it over we can sum it up in a few words: If you find happiness in the world, share it, and more will come your way.

Richard and Kathy Verlander are proud parents, youth development and animal welfare advocates, and authors. Rocks Across the Pond *chronicles their family experiences raising sons Justin and Ben, who both advanced to play professional baseball.* The Shelter Gang and Their Secret Adventure *is a children's book about cats, dogs, and baseball; it's a tale of hope, acceptance, perseverance, and love. The Verlanders support teachers, coaches, and all persons working with youth. In addition, they advocate for humane animal treatment.*

THE FAST AND THE FURRIEST

By Heather Weidner

Cassidy Green just wants to keep her racetrack business from crashing. When an altercation breaks out between two race teams at the driver meeting, it adds one more problem to her already full plate. Cassidy gets more than she bargains for when Oliver, her Rottweiler, finds one of the star drivers dead in her garage. She hopes her fuzzy director of security will help uncover clues to reveal the killer before the bad publicity drives business into the wall.

Originally from Virginia Beach, **HEATHER WEIDNER** *has been a mystery fan since Scooby-Doo and Nancy Drew. She lives in Central Virginia with her husband and a pair of Jack Russell terriers. Her short stories appear in the* Virginia is for Mysteries *series,* 50 Shades of Cabernet, *and* Deadly Southern Charm. Secret Lives and Private Eyes, The Tulip Shirt Murders, *and* Glitter, Glam, and Contraband *are her novels in the Delanie Fitzgerald Mysteries, and her novellas appear in the Mutt Mysteries.*

She is a member of Sisters in Crime – Central Virginia, Guppies, James River Writers, and International Thriller Writers. Through the years, she has been a cop's kid, technical writer, editor, college professor, software tester, and IT manager.

Website: www.heatherweidner.com

CHAPTER ONE

"I see you were attending to more important things," Uncle Henry said to Cassidy Green as she slid in an empty plastic chair in the back. Some of the drivers and crew members turned around to stare at her as her uncle continued to plow through his list of race violations to avoid. The participants settled back in their rows of chairs, set up like a classroom.

Cassidy smiled. She had hoped to sneak into the driver and crew meeting without anyone noticing. Her uncle held court there each race night at the Amelia Speedway. She kicked her legs forward, hoping to relax for a few minutes. She needed a reprieve from the normal chaos of keeping the track running

Thirty minutes later, her uncle wrapped up his PowerPoint slideshow of rules for the different races that included late model, grand stock, modified, and U-CAR. No go-cart, sprint, or midget racing this evening. Cassidy liked the latter because it often gave younger drivers a chance. At least they had U-CAR, an acronym for You Can Afford to Race. This opened up the field to guys who didn't have sponsors or deep pockets.

Uncle Henry, who loved racing as much as her dad had, talked about the forms and waivers he had available at the front table. Cassidy ran the day-to-day operations of the track, while her uncle, a retired postal inspector, took care of the garage, rules, and inspections. Cassidy had inherited the lion's share of the track after her father's death two years ago and had spent that time learning the ins and outs of maintaining the business that were a lot different than her previous job as a marketing manager.

Uncle Henry's spiel ground to a halt when a high-pitched squeal echoed through the meeting room. "There you are." Cheri Ellis made a beeline for her driver husband Donnie. She waved a pair of bubble-gum pink stilettos that matched her long fingernails. "Look what I found, in my minivan of all places."

Donnie jumped up. His brother Dickie, his crew chief, joined him. Both brothers had a deer-in-the-headlights look as Cheri continued to advance toward them. She waved the shoes high above her head.

Before Donnie could explain, Mandy Jenkins rose from her seat next to her brother, a driver for another team. "That's where they went? I've been looking for those everywhere. Did you happen to find a matching thong?" Mandy titled her head so that her long blond hair draped over her shoulder like a stole. She waved her hand with its perfectly manicured hot pink talons in Cheri's direction.

Cheri shrieked like a banshee and launched herself at the younger woman. She got in a good swing to the jaw while Mandy returned the favor with a few scratches and some hair pulling before two groups of men pulled them apart. Dickie and his son Richie grabbed Cheri and dragged her, kicking and screaming toward the door. For a petite woman, she created quite a ruckus. Donnie turned toward the door and then to Mandy. Then he looked toward the door again like he was going to bolt. Mandy whispered something to him. Donnie picked up a folder next to him and tore out of the room.

Uncle Henry rapped his fist on the lectern and adjusted his reading glasses. "Settle down, boys and girls. Show's over. Time to hit the track. Make sure to fill out your waivers and let me know if you have any questions. The inspectors will be around about thirty minutes before the flag drops. Meeting adjourned."

The remaining men murmured, gathered their things, and headed toward the garage and infield area. Cassidy smiled at her uncle from the back of the room. "Race day always brings out the emotions."

He returned a half-smile. "Very true. And some of these young stallions don't know how to maintain their personal lives. Hopefully, Donnie's racing life is better than his married one. I'll swing by on my rounds and make sure he understands that he needs to get this under control."

"I'm heading back to the office to check on tonight's attendance numbers. Let me know if you need me," Cassidy said.

"You might want to give the security crew a heads up on Donnie's women in case the catfight spills over in the stands later. I'm headed over to check on the car inspections."

"Hopefully, they'll cool off a bit, but it sounds like a plan. There's always some kind of excitement at our speedway," Cassidy said with a smirk.

After a chat with the security team, Cassidy noticed Mandy sitting in the front row of stands near the starting line with two of her girlfriends, regulars who flirted with the drivers or anyone who resembled a driver. All the gals were overdressed for a summer night at the racetrack. Cassidy wondered how they walked without turning an ankle in four-inch stilettos on the graveled paths. Security might have their hands full this evening.

Mandy didn't look like she had been involved in an altercation a few minutes earlier. The heavy makeup and hair looked model perfect. The girls chatted and laughed, oblivious to anyone around them.

Chapter Two

A sharp *rat-a-tat-tat* echoed through the back office. Cassidy's Rottweiler Oliver raised his head and stared at the door. Before she could answer it, the staccato knocking repeated. Louder and faster. Oliver let out a low growl.

Cassidy opened the door, and a sparkplug of a man stopped in mid-knock. "May I help you?" she asked.

"That snippy girl at the concession stand told me to go to the office and ask for Mr. Oliver," the man said. "And that pompous driver Donnie, Donnie Ellis was there, and he had the gall to shove me out of line before I finished my discussion with your staff person," he said as he hiccupped.

"I'm Cassidy Green, the owner, and that's Mr. Oliver," she said, pointing to the dog who sat on high alert on his bed. All one hundred and ten pounds of muscle twitched as he waited for Cassidy's signal.

The red-faced man took a step back. "I, uh came here with some friends. I ordered a round of beer for the gang, and your girl wouldn't sell me more than two at a time. And that stupid driver . . ."

"Yes. That's policy. The Amelia Speedway is a family establishment, and we follow all ABC laws. I'm sorry that it caused you an issue, but we need to ensure that we're following the rules for adult beverages," said Cassidy, as she pushed a strand of her long red hair behind her ear.

He let out a harrumph and glared at Cassidy. "I don't appreciate your staff's tone. There was attitude and eye rolling! And that idiot driver."

The yeasty scent of beer wafted toward Cassidy as the man spoke. "Mr, uh."

"Smith. Jerry Smith."

"Mr. Smith, I will talk to my team and the volunteers about customer service. But in this case, it is up to the snack-bar staff to follow all rules pertaining to alcohol sales."

Jerry Smith turned abruptly and threw his hands in the air. "Then I'm just going to have to find new entertainment."

"I'm sorry that you feel that way."

Oliver let out a low, guttural growl as she shut the door.

"Thanks for being Director of Security, Oliver. The team knows to send the tough cases over to you." Cassidy patted his soft, furry head. "I'll have to order you a name plate for the door." The large dog, who was a big baby when he wasn't at work, curled up on his bed as Cassidy returned to her attendance spreadsheet.

After the last grand stock race, Cassidy pulled her long red curls in a loose ponytail and whistled for Oliver. She clipped his leash in place, and he followed her out the back door to the racetrack's golf cart. Jumping in the shotgun seat, he was ready for his ride around the track and garage area. The garage had six carport-like stalls for inspections and engine work that could not be done on the track.

Cassidy inherited the small, oval track built in the 1960s by her grandfather. When her father passed away, she quit her marketing job to run the raceway. Uncle Henry, who owned the large white farmhouse on the other side of the racetrack's fence, held a small stake in the venture. In addition to managing the drivers and officials, he liked to think of himself as the head groundskeeper, faithfully mowing all the grass twice a week with his tractor.

Cassidy had grown up at the track but had no idea of the workload until she took over the daily operations. Her biggest problem lately was keeping gate numbers up. The facilities, only used in warmer months, still had to be maintained year-round. Attendance had been off since the last downturn in the economy.

There wasn't much left in the reserves. She needed something to happen to get spectators back to the track.

She pushed thoughts of empty seats in the stands away, and she and Oliver tooled around the ticket booth and concession and souvenir stands. On their right the large clapboard building, where Cheri and Mandy had an earlier altercation, stood dark. Cassidy waved at one of the security guards who patrolled the area and shooed guests toward the main entrance. It always took a few hours to vacate the grounds.

The infield had a ghostly feel under the tall halogen lights on telephone poles. All the race cars, trucks, and emergency stand-by vehicles had left. A few fans lingered around the flag stand. The souvenir shack had shut down, and concessions staff scurried around performing closing procedures.

Empty cups and wrappers littered the area below the stands. It always surprised her that people couldn't be bothered to use the trash bins. Volunteers would arrive tomorrow to pick up the trash. Cassidy paid civic groups a donation, and they provided the cleanup crews. Tomorrow, a group of ROTC members would work to raise funds to put flags on all the veterans' graves in the county.

She and Oliver drove by the garage, where the inspections and any emergency fixes occurred. The lights illuminated the bays. All of the crews had left except Donnie Ellis's. His blue, late-model Taurus, covered in sponsor stickers, sat alone in the third bay. His matching car trailer and truck that advertised their Greased Lightning race team sat under a light pole near the edge of the garage. She wondered where the Ellises were and why their vehicles were still parked near the garage.

Donnie and his brother Dickie had formed a race team with their dad when the brothers were teens. They had dumped a lot of money into the maintenance of their car that had a pretty good winning record at small, East Coast tracks. Donnie didn't mind reminding everyone he came in contact with about his winning record and how great he was. In her teen years, he had hit on her several times. Now as an adult, the come-ons were more subtle, but still as sleazy. Oliver did a good job at keeping him at least a leash distance away.

By the time they looped around the track, only a few fans remained. "One more lap, Oliver, and then we're done for the evening. Uncle Henry and security will have this place cleared and locked up soon." Her dog let out a whine that sounded like a sigh and stretched out on the front seat of the golf cart with his flat head on her lap.

Donnie's race car and trailer still sat in the now darkened garage area. She keyed the squawk button on her radio. "Security. This is Cassidy. Donnie Ellis's car is still in the garage."

The radio crackled. "Ten-four. Engine trouble. He'll be back tomorrow to get it."

"Thanks. Goodnight." She released the squawk button and turned to her golf-cart companion. "Well, Oliver, let's head home and see what's on the DVR."

The rottie raised one eyebrow in agreement, especially if TV night meant snacks.

CHAPTER THREE

Cassidy's stomach growled and reminded her that the lunch hour had passed. Mondays were usually quiet at the track, but she'd been buried in the accounting files, so the day flew by. Her cell phone vibrated across the desk. Oliver raised his head from his napping place.

A woman on the other end launched into a panicked, high-pitched rant as soon as Cassidy picked up.

"Hey, it's Cheri Ellis. I'm worried sick. Donnie didn't show up for work today. That's not like him. I haven't seen him since Saturday night. Could you tell me if he's there? This is not normal. He never misses work."

"I'll check the track and call you back. Is this number good to reach you?"

"Yes. It's my business cell. You know, for my custom interior designs." Cheri clicked off.

"That's odd," Cassidy said to Oliver who raised one eyebrow in response. "He's been gone since Saturday, and she's concerned because he missed work today?" The rottie raised his other eyebrow. "Come on, boy. Let's go check the grounds."

Cassidy clicked Oliver's heavy-duty leash to his spiked leather collar, and they set off around the concession area to the stands. When they rounded the corner near turn four on the track, Donnie's shiny midnight blue truck and car hauler glinted in the sun, and his race car sat alone in the open-air bay of the garage, where he had left it on Saturday night.

Cassidy pulled her cell phone from her back pocket and pressed Uncle Henry's contact. After the second ring, he answered. "Hey, kiddo. I'm painting the porch swing. What's up?"

"Sorry to bother you. I got a frantic call from Cheri Ellis. She hasn't seen Donnie since Saturday's race. Have you heard from him? His car and vehicles are still at the garage."

"Nope. Security said he had engine problems, and that they'd be back on Sunday to get it."

"Cheri's concerned that he didn't show up for work today."

"I'll get Dickie on the horn," he said. "Call you back in a sec."

Cassidy clicked the button and pocketed her phone. It was odd that they'd leave their racing vehicles without a second thought, like forgetting a sweater or a pair of sunglasses.

When she gave the signal, Oliver led the way to the garage. He sniffed around the back of the race car and then tugged on his leash zeroing in on the right front wheel well. He almost pulled Cassidy off balance in his quest to get near the car.

"Heel, Oliver."

The dog sat reluctantly on his back haunches. Every few seconds, he looked at the front of the car and let out a shrill whine.

"The jacks are still in place." She tugged his leash. "Come, Oliver." Directing him to the back of the car, Cassidy walked around to the driver's side. A large oil spill oozed out from under Donnie's race car. "This is a total disaster. I don't know who Donnie thinks he is, but he can't walk away and leave a mess like this. And he forgot all that junk." She waved an irritated hand toward the oil cans and shock absorbers scattered across the counter.

Her phone buzzed. 'Hey, Uncle Henry. Anything new?"

"Dickie'll be by tonight after work to get the car."

"There's a huge mess in the garage. There's oil all over the floor," she said.

"I'll meet Dickie when he gets here and see how he plans to get the garage cleaned. If not, they don't race next week," he said.

Oliver let out a pitiful whine and walked around to the car's grill. Cassidy stepped around the front fender to guide him back.

A pale hand stuck out from under the car. Cassidy screamed.

"What's wrong?" Uncle Henry asked.

"Oliver found someone under the car. Could you come over here now?"

"He found what?" her uncle asked.

"There's a hand sticking out from under the car," she said. Looking underneath, Cassidy sputtered, "And it's connected to a body. Donnie Ellis's body." She recoiled by taking a couple of steps backwards.

"Stay there. I'll be right over." The phone went silent.

Cassidy yanked on Oliver's leash and led him away from the stall and Donnie's race car. She took several deep breaths to control the lightheadedness. Feeling slightly better, she dialed 9-1-1.

"9-1-1. What's your emergency?"

"This is Cassidy Green at the Amelia Speedway. My dog and I found a body under one of the race cars. I need the police."

"Where are you?" the dispatcher asked.

"I'm in front of the garage area at the far end of the track. The body is on its side. Kinda curled up."

"Are you okay? Are you in any danger?" the dispatcher asked.

"I'm fine. I'll wait here for the police." Cassidy ended the call and lowered herself to the asphalt next to Oliver. She patted his back. He leaned in toward her.

"Well, Oliver, when I said I wanted something to change around here, this isn't what I had in mind. What are we going to do? There's a body in our garage."

Chapter Four

All kinds of emergency vehicles descended on the track. Cassidy, Henry, and Oliver stood out of the way as the sheriff and his two deputies approached the area. Several state troopers cordoned off the area and huddled in the garage. A forensic vehicle and a gray van drove through the back gate and parked next to the collection of police vehicles.

They took photos and measurements from every angle.

Cassidy was getting antsy to check on the office when three men guided a gurney with a sheet over it to the van. A melancholic feeling washed over her, and she was saddened by the loss of life. Thoughts of death quickly morphed into her concern about the track's reputation. She shook off the worried feeling.

Sheriff Watkins hitched up his pants and made his way over to where they sat.

"Hey, Cassidy. Hey, Henry," Sheriff Watkins said. "I'm going to need a list of everyone you know who was here on Saturday night. And the team is going to need to talk to you both."

"I'll pull a list of the drivers and staff from my computer and make some coffee," she said. "And you're welcome to use the office."

"We'll be over in a minute." He looked back at the garage.

"This doesn't look good for Cheri," Henry said as they walked out of earshot of law enforcement. "The majority of the people on the list you're going to give him are going to tell him about how she stormed the drivers' meeting and made a scene," he added.

"But why would she kill him?" Cassidy asked. "He's been a philanderer as long as I've known him. Saturday wasn't anything new."

"But this time it was very public. Cheri didn't have time to cover it up or pretend she didn't know." He rubbed the slight gray stubble on his chin.

Cassidy unlocked the back door to the office and logged into her computer. The phone on her desk blinked red with messages. When she punched in her voicemail password, the mechanical, sing-song voice told her that there were fifteen waiting for her. She jotted down notes on a legal pad as Uncle Henry made coffee.

"We've had a boatload of calls from reporters about Donnie Ellis. Print and TV. I'm not prepared for a public relations nightmare. I'm going to talk to Sheriff Watkins. My plan is to refer everything to his office. I don't think we should comment on this. And how did the reporters know it was Donnie? The police haven't made a statement yet." She tapped her pen against her legal pad.

"I ignored all the TV vans outside in the parking lot," Henry said. "They must have picked up activity on the emergency scanners. It's a small county. People talk."

Cassidy let out a heavy sigh and sank into her office chair. "I'm sorry that he's dead. No one deserves that, but we don't need a scandal right now when business is slow. What if people stay away because they think it's a dangerous place?"

"Or the opposite could happen. Morbid curiosity could bring them in by the droves," he said with a slight grin.

A knock at the back door interrupted their conversation and put Oliver on high alert. "Stay," she ordered.

The dog lay back down, but watched Uncle Henry let Sheriff Watkins and two others in.

"Hey, y'all," the sheriff said. "You know Charles, and this is Trooper Hendricks from the state." They shook hands all around.

Cassidy pointed to the small, white table near the kitchenette. Charles and Uncle Henry pulled out chairs and sat, while the others leaned against the wall and the counter near the microwave and refrigerator. Today, even the red and white gingham curtains couldn't perk up the somber mood.

"Coffee's ready. Any takers?" Henry asked.

Charles, who Cassidy had known as Chuckie in school, and the trooper shook their heads. The sheriff said, "Black would be great."

After everyone had settled in, Trooper Hendricks began the questioning. "Tell us how you discovered the body."

Cassidy caught her breath. It felt cold to refer to Donnie that way. "Cheri Ellis called this afternoon. She was a hot mess because she hadn't seen Donnie since Saturday's race. She wanted to know if he was at the track. Oliver and I walked over to the garage where he had left his car and truck. Oliver was interested in the bumper, and I was curious about the huge spot on the floor. When I walked around the vehicle, I saw a hand sticking out from under the race car."

"Have you called Cheri Ellis back?" Sheriff Watkins asked.

"No. I got kinda sidetracked. But word is already out. I've received a bunch of voicemails from the media, and Henry said that there were camera crews outside the gate," Cassidy said.

"We'll head over to talk to Cheri and Dickie after we wrap up here," Sheriff Watkins said. "The forensic team should be done with the crime scene later today."

Henry shifted in his chair. "When can the family get their car?"

"As soon as we're done. Have you noticed any strange behavior or anything out of the ordinary lately?" Sheriff Watkins leaned forward.

Henry said, "Cheri Ellis stormed into the drivers' meeting on Saturday and had an altercation with another young lady. What's her name, Cassidy? She's Boogie Jenkins's little sister."

"Mandy. Mandy Jenkins," she said.

"Yes, that's her," Henry replied. "It was a good catfight. Dickie and the Jenkins boys had to separate the girls. They got into a knock-down, drag out over old Donnie. I don't think I've ever seen that boy speechless before. He stood there like a deer caught in the headlights."

"What happened after that?" the trooper asked.

"The drivers and the crews reported to the track. I'm not sure where Cheri went," Henry said. "After the grand stock race, the last one for the evening, Dickie told the race officials that Donnie had engine trouble, and they were going to leave the gear in the garage bay. They had planned to get it on Sunday, but nobody ever showed up. I called Dickie today to check on it, and he said that he'd be out here after work. He thought Donnie was going to come by and get it. Dickie said that his brother had been really busy over the weekend."

"I saw Mandy and her friends in the stands during the races," Cassidy added.

"Anything else unusual that evening?" the trooper asked.

"No, that's about it," Henry said. "It was a normal race day except for the wife and the girlfriend fight that interrupted my driver meeting."

"I'm going to need the list of folks that you know who were at the track," the sheriff said.

"I'll pull that together and email it to you. There were probably about another two thousand spectators I have no way of tracking," Cassidy said.

The sheriff nodded and passed her a business card. "Okay. The investigation continues. Don't let anybody back in the garage area until we finish with the crime scene. Dickie can get his belongings later tonight when we're done. If you remember anything else, call me," he said, rising.

Cassidy cleared her throat. "We're getting a lot of calls from reporters and interested folks. I'm going to refer them to your office if that's okay."

The sheriff nodded, and Charles pushed away from the table. The police followed the sheriff out the door.

When the door closed, Henry said, "I overheard some of the forensic people out back. Donnie had been hit on the head, and somebody hid the body under the car. They couldn't say for sure when he died, but they guessed that he'd been dead less than thirty-six hours."

"Probably the night of the race," she said, trying to shake the gloomy feeling that enveloped her. "So, what's next?" Cassidy asked, putting the mugs in the kitchenette's small sink.

"Dinner? I've got a lasagna in the freezer," he said. "A change of scenery would do us both good."

"Sounds perfect. I'm starving."

Oliver stood up to make sure he was invited, too.

Chapter Five

After lunch the next day, Cassidy stood and stretched. Oliver raised an eyebrow and returned to his nap. She needed a break from going through the emails and listening to the voicemails from reporters and curious friends. "Come on, Oliver. Let's take a walk."

He stood patiently at the back door waiting for her to attach his leash. They walked around the track, enjoying the warm afternoon. The pair rounded the corner and the sight of the empty garage caused her to pause. The forensic team had released the site last night, and Dickie and some of his guys retrieved the race car and Donnie's truck.

Oliver pulled on his leash, and Cassidy followed him to the empty bay with the large oil spot, the only reminder of this weekend's tragedy. The sheriff had said that Donnie was found in the fetal position on a mechanic's creeper, the flat-wheeled cart crews used to slide under cars. They felt the head wound was probably the fatal blow, but they'd know more after the autopsy. Cassidy shook off the glum feeling.

For some reason, Dickie and his gang had left the oil cans and the shock absorbers on the counter again. She made a mental note to contact him about picking up his stuff.

"Let's keep walking, Oliver. We need to get our steps in."

The dog trotted out of the garage stall toward the scoreboard between turns three and four.

After their brisk walk, Cassidy booted up her laptop and put together a spreadsheet of who she knew was at the track on Saturday for the sheriff. She frowned. Cassidy hoped Donnie's demise won't scare off spectators.

Several taps on the back door caught Oliver's attention. Cassidy opened it.

Cheri Ellis barged in, flashing her red leather Michael Kors bag and matching fingernails.

"I don't know what I'm going to do. Stuff just keeps piling on. Donnie could be such a jerk, but there was another side that not too many people saw. I can't believe this has happened," Cheri said.

"Cheri, I'm so sorry," Cassidy said. That's all she could get out before the woman launched into her tale.

"I still can't believe he's gone. There was so much we had planned to do. And the sheriff and his team came by yesterday. They made such a big deal of my disagreement with that track hussy. It was just me blowing off some steam." Cherri pulled a tissue from her oversized purse and daubed her eyes, smearing her heavy eyeliner. "I think I'm going to be arrested," she whispered.

Cassidy patted Cheri's arm. "The police were here for a long time yesterday, too. It doesn't seem real."

"Things were starting to turn around for us." Cheri sniffed. "And my business is doing fantastic. Everything will crumble if I get arrested. I can't even think about it right now. This is so unfair. And the timing is so bad."

Cassidy furrowed her brow. Cheri seemed to be more concerned about herself than about the loss of Donnie.

Cheri babbled on. "Everybody knows what happened with that witch. She and her floozies flit around your track and try to latch onto any driver with a pulse. After the race, I stopped by the garage on my way home. Donnie was there banging on the car's engine. We had an argument and probably said some things that weren't PG-13. I hope no one complained. But it was worth it. He apologized for all of the philandering. And I believed him. He meant it this time. From now on, it would be just the two of us. We were even talking about a second honeymoon," she said, dissolving into sobs.

"Here, sit down," Cassidy said, pointing to the table area.

Cheri sat in the seat that Cassidy pulled out for her. When the sobbing eased, Cassidy asked, "Did you tell the sheriff all this?"

"Yes, but I didn't get the sense he cared. I don't think it's going to help. My friend Mary Louise talked to Chuckie's momma, and she said that the police were going to arrest me for murder because I don't have an alibi, and thanks to that little hussy, everybody in town thinks I did it. But I didn't do it," she wailed.

"Where were you after the race on Saturday?" Cassidy asked.

"I went home and soaked in my tub. I got tired of waiting on Donnie to show up, so Coco, Chanel, and I went to bed."

Cassidy smiled. She remembered seeing photos of the pampered chihuahuas on Facebook. Both looked like toys compared to Oliver.

"So, no alibi? No phone calls or texts? Anyone who can vouch for you?" Cassidy asked.

"Just my two sweetie babies," Cheri said, rolling her eyes.

"Have you talked to a lawyer?" Cassidy asked.

"Yes. But he didn't strike me as being all that helpful. He kept telling me to be patient. He's not the one facing arrest. Cassidy, I need your help. You know everything that goes on around here. If I get hauled in, the police will stop investigating, and Donnie's killer will get off scot free." After she recovered from a sobbing fit, Cheri continued, "I talked to Donnie about nine fifty. I know 'cause I checked my texts right before I got to the garage. Anyway, we kissed and made up. He said he'd be home as soon as he could. I was stunned and furious when he didn't come home that night. I thought he played me for a fool again. But now I know why he didn't come home. He really did love me. Promise me you'll help me find out who did this," she wailed.

Cassidy let out a sigh that she hoped Cheri didn't hear. "I'll see what I can do. I'm sure the truth will come out." Cassidy could kick herself for volunteering to help Cheri. She had no business poking around in the sheriff's case, but it had happened on her property. Curiosity got the best of her.

"Oooh, that's great news." Cheri hugged Cassidy. "I don't

know what I'll do if the police come after me."

That evening, Cassidy flipped on the local news while she fixed a salad for herself and a bowl of chunky, meaty bites for Oliver. The anchors chattered about the headlines and teased that new information on Donnie Ellis's murder would be next after a commercial break. She stopped chopping vegetables and turned up the sound on the TV in the living room.

After the commercial break, the camera switched to a live report in front of the track gates. "Thanks, Dean and Misti. I'm here at the Amelia Speedway, the site of local legend Donnie Ellis's mysterious death after the race on Saturday night. Police have not released any new information. However, I have several anonymous sources who say that there is a suspect, and an arrest is imminent. I will bring you more details as soon as they occur. Live in Amelia County, this is Wendy McGann."

Cassidy turned the sound down. She wondered if she should even get involved with this mess. She half-heartedly hoped that the story would die down, and they could get back to a normal schedule. Cassidy picked at her salad. Oliver hadn't lost his appetite. He wolfed down his meal in seconds and looked around for more.

She took what was left of her dinner to the living room and curled up with Oliver on the couch to watch *Vera* and *Queens of Mystery*.

Cassidy woke up to the eleven o'clock news blaring the announcement of Cheri Ellis's arrest. Cassidy sat bolt upright. Wow. Cheri was right. She was their main suspect.

The same reporter, standing in front of the sheriff's office, prattled on about the police taking Cheri in custody this evening. She noted the police were currently at the Ellis home. The reporter promised to stay on the story and have more details during tomorrow's morning news.

Too wide awake to sleep now, Cassidy grabbed her tablet and rummaged around the kitchen junk drawer for a notebook and pen. She spent the next few hours jotting down anything on social media about Donnie, Dickie, Cheri, and Mandy. What had she gotten herself into?

Chapter Six

The next morning, Cassidy showered and dressed in record time. She grabbed a muffin and her notebook. "Oliver, you guard the house today. I have a couple of errands to run, and I'll be back soon." She kissed him on the top of his head.

Cassidy stopped by the office to check messages. The phone's red light pulsed to an imaginary, fast beat. "Fourteen reporters from all over asking for a comment," she said to no one. Cassidy chose to ignore all of them. What would attendance would be like on Saturday?

After skimming her email that contained another six queries from reporters, she locked the office and jogged to her black Jeep Wrangler. Doing a U-turn in the gravel, Cassidy decided to go out the back exit in case any reporters were camped out in the parking lot.

Cassidy cranked up the radio to a classic rock station and rolled down the Jeep's windows. The tunes were perfect for the curvy back roads leading to Amelia's business district. Ten minutes later, she drove by a town square, surrounded on three sides by the courthouse, sheriff's office, and jail. Parking was at a premium. Camera crews had staked out every foot of the empty space on the grassy area outside the courthouse, filling every space under the pecan and oak trees that had probably been there when the troops marched through on their way to Appomattox.

Making a right turn at the corner, she wended through the

streets, trying not to hit any pedestrians who were gathering in the square for a view of what was going on. Cassidy hadn't seen this many people in town since the Christmas parade.

Last night, Cassidy had found Mandy's address, favorite bar, and her place of employment. After several more turns and more slow traffic, she pulled in the lot by the Captain Dollar. Mandy had diligently posted her activities on her social media sites and wasn't too concerned about who could see the posts.

Cassidy opened the glass door to the discount store. A bell bonged somewhere inside. Wandering around, she looked at the items for picnics and summer fun. By the time she got to the kitchen aisle, Mandy sashayed up the aisle from a backroom and headed to the customer service area. She busied herself with straightening the counter.

Mandy looked up and glared as Cassidy approached.

"Hi, Mandy." After a pause with no response from the young woman, she continued, "I'm Cassidy Green from the speedway."

The young woman shrugged. "I know who you are. I'm having the worst time. I haven't had much sleep lately. Reporters keep calling and knocking on my door. I'm hoping this will be over soon." She waved her hand, sporting nails in two shades of pink and a bandage around one of her fingers.

"I'm so sorry. I know it was quite a shock. We're still reeling at the track. Nothing like this has happened around here before," Cassidy said.

"Donnie was such a wonderful guy. He was so generous and kind. That woman didn't deserve him. I'm glad she's going to get what's coming to her," Mandy said, curling her lip.

"How long had you known him?"

"About a year or so. We'd been dating seriously for about three months. He was going to leave her, and I guess Cheri decided that if she couldn't have him, no one would." Mandy wiped the corner of her eye with her fingers. "We were going to get married." She sniffled and rubbed a silver ring with a pink heart stone on her left hand.

"I'm terribly sorry," Cassidy said again, staring at the young girl. "Did you hurt your hand?"

"Uh, no," she said, looking at her fingertips. "I broke some nails and haven't had time to fix them perfectly. This is just a quick repair. Oh, Channel 8 did an in-depth interview with me yesterday. It's going to air tonight. Make sure you watch it." The waterworks ended abruptly.

Interesting. Mandy had accelerated from rage to tears to excitement in ten seconds flat. "I'll be sure to catch it. See you around," Cassidy said.

"Saturday. I'll be at the track this weekend. See you then." Mandy returned to sorting returned items into bins.

Cassidy stopped at home to pick up Oliver. Both of them needed a good walk.

She attached his leash and let him lead the way around the oval track. He spent quite a while sniffing the grass under the scoreboard at the back of the track. When he got tired of chasing June bugs and grasshoppers, he ambled over toward the garage area. That oil spot stood out on the light concrete floor.

Oliver tugged on his lead and sniffed the area where Donnie's car had sat over the weekend. His head jerked, and he sniffed the concrete and under the storage bench.

"What's on your nose?" she asked, picking off a hot pink plastic piece that had stuck to his damp nose. "Weird. That looks like a fake nail. Where'd you get that?" Oliver sat obediently and turned his head as she talked.

"I'll set this here by the junk Donnie left." Cassidy arranged the oil cans and slid the three, shiny black shock absorbers side by side in a row. She opened the cabinet below and poked around. A cardboard box, shoved in the back corner, sat alone in the cabinet. The box didn't close completely due to a fourth shock absorber poking out of the corner. Cassidy pulled it out to get a better look. This one was like the other three except that it had some gunk on the end. She snapped a couple of pictures with her phone and then took one of the fake nail for good measure. It was odd to find it here in a male-dominated place. What woman had been hanging around here and why? Was it a rendezvous with one of the drivers?

Cassidy put a call through to the sheriff. After three rings, the sheriff's stern voicemail started. At the beep, she said, "Sheriff Watkins, this is Cassidy Green. I've found something in the garage that I think one of your investigators needs to check out. It may relate to Donnie's murder."

She clicked off and nosed around the garage to see if anything else had been left.

A few minutes later, her phone rang.

"Ms. Green, this is Trooper Hendricks. The sheriff forwarded me your message. Are you at the track now?"

"Yes, sir. I'm at the garage near the back gate," Cassidy said.

"I can be there in about fifteen minutes." She heard his radio in the background. "See you in a few." The phone went dead.

Cassidy swung the metal gate open, and the trooper's navy and gray cruiser drove in, kicking up dust and gravel. No reporters this time, thank goodness. She hurriedly locked the gate and trotted behind the car to the garage bays. The tall officer stepped out of his car and put on his Smokey Bear hat. "What did you find?"

"Over here. Oliver, my dog, found a pink plastic thing that looks like a fake nail." Cassidy pointed to the workbench. "I poked around in the cabinet, and that box in the back had a fourth shock absorber. When I pulled it out, it had gunk on it. Not regular car gunk."

"I'll have to check the original photos and report, but I don't remember any boxes being in that work area the day the body was found." After a quick jog to his cruiser for a black briefcase, he pulled on rubber gloves and sorted through the box that contained several empty oil cans, two empty smaller boxes, and the shock absorber, a match for the other three.

She and Oliver watched as he photographed the area and each item. He dropped the items in evidence bags and labeled them. She wondered if any of this would help Cheri.

After the trooper had sifted through everything in the garage area, he made some notes in a small black notebook. "Thank you for calling this in." He capped his pen and closed his notebook. "Let me know if you find anything else." He put the evidence and his briefcase in the trunk.

"Thanks for the quick response," she said, smiling.

After relocking the back gate, Cassidy called her uncle. When his voicemail beeped, she said, "Uncle Henry, Oliver and I found some things when we were poking around the garage. That trooper came by and cataloged them. Call me when you get a minute."

Back at her office, Cassidy refreshed Oliver's water bowl and poured herself some iced tea. Before her laptop booted up, Uncle Henry, in grease-stained coveralls, burst through the back door. "I got your message, kiddo. What's up?"

"Oliver and I took a walk this morning, and he was sniffing around the garage. He found a box under the workbench. It had a shock absorber sticking out at a wonky angle. It matched the three that were lying on the counter. Were they Donnie's?"

"I think so. Did you get a good look at shocks?" he asked.

"They were oversized and black." She held her phone for him to see the picture. "The trooper said that he didn't remember any boxes under the counter when the forensic people worked the scene."

"Interesting. Yep. They're a match. You know how the crews get when they're working on cars. They are in their own little world. But they still should have cleaned up their mess."

"The gunk didn't seem like oil," she said. "I didn't want to make wild-eyed guesses to the police, but it looked like dried blood."

"Do you think it was the murder weapon?"

"I don't know." She shrugged. "Oliver found a pink fingernail back there too."

"Why would someone hide it in plain site or return it to the crime scene? It doesn't make sense. You could chuck it out the window on a lonely road, and no one would ever find it."

"I dunno. Maybe someone was in a hurry or didn't care," Cassidy said, thinking of Cheri. Would she be strong and tall enough to swing a shock absorber and take down a sturdy guy? The sheriff didn't seem to believe her kiss-and-make-up story. And the fingernail was an odd find in a garage. It looked like everything pointed to Cheri.

"I'm going to call Dickie and have him come over to the

garage to chat tonight. You wanna be there?" her uncle asked.

"I'd like to hear his explanation for all of this. You gonna let them race this weekend?" she asked.

"We'll see what he has to say."

Too bad they didn't have cameras around the outbuildings. That might be an investment that she should think about. It would be nice to know who was skulking around the track and hiding what might be a murder weapon on her property.

Chapter Seven

Around seven o'clock that evening, Henry texted Cassidy that Dickie and Richie were waiting near the garage. She snapped on Oliver's collar, and they walked the short distance from the office.

The three men stood in a semicircle when she and the dog approached. Dickie moved gravel around with the toe of his cowboy boot as he stared at the ground. Richie leaned over to pet Oliver who sniffed his hands and his shoes.

"Hi, all," Cassidy said. Oliver moved over and sat next to her. "I'm sorry to hear about Donnie. We are all very sorry for your loss."

Dickie still hadn't looked up. "We're here chatting with your uncle about racing this weekend. I want to take over the ride. Richie here will run my crew," he said in a low tone.

"I think it's good to honor your brother's memory," Henry said. "We'll have a moment of silence and a prayer of remembrance. I'll get Pastor Brown to say a few words when he does the invocation."

"That's mighty nice of you." Dickie looked up for the first time. The man had aged ten years in the last few days. Dark bags hung under his eyes, and the parentheses wrinkles around his mouth looked deeper than Cassidy remembered.

"Right now, we need to talk about the mess in the garage. There's still an oil spill and all that stuff y'all left. You know anything about all that equipment?" Uncle Henry shifted his weight from one leg to another.

"The oil was for the leak Donnie had in the last race. It must have spilled over onto the floor when he drove in here," Richie said.

"Must be." Dickie stared down at his boots again. "And I was going to replace the shock absorbers before we trailered the race car, but Donnie told me not to mess with it. I left them on the counter. I thought he'd get them. It won't happen again. I don't know where the box came from," he said, almost in a whisper.

Uncle Henry's lips were pursed. He paused for a moment. "Well, I reckon that's good enough. I'll work on that oil spot tomorrow. It's probably good and soaked in. I'll see you on Saturday."

The two men climbed into Dickie's red Chevy Silverado. From the passenger seat, Richie saluted with two fingers as they drove out of the back gate.

Interesting that Dickie mentioned the shock absorbers. Uncle Henry didn't say what type of equipment it was.

When the dust settled, Cassidy said, "Why was he acting so weird?"

"Dickie's usually more of a chatterbox. Maybe he's tore up over his brother's death," her uncle said.

She shrugged. "Could be, but I think there's more to it. I'm going to see what else I can dig up."

The next morning, Cassidy called her hairdresser Bev at the Clippity-Do-Dah out on the bypass to see if she could get an appointment. Cassidy didn't need a haircut, but she did need some information. The gals there always had their fingers on the pulse of what was going on within a hundred-mile radius of the county.

She patted Oliver and said, "You're on guard duty. I'll be back soon. Hopefully, with some something that can help Cheri." She wasn't close to Cheri, but she did feel obligated to help her since the woman had asked. And the murder had taken place at her track, so she had a right to know if it was an isolated incident or whether she had something bigger to worry about.

The dog licked his chops and ambled into the kitchen to finish his breakfast.

Cassidy pulled open the screen door and entered the parlor of the house that had been converted into Bev's hair salon. A strong whiff of chemicals and lemon cleaner greeted her at the door. When Bev looked up from cutting an older woman's hair, Cassidy said, "Thanks for squeezing me in on short notice."

"Not a problem, hon. Have a seat over there, and I'll get to you after Alice here and then Kristi." She pointed to the sinks in the back. Kristi, a cashier at the Stop 'n Shop, and Bev's daughter, Lila, waved from the back area.

The chatty conversation came to an abrupt halt when Cassidy sat down in one of the pink padded chairs in the front room. The women stared at her like they were waiting for something.

"Oh, y'all quit it," Lila said. "Hey, Cassidy. Sorry for the stares. We've all been glued to the news lately. Tell us what you know. You had a front row seat to a celebrity murder. I heard you found the body." She returned to rinsing Kristi's hair. The water swooshed out of the nozzle.

Cassidy smiled a half-smile. "I don't know about that. Actually, Oliver, my dog, found him. He was sniffing around Donnie's car."

"It's a terrible situation," Alice, the older woman, mused, dabbing the corners of her eyes with her pink smock.

"It is. I feel for his family." Cassidy shifted in her chair.

"Tell us," Bev said. "Did Cheri really get in a fight with that little girl Mandy who works at the Captain Dollar?"

"Uncle Henry's still miffed that they interrupted his driver meeting," Cassidy said.

"That must have been something. I'm sure the sparks were flying. You had a ringside seat to your own lady wrestling event," Lila said over the swishing of the rinse water.

"Something like that. Say, does Cheri or Mandy get their hair or nails done here?" Cassidy asked.

"No," Lila said with a huff. She pushed Kristi's chair into a seated position and wrapped a towel around her long hair.

"Cheri thinks she's too good for Amelia," Bev said. "Miss high and mighty has her hair colored and nails done in Short Pump, where she does her shopping," Bev said. "As for Mandy, I've never seen her in here."

"She does her own nails," Lila said. "Mandy has one of those side hustles where she sells wraps and press-on nails. They never work right. They're always falling off." She pointed Kristi to the vacant chair next to Bev.

Cassidy raised her eyebrows. She would have to look into Mandy's side business.

"So, tell us. What did the police say?" Kristi asked. "Rumor at the Stop 'n Shop is that Cheri killed him when he told her that he was going to leave her for Mandy. The wife didn't want to be traded in for a younger model."

"I don't know the details of the love triangle. When we found the body, we called the police. The sheriff, his team, and some forensic folks took over my garage for hours. They finally let Dickie come and get the car."

"Did Dickie or Richie get in on the fight?" Lila asked.

"I don't think so. They helped separate the girls when they went at it," Cassidy said. "Why?"

" 'Cause Dickie and Mandy dated before she took up with Donnie. They met at the Iron Horse Tavern, and they were a thing for a while. I know it broke Dickie's heart, but he never said anything when she took up with his brother. I thought he might of come to her rescue or something," Lila said. She wiped out the sink and straightened the wash area.

"Dickie and Mandy?" Butterflies awoke in Cassidy's stomach. That might be an angle worth pursuing. She cleared her throat.

"Yep. Mandy's closer to his son's age, but she fed Dickie some line about liking mature men with steady jobs. Then that girl dumped him like a hot potato for his younger, married brother," Lila said.

Alice paid Bev for her haircut, and Kristi took her place in the stylist chair.

"This is too good to miss," Alice said, pulling up a chair in the lobby area and settling in like she was watching a favorite television show.

"Come on back, Cassidy. I'll get you shampooed while Mom works on Kristi," Lila said.

After her time at the wash station, Lila wrapped Cassidy's hair in a towel turban.

"Come on up," Bev said. "You can sit in this chair while I finish up with Kristi." She patted the chair next to her.

Cassidy slid into a silver-and-black swivel chair and waited for the barrage of questioning to start again. Surprisingly, the conversation turned to upcoming weddings and summer vacation plans. As the women chattered, Cassidy's mind wandered to the news of Mandy and the two Ellis brothers. The brothers always seemed to get along. She wondered if there was any deep anger over the love triangle. Sibling rivalry that went too far?

Chapter Eight

On Cassidy's way out of the Clippity-Do-Dah parking lot, Uncle Henry called. "Hey there," she said.

"Didn't know when you were coming back, so I wanted to make sure I told you that Trooper Hendricks stopped by while I was mowing the grass. I gave him your cell number."

"Thanks. I'm going to run a few errands and grab lunch. Do you need anything?"

"Nope. I'm good. See you later, alligator," he said.

After a stop at the drug store and the post office, Cassidy pulled into a parking spot in front of the Isle of Capri, a family-owned Italian restaurant. The restaurant on the busy Patrick Henry Highway had begun its life as a house. Owners through the years had added on a variety of additions until the building was a mishmash of different architectural styles. Even though the parts didn't match perfectly, it was the place in the tri-county area for pizza and cannoli.

The tiny brass bells jingled when she opened the front door. "Hi, Erlene," Cassidy said to the tall woman behind the counter. "Long time no see."

"Hey, sugar. Grab a seat anywhere, and I'll be right with you. How's Henry? I haven't seen him in ages."

"He's as busy as ever. It's hard to keep up with him." Cassidy found the only empty table in front of a bay window. She ordered a salad and a slice of cheese pizza. While waiting, she checked email and the track's social media accounts. A shadow crossed her table. She turned her head to see what moved.

Trooper Hendricks took off his Smokey Bear hat and stood across from her.

"Oh, hi," Cassidy said. "Uncle Henry said he talked with you this morning."

"Good afternoon." He rocked back and forth slightly on his heels.

"Have a seat." She motioned to the empty chair across from her as Erlene dropped off her iced tea.

"I see someone has joined you," Erlene said. "What can I get you to drink?" She placed a well-worn menu in front of the trooper.

"Iced tea is fine, and I'll have the meat calzone." He handed the unread menu back to the waitress.

After Erlene collected the menu and retreated to the kitchen, Cassidy asked, "So what brings you to Amelia this afternoon?"

"It's part of my regular patrol, but today, we're still working on the Ellis case," he said, getting comfortable in the wooden, straight-backed chair. His thick, leather gun belt creaked when he moved.

"Even with Cheri in custody?"

"We're always working leads." He scanned the room. His eyes darted from person to person.

"Anything new you can talk about?" she asked.

"I got some preliminary reports back on what you found yesterday. There was definitely hair and blood evidence on the shock absorber."

Cassidy's eyes widened and butterflies banged around her insides. Her hunch had been right.

The waitress brought his iced tea and handed him a straw. Cassidy's thoughts bounced around her head like ping pong balls. It still felt surreal that a murder happened at her track.

A few minutes later, Erlene broke the silence by dropping off their meals. Trooper Hendricks dug into his calzone with gusto.

After a few bites, the trooper continued, "I went back through my notes. That box you found wasn't in any of the reports or the photos. Someone put it there after we released the crime scene."

Cassidy took a deep breath to try to suppress the adrenaline. Her mind started clicking through who had been on the racetrack property after the races and over the weekend. "What does this mean?" she asked.

"We're still exploring all leads." He stared at her.

"So, do you think it's someone Donnie knew?"

"We're still exploring all leads," he repeated. His stare bore into her and made her nervous. But he did have pretty hazel eyes.

"You'll have to check with Uncle Henry for the names of the guys who came with Dickie to retrieve the truck and hauler. He met them at the back gate."

"Your uncle gave me the list when I talked with him."

Of course, he was way ahead of her. "I found out some bits of gossip this morning when I got my haircut. Don't know if they're helpful, but they're definitely curious. Mandy and Dickie were an item before she dated Donnie."

The trooper sat straighter in his chair. "That is interesting. Anything else?"

"The gossip vine seemed to think Dickie took it pretty hard when Mandy dumped him for his younger, married brother. I hadn't heard any stories about that. It surprised me. They must have kept it hush hush. I never saw them together, but I wasn't watching for it either," she said, taking a bite of her lunch.

He jotted something in his black notebook and recapped the pen. After a couple of bites, his lunch had disappeared.

Cassidy nibbled her pizza crust and pushed the plate away. "The gals at the salon had a lot to say about Cheri and Mandy and their beauty regime. The shop owner, Bev, said that Cheri wasn't a customer. She had her work done at a fancy salon in Short Pump. I got the feeling that Cheri wanted folks to know that she frequented swankier venues. Bev's daughter also commented that Mandy wasn't a client either. They said that Mandy had one of those side businesses that sold nail wraps and press-ons."

He made more notes and pocketed the pen and notebook. When Erlene caught his eye, he signaled for his check.

"Thanks for the information. If you think of anything else, call me." He pushed a business card across the table.

Trooper Hendricks paid his tab at the counter and disappeared through the front door. Good news for Cheri. The trooper, who seemed very nice when he wasn't staring through her, was still following up on leads. But who left that box under the workbench with the dirty shock absorber? And why, like Uncle Henry posed, hadn't they just thrown it away somewhere? She could hardly wait for the next race weekend to do some more digging.

Chapter Nine

The lines of patrons wound around the ticket booth when Cassidy stopped by to check on the staff. Always a good sign for a Saturday night race. She made the rounds by the concessions and the souvenir shack. She picked up a few stray pieces of litter and watched the crowds gather at the snack counters. She glanced at her watch and hiked over to the meeting room to get a good seat for Uncle Henry's drivers' meeting.

Earlier in the week he had mentioned that Dickie Ellis, his son Richie, and two of the crew, Jimmy Thomas and Elton Cox, had been the ones to retrieve Donnie's car and truck after that fateful night. She wanted to secure a good spot to keep an eye on all of them. It seemed more plausible to her that a man could have probably swung that shock absorber hard enough to do in Donnie. Cheri was spunky, but maybe not tall enough to do that kind of damage to her husband.

While Cassidy checked her emails, the drivers and crew filed in and found seats. She stood, stretched, waved at a couple of friends, and then slid in the seat behind Dickie Ellis.

Uncle Henry took his place at the front of the room and started his weekly presentation about tonight's races. Technically part of her brother's race team who often attended the drivers' meetings, Mandy was nowhere in sight.

After the meeting adjourned, Cassidy remained in her seat until the Ellis group filed out. Mixing in with the other drivers, she tailed Dickie to the infield and their trailer. Lingering long enough to greet the crews, Cassidy then circled back to the Ellis camp. Oil, rubber, and exhaust fumes lingered in the air. It smelled like home.

"Hi, y'all. Ready for tonight?" She stepped closer to the car. The crew buzzed around like bees, turning bolts and checking coolant levels. The heat from the warm asphalt seeped into her sneakers.

"Hey, Cassidy." Richie Ellis stepped out of the preparation frenzy. "We're ready. Dad's got a good shot tonight. Hey, where's Oliver?"

"He's hanging out in the office tonight. He'll come out and visit when the crowds die down." She lowered her voice and asked, "How's Cheri doing?"

"Not sure. I don't think anyone from our side has been to see her. My grandma never liked her, and the arrest is proof to most of the family that she's no good." He removed his ballcap and wiped his forehead with his sleeve.

"I'm sorry about what happened."

"Me too. But for now, we're gonna concentrate on racing," Richie said. "Yep. I still can't believe Uncle Donnie is gone. I keep waiting for him to come sauntering around the corner, whistling some tune and telling some lame dad joke."

"I've got to be heading back," Cassidy said, loud enough to be heard over the nearby engine noise.

She crossed the track at the starting line and walked slowly by the stands on the lookout for Mandy and her crew. The gals stood out on the front row, wearing brightly colored sundresses and matching heels. All had on enough makeup for a modeling photoshoot.

Cassidy stopped in front of the young women and waved at Mandy who nodded in her direction. "Hey, Mandy," Cassidy said, yelling to be heard above the crowd noise. "Somebody told me you sell nail supplies. Do you have a card?"

Mandy almost tripped in her hurry to make her way down the aluminum steps. "Hi, Cassidy. Are you interested in my Glitterbomb Nails? I do parties or individual orders. Here's my card," she said, fishing it out of her phone case. "Text or email me, and I can set you up. I've got some good specials going on."

"Thanks," Cassidy said, staring at the gaudy business card. "I really need to do something about my nails. They're too short for a manicure."

"I can fix that," Mandy said. She waved her left hand with mostly perfect, pink nails. Her other hand sported a bandage on one of her fingertips, and another was in a different shade of pink. "Text me, and I can come over and give you a demo."

"Thanks. It's for me right now, but if it works out, maybe we can throw a party later," Cassidy said.

"Ooooh, sounds great," Mandy cooed. "I'll be waiting for your call. See you around." She turned and made her way back up the stands to her seat.

Cassidy pocketed the card and walked toward the white cinderblock snack bar. Lines snaked around the small buildings. Another smaller line circled the souvenir shack. Popcorn, cotton candy, and fried-dough aroma drew spectators in like a magnet.

Rounding the corner, she almost bumped into a tall man in a black shirt with the sleeves rolled up to his elbows. He had a hot dog and a soft drink in one hand. She thought she recognized him but couldn't place him until he spoke.

"Hey, Cassidy. I'm checking out your menu here."

"Trooper Hendricks, how are you? I didn't recognize you in your civvies. What brings you out this way on your day off?" Cassidy asked.

"Hey. Call me Todd. I thought I'd catch the races when I had some free time."

"I hope you enjoy it. We should have lots of excitement tonight with the late models, grand stocks, modifieds, and the sprint car races. If you need anything, let me or my team know."

"Will do." He smiled. "I'm looking forward to it. Plus, I heard you had the best hot dogs this side of Richmond."

"The chili is good too. Rita makes it from her mother's secret recipe. It's perfect if you like to spice up your dog. Enjoy your evening."

The tall officer melted into the crowd. He looked a lot younger in his street clothes. One drink and one hot dog.

Interesting.

Still wondering if the trooper had an ulterior motive to be at the track tonight, Cassidy made her way through the throngs of people to the office.

The sun slid closer to the horizon in the west. Cassidy stood, stretched, and patted Oliver on the head. "Be good and guard the office. I'll be back as soon as I can." She slid her phone in her back pocket and slipped out the door. Cassidy caught a glimpse of two TV mobile trucks in the parking lot. Maybe all the news coverage wasn't bad for business after all.

Moving through the crowds, Cassidy inched closer to the fence near the flag stand. Uncle Henry and Pastor Brown climbed up on a small reviewing stand. The two Amos sisters followed. After the invocation and a moment of silence for Donnie, an ROTC color guard presented the flag, and the two middle-aged sisters, who run the music program at the Baptist church, sang the National Anthem.

Jason, the voice of the Amelia Speedway from high atop the stands in the press box, took over and announced the first sprint race and the teams. Cassidy stood along the fence as the tiny sprint cars zipped around the track like dragonflies on a summer afternoon. The race among the top three challengers came down to a few inches at the finish line. The crowd was on its feet when the checkered flag dropped.

Between races, Cassidy walked around the track's outer perimeter to the garage area. Not seeing anything out of the ordinary, she retraced her steps in the opposite direction. Dickie, in his race suit, stood at the bottom of the stands talking to Mandy. The young girl shook her head furiously. He waved his arms around.

Cassidy moved in closer to try to catch what they were saying, but before she heard a single world, Mandy stomped off toward the concessions, and Dickie turned toward the garage area. After a moment of hesitation, Cassidy trailed Dickie to his truck. She ducked behind a nearby car trailer and peeked around the corner to see what he was doing.

He climbed in his truck and sat there, staring out the front window for a long time. Then he banged his fists on the steering wheel. He reached over and pulled a flask out of the glove compartment and took several swigs. Dickie wiped his mouth with his sleeve, checked his hair in the mirror, and climbed out of the truck.

Before she could say anything about his drinking, he slipped around the trailer.

Cassidy followed him to where his race car was parked.

Richie ran out to meet him and yelled, "Hurry up. The grand stocks are up next. We need to get this moved and in place. You ready?"

Dickie nodded.

The men disappeared into the rows of parked cars waiting for the upcoming races.

What was the Dickie/Mandy thing all about? She wandered back to the stands to locate Mandy and see if anything else developed.

Chapter Ten

Cassidy climbed the aluminum steps in the viewing stands and settled in a spot in the row behind Mandy and her entourage. Mandy spent the entire time on her phone. The other two chatted for a few minutes, but Cassidy could only hear snippets of their conversation about boyfriends and the gifts they bought above the engine noise.

The flag dropped for the grand stock race. Cars whizzed by, making it more difficult to eavesdrop on the women. Dickie's blue Taurus, which started in fifth pace, zoomed past two cars. He dodged in and out of traffic to pull into second place behind Boogie Jenkins's red Monte Carlo. For several laps, they raced nose-to-tail, in and out of lapped traffic. The crowd roared and stood to watch the two battle it out for first place.

Fifteen laps into the thirty-lap race, the two cars caught up to a pack of slower cars that didn't move out of the way fast enough for those on the lead lap. Dickie accelerated and slammed into the back of Boogie's Monte Carlo, sending it fishtailing into the outside wall. The crowd gasped as the yellow caution flag came out. Boogie's crew jumped the fence. A wrecker sped out from pit road. Before they could assist, Boogie restarted the car and pulled into the pits.

Boogie's team went to work on the car while the officials checked the track for debris.

Three laps later, the flagman restarted the race with Dickie as the lead driver.

On lap twenty-two, Boogie's crew got him back out on the track. Some of the crowd cheered when the red Chevy left the pits. Others booed. He darted around cars on his way from the back of the pack.

On lap twenty-four, Dickie had a serious challenger. In a surprise move, Boogie had pulled within two car lengths of the leader.

With some intense racing around turns two and three, Boogie launched his car into second place.

Dickie got bogged down in lapped traffic. The crowd let out a collective gasp. Boogie closed the gap between cars and then zinged his car into first place. The crowd erupted in cheers.

Only a few laps left.

The announcer talked a mile a minute as the cars raced around the track. Dickie kept his car inches from the bumper of Boogie's red car. After turn one, Dickie bumped the rear of Boogie's car, sending him into the jersey wall. The car's radiator collapsed. Steaming water and oil flooded the track. Dickie slid across the finish line to win the race.

His team stormed the track.

The announcer cautioned fans to wait and see how Boogie Jenkins faired. The netting on the driver's side came down. The EMTs rushed in. Boogie slowly climbed out of the car. The crowd erupted in applause.

Dickie's team celebrated as he drove the car to the garage area for the after-race inspection. The track crew cleaned up the spill and readied the track for the next race.

Cassidy walked around to the garage area, where things were getting heated between the Ellis and Jenkins's teams. Her security team had already marshalled around the two teams in case words turned into an all-out brawl. Boogie shouted at Dickie and his crew chief.

Dickie waved dismissively at the string of obscenities that Boogie spewed.

Uncle Henry took charge and shepherded Dickie's team into one of the bays. Two off duty deputies moved Boogie's team to the far side of the garage. Cassidy's security team kept the curious gawkers at bay.

After a meeting with the race officials, Jenkins's team filed out and loaded their crumpled car into their hauler. They left before the inspectors finished with the Ellises.

Twenty minutes later, Dickie's crew wandered out of the garage area. Two deputies followed Dickie to his truck.

The crowd around the garage dissipated. Most people headed back to the stands to watch the rest of the evening's races.

Dickie, still in his race suit, walked toward Cassidy. He nodded without speaking and strode toward the front gate. She picked up the pace to keep him in sight.

Fans in the crowd called out and cheered his victory. Dickie played to the crowd with waves and fist pumps. He stopped abruptly in front of the stands where Mandy and her gals were perched. He yelled her name twice before she bellowed, "What?"

"We need to talk," he yelled.

"I'm done talking. I'm trying to watch the race," she said, turning her head.

"Oh, go on and talk to him," a guy yelled from another row.

Mandy turned her head and said something to the man that Cassidy couldn't hear. Then she got up and stomped down the aluminum steps. Mandy and Dickie walked toward the snack bar. Cassidy let a few people get ahead of her before she trailed the couple.

Mandy sat on top of one of the wooden picnic benches. Dickie's arms, laden with popcorn and two beers, joined her.

Cassidy moved to the corner of the concession building where she could use the wall for cover and still spy on the couple. Unfortunately, she couldn't hear what they were saying.

Before Cassidy could move closer, a hand touched her shoulder. She jumped and stifled a squeal. She turned. Todd Hendricks stood behind her.

"Sorry. I didn't mean to scare you. You didn't respond when I called your name."

Cassidy smiled. "I'm watching Dickie and Mandy. The crews separated Dickie and Boogie after the wreck at the end of the previous race. It seems like Dickie and Mandy are being more civil than he was with her brother," she whispered.

Mandy jumped off the table, threw her hands in the air, and then stormed off. Dickie looked perplexed. He glanced around and then dumped their trash in the can. So much for civility.

"I'll follow him. You see where she goes," the tall trooper said as Mandy blended into the crowd.

Cassidy followed Mandy back to the stands where she returned to her favorite seat. Cassidy climbed up and squished between two people in the row behind Mandy and her gang. She leaned forward slightly to hear their conversation.

"You okay?" her brunette friend asked.

Mandy shrugged. "It's Dickie again. He wants to have dinner later or go away for the weekend. I told him it's too soon. And that I didn't appreciate him putting my brother in the wall twice tonight. Boogie'd have a fit if I went out with Dickie again."

"He's too old for you. You can do so much better. Why won't he just go away?" her other friend said.

Cassidy couldn't make out Mandy's reply.

The girls returned to their cell phones.

The race ended. One more race on the docket for the evening.

Cassidy hurried down the stairs on the other side and hoped the gals wouldn't notice her. At the bottom of the stands, she spotted Mandy descending the stairs like she was in a beauty pageant. She did every pose from the red-carpet walk except the queen wave to the crowd.

Cassidy picked up her pace in order to keep up with the girl in stilettos. The crowd thinned out near the garage, and Cassidy had to adjust her gait again so it wasn't that obvious that she was following Mandy.

Mandy seemed to know where she was going. She headed to the first garage stall.

Cassidy tucked herself in the corner of the building. She hoped the edge of the wall kept her hidden from Mandy's view.

Dickie entered the stall a few minutes later. From her hiding spot, Cassidy got a glimpse of each of the speakers' profiles. She glanced around, but Trooper Hendricks was nowhere in sight.

"What do you want? Why do you keep texting me?" Mandy asked.

"You won't give me a chance. I just want to talk. What can that hurt?" He took a step towards her.

"Listen, it's too soon. I'm not ready to go out with anybody. And I'm sure my brother is furious at you for your stunts tonight. Let's let things calm down for a while." Mandy took a few steps backward.

His face reddened. He threw his hands in the air. Then he pounded his fist in his palm. "I helped you. I risked everything to help you, and this is how you repay me? My family will not understand any of this."

Cassidy let out a breath she didn't know she was holding. She wondered if she should intervene and try to diffuse the situation.

"Friends help each other. I was in a bad situation, and I didn't know what to do with that stupid car part," she said.

Cassidy fished her phone out of her pocket and set it to record. She hoped the microphone would pick up the voices from her hiding spot.

"What if I told the police what I know? I've been silent so far. But if you continue to ignore me, I may be forced to talk to the sheriff. He might be interested in what I know," he said.

Cassidy's heart pounded. She took a deep breath to calm the jitters. What was Dickie alluding to?

"So, you're going to blackmail me into dating you. That's kind of desperate, even for you, Dickie." Mandy's voice rose an octave.

"It's not like that," he whined.

"That's what it sounded like."

"Baby, it's not like that. I miss you. You know I'd do anything for you. I've already proven that."

"Then start by keeping your mouth shut. We're in a good place right now. Neither of us needs the hassle. Let things die down, and we'll see how it goes."

"Sheriff Watkins thinks it's Cheri, and it will stay that way, unless you start ghosting me again," he said. The tone of his voice changed.

Cassidy's heart skipped a beat. She wanted to call the police, but she didn't want to interrupt the recording.

"You're threatening me," she hissed. "It was an accident and you know it. I didn't know what to do. I didn't mean to hurt him. I needed your advice."

"It didn't look like an accident. When I walked in, you were screeching at him because he broke it off. I heard him tell you that he was going back to Cheri, and you flew into a rage."

"I was defending myself. Your brother came at me, and I hit him with what was nearby. We were going to get married. He didn't love her. And . . . and it was an accident," she sputtered. "I hit him. He wobbled, and when he fell, he hit his head on the cement floor and bled all over the place. I had to use the oil to cover it. It was everywhere. I've never seen so much blood, and I went to medical assisting class for three months."

"Oh, right," he said. "He came at you, and you hit him in the back of the head. Mandy, that makes no sense. You know what you did, and I was stupid enough to help you cover it up. I fall for your sweet talk every time. I love you. I even hid the shocks for you."

"And you didn't do a good job of that either, Captain Obvious. Now, you listen to me," she hissed, shaking a finger in his face. "If you talk about this to the police or anyone, I'll tell them that you stalked me, and I was afraid of you. I'll tell the sheriff that you threatened me, and I was afraid for my life. I'll tell them that you did it and tried to blame it on me." She sniffed. "Why couldn't you leave it alone? The police think it's Cheri."

Cassidy couldn't believe what she heard. She steeled her resolve and stepped around the corner. "Hey, y'all. How's it going?" She hoped she sounded confident.

Mandy's head turned to look at the interloper. "What do you want and what did you hear?" Mandy snapped. "This is none of your business. We are having a private conversation that does not concern you."

"Calm down," Dickie said.

"Don't you tell me what to do. You are one to talk." Mandy sneered. "You're both wasting my time. I've gotta get out of here."

"Mandy, we can find someone to help you. We'll find

someone who will listen," Cassidy said in a soothing tone.

Mandy's head turned so fast Cassidy thought it was going to snap her neck. "You witch. You were eavesdropping on our private business. You need to butt out," she hissed and lunged at Cassidy.

The smaller woman knocked Cassidy backwards and toward the side wall of the open-air garage bay. Mandy started swinging as she came down.

Cassidy grabbed the smaller woman's wrists, trying to stop the blows, and she hooked her leg around Mandy and flipped her over on the cement floor. They struggled until Cassidy finally pinned her down. Several of Mandy's fake nails hit the floor.

Dickie stood nearby with his mouth hanging open. He took a step toward the women.

"Freeze," called Trooper Hendricks.

Mandy and Dickie looked toward the opening of the bay.

"Put your hands where I can see them," Trooper Hendricks said. "Hands behind your back. Now," he said to Dickie. The trooper cuffed him.

The trooper helped Cassidy up and then zip tied Mandy's wrists behind her. He pulled her to a standing position. Cassidy had never seen Mandy so disheveled, and then had a moment of panic when she wondered what she looked like.

"What is going on here?" Mandy demanded. "Who are you? This is stupid. You can't cuff us. We were talking. I'm going to scream."

"Calm down. It didn't look like you were chatting. I'm Trooper Hendricks from the Virginia State Police, and you're both under arrest for the murder of Donnie Ellis."

"You have no proof," she said squirming. "You can't go around making false accusations."

"I heard your entire conversation," he said.

"I'll deny it," Mandy said with a smirk. "I'll say you forced me into it, and I was so afraid." She sniffed.

"I heard it too," Cassidy said. "And I recorded it." She waved her phone in the air.

"I thought we were friends." Mandy screeched and tried to

lunge at Cassidy.

Trooper Hendricks pulled her back. "Settle down," he commanded.

Within minutes, Cassidy's team arrived along with the two deputies. They put Dickie and Mandy in the backseats of two different cruisers.

"Thanks for your help. Can you send me your video?" Todd Hendricks asked.

"Will do. Your timing was perfect," Cassidy said. "But you're in civilian clothes, where did the cuffs come from."

"Former Boy Scout. I'm always prepared. You never know when you're going to get called in."

Cassidy smiled and slid a stray curl behind her ear. She hoped she didn't look like she had been rolling around on the garage floor.

"Something wasn't right with this case," Todd said. "The timelines didn't add up. The pink nail was important. Cheri didn't wear press-on nails, and none of her nails were damaged or missing when we interviewed her. It looked like Mandy tried to repair hers, but the nail color was off."

"Oliver uncovered that clue," Cassidy said. "He's my Director of Security."

Todd laughed. "I've got to head to the sheriff's office with these two. One of the deputies will need to get your statement. Deputy Hawkins, could you get Ms. Green's story?"

"Not a problem," Charles said as he hiked up his pants and sauntered over. He pulled out a notebook and asked her to explain what happened.

After Cassidy detailed the events of the night as best as she could, Charles said, "Thanks. I'm sure Trooper Hendricks will be in touch if he has any more questions."

Uncle Henry stepped into the garage bay. "The garage was kinda crowded. You seemed to have had more action back here than we did on the track."

"What a night. Lots of passion on and off the racetrack," she said. "I got lucky that I recorded their discussion of how Mandy killed Donnie. And Dickie helped her cover it up."

"So, she slugged him," he said.

"With the shock absorber. He fell and hit his head on the concrete. And then she got Dickie to help her hide the body."

"Love makes you do some strange things. This takes the cake. You never know what people are capable of," her uncle said.

"The place is clearing out pretty well. I'm going to go check on the office and Oliver. He deserves a big bone for cracking this case."

"Come on, I'll walk you back to the office. If you thought Donnie's murder brought a lot of attention, wait until folks get wind that you and Oliver helped solve the crime and bring Mandy and Dickie to justice." He draped his arm around her and hugged her. "I'm proud of you. And your dad would be too. You had everything under control, even if you look like you've been wrestling a pig."

"Thanks. I think. Hopefully, something good will come out of all of this like our attendance numbers soar for the rest of the summer," she said with a wink.

THE END

PAWSITIVELY SCANDALOUS

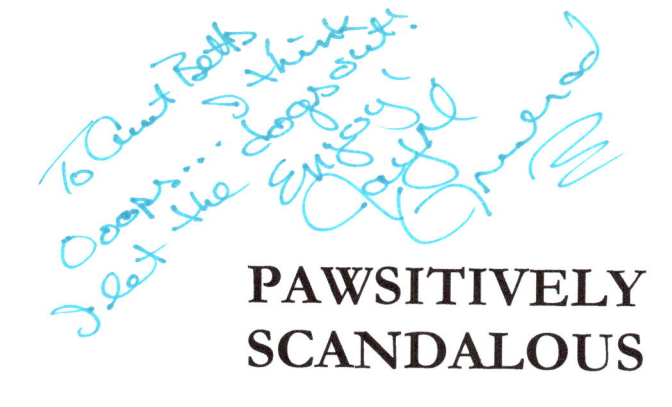

By Jayne Ormerod

Pilar Pruitt and her black Lab Natti live in a community that has not had so much of a whisper of a crime in over 60 years. So, it's disconcerting when a neighbor is hauled off in handcuffs by the police for crimes unknown. But it's downright alarming when another dear friend is found dead. Pilar and Natti start digging deeper into residents' pasts, and the things they find are pawsitively scandalous!

JAYNE ORMEROD *grew up in a small Ohio town then went on to a small-town Ohio college. Upon earning her degree in accountancy, she became a CIA (that's not a sexy spy thing, but a Certified Internal Auditor.) She married a naval officer and off they sailed to see the world. After nineteen moves, they, along with their two rescue dogs Tiller and Scout, have settled into a cozy cottage by the sea. Jayne is the author of the Blonds at the Beach Mysteries,* The Blond Leading the Blond, *and* Blond Luck. *Her stand-alone anthology,* Goin' Coastal, *is a collection of four short mysteries set along the shore. She has contributed seven short mysteries to various anthologies to include joining with the other* To Fetch a Scoundrel *authors in* Virginia is for Mysteries, Volumes I *and* II, *and* 50 Shades of Cabernet.

Website: www.JayneOrmerod.com

CHAPTER ONE

What's in your Yeti today?" my friend and neighbor Ryleigh Duncan asked as I approached the community dog park.

My Mona Lisa smile accompanied by a devilish wink let her know she was in for a treat.

I parked my gallon jug of adult beverage on the park bench and then bent to unsnap the leash from my dog Natti's collar. Ryleigh's sheepadoodle Chewy (short for Chewbacca, whom he'd resembled as a pup) greeted my black Lab/mix in the traditional manor of dogs. Off they ran, frolicking through the grass.

I picked up the Yeti and gave it a shake. "Let's wait until the others get here."

"Maybe I can guess, then. What's the occasion?" Ryleigh asked.

I create a custom cocktail for each of the events I cater. What makes my party planning business special is the personalized concoction based on the clients' preferences. And then I give the drink a unique name. But nothing, and I mean nothing, went out to the client until I'd run it through a taste testing by my fellow Friday afternoon Yappy Hour participants. Yappy Hour, for those who have never heard of it, is an opportunity for dogs to burn off energy while their owners enjoy a refreshing drink. Oh, and there may be a wee bit of gossip while we sip. Just a wee bit.

Ryleigh waved jazz hands in front of my face, her two dozen or so bangle bracelets jangling with the motion. "I'm feeling a Star

Wars wedding." Yeah, Ryleigh could get a little "woo-woo" at times. She was, after all, a descendant of Gypsies and claimed to have clairvoyant powers. She dressed exclusively in loose fitting natural fibers from whatever color palette suited her mood. Today she wore dull earthy shades in stark contrast to the vibrant greens of summer in the park.

"Star Wars is so 2015. I did that for Janice and Gary's wedding. Remember?"

"Ah, yes. The infamous Nookie Wookiees. I have a vague recollection." She smiled sheepishly.

Let's be honest. That concoction had knocked the tall wispy woman on her butt. "Today's drink is to celebrate somebody's book launch."

"So, a book-ish cocktail."

"Did someone say cocktail?" neighbor Tilda Young interrupted us. "Count me in!"

I don't' know how Tilda does it. She's like a ghost, appearing out of nowhere. I think her diminutive five-foot stature and ethereal 90-pound weight makes her light on her feet. Her mop of curly white hair and wardrobe choices that lean towards monochromatic colors helps her blend into her surroundings.

"Hi, Tilda." Ryleigh and Tilda hugged like two sisters who hadn't seen each other in decades, despite their morning constitutional a few hours ago. The two do a few laps around the neighborhood every day. They call it their exercise, but I think if they raced a snail, the snail would win.

"Hi, Tilda," I said. I couldn't help but notice that Tilda was a little unsteady on her feet. Not unusual. She proclaims to love God but admits to drinking a little. Sometimes too much. "Where's Hooch?" I asked. Hooch was her eleven-year-old black Scottie, a constant companion. Probably no need to explain the inspiration for his name.

"At the groomers," Tilda said. "He rolled in stinky juice from the garbage truck this afternoon. He smelled so bad I didn't even let him in the house. He's mad at me. Thank goodness Scrub-a-Dub Dog had a cancellation. He better come home smelling like a rose, or he's sleeping in the garage tonight."

I hoped not. Hooch banished to the garage meant he would howl all night, keeping the entire neighborhood awake.

More dogs arrived. The sounds of playful pups made it hard to think, let alone carry on a conversation.

Tilda sidled up to my elbow and stared pointedly at my Yeti container.

"Can I interest you in a drink?" I asked. The question was superfluous. To my knowledge, Tilda has never refused a drink. Ever.

Before I could twist off the cap, Geoffrey Burnside, retired city councilman and current muckety-muck in the dog agility circuit, elbowed his way between Tilda and me. He held his grizzled face a mere few inches from my own. "Pilar. We need to talk. Now."

That was odd behavior, even for Geoffrey, who was known for his gruff ways.

He took me by the elbow and culled me from the crowd of neighbors. I handed my thermos to Ryleigh to do the honors of pouring tastes for the Yappy Hour crowd.

Once safely across the street and away from the cacophony of yips and yelps, I asked, "What's up?"

"I'm bringing a new dog home, and I want to host a puppy shower. This pup is descended from royalty. A Cavalier King Charles spaniel with royal canine lineage."

I'd never seen Geoffrey agitated, but he was worked into a state now as he raked his fingers through his hair and scrubbed his face with his hands. "I'm trying to create a huge buzz. I've invited writers from *Fancy Dog* and *Champ!* magazines. I'm hoping you can get the local media to cover it, too. I'll pick up the pup at the airport at two on Friday. Please arrange for a police escort from the county line to the party. Can you handle that?"

Police escort? Was this guy serious? I looked at his face. He was serious. "Of course." I spread my arms out as if holding a six-foot sub sandwich. "Pruitt's Party Planning at your service. A few questions to get me started. Where will the party be? How many dogs? Will there be people invited, too? And what's your budget?"

"I want this big—bigger than I can accommodate at my home. The dog park will be the perfect venue. I'll send you a list of our agility circuit associates, probably about forty strong."

"You know the rules, no private parties in common areas. You'll have to invite all the dogs in the neighborhood."

Geoffrey's upper lip curled and his nose scrunched as if he'd just gotten a whiff of a pile of doggie waste baking in the summer sun. Talk about a dog snob! He lived right across the street from the dog park, yet he and his Australian shepherds Holey and Moley rarely graced us with their presence. Nationally ranked agility course champions, you see, and much too good to rub noses with the "ruff-raff," as he called our mutts.

But deep down, Geoffrey was a rule follower. "Okay, invite the neighborhood mutts if you must. Budget wise, sky's the limit. This is the launch of my new venture into breeding."

We discussed a few more details, and then he rushed into his house. That's one thing about Geoffrey, despite his roundness, he got around pretty fast. I have never met someone who was always, always, always rushing around like his hair was on fire.

A puppy shower would be a first for me. I would have to reach deep into my bag-o'-tricks to come up with something truly unique. Something worthy of national magazine media coverage. In one week.

I returned to the melee of dogs and drinkers. By this time, there were more than a dozen pets running and yapping while their owners enjoyed my newest intoxicating adult beverage.

I caught the tail end of Tilda's latest bit of salacious gossip. Something about a tangled love triangle. Right here on Grant's Garden Square? No way.

"Paws-itively scandalous," Tilda said as she made her way through the group, bumping fists with anyone who offered theirs. This was all accompanied by her trademark "*Woof, woof, woof!*" Everyone smiled at her antics, even though we'd seen them hundreds of time before.

You could never trust what Tilda said, though, especially after she got a few sips of liquor in her. A retired school teacher with nothing to do all day, she spent her days watching soap operas. It wasn't unusual for her to sometimes confuse Brookville, North Carolina, reality and Hollywood, California, fantasy.

I poured myself a bit of my Book Buzz brew—a mix of vodka, Cointreau, cucumber, mint, and club soda. I raised my cup to my mouth but stopped mid-air when the sound of sirens broke the air. That set the dogs to barking and cavorting even more. It was more unsettling than hearing a pack of coyotes howling at the moon. The hair on the back of my neck snapped to attention. I hate when that happens.

Four police cars, lights flashing, and two menacing-looking black SUVs pulled up across from the park. At first, I thought (kind of hoped) they might be heading for Geoffrey's unit. But with guns drawn, they stormed the steps to the townhome next to Geoffrey's, the one belonging to Mr. Kinney Copeland.

What in the world?

Once the sirens silenced, the dogs stopped howling and went back to romping, oblivious to the police drama playing out right under their noses.

The neighbors were not as oblivious. We stood in stupefied silence. Watching. Waiting. When the front door opened, two uniformed officers led a handcuffed Kinney down his steps. With his head held low, he shuffled to the curb. A burly officer shoved Kinney into the backseat of the cruiser.

Tilda dropped to the ground in a dead faint. Or a drunken stupor. I wasn't sure.

I looked at Ryleigh, and she looked at me.

"Well, well, well," she said. "What do you think that was all about?"

I shook my head. I didn't know, but with our community as small as it was, it wouldn't be long before we knew every last dirty detail.

CHAPTER TWO

The chatter started, sounding like a swarm of carpenter bees trapped in a building. Suppositions and wild guessing commenced, with neighbors talking over each other in increasing volume. I was impressed with their imaginations. The list of "I bet it was . . ." crimes ran the gamut from embezzlement to child pornography to selling secrets to Russian agents. For gawd's sake, people! The police car hadn't even turned the corner yet, and they already had Kinney tried, convicted, and sentenced to life in prison.

Neighbor Babs Newsome was an RN, and had Tilda up and walking. Turned out her collapse was a mere dog-avoidance maneuver that had ended in a tumble. Lord knows, I've had my share of those. Tilda would be fine.

The chatter got louder. The dog romping got noisier. The beginning stages of a headache pinged right behind my eyeballs. Time to head home. I had work to do, anyway, if I was going to pull off the Puppy Shower of the Century by next Friday.

"Natti," I called to my dog. Natti was short for Natural Light, as in the brand of beer. For the record, he'd already been baptized with that name before he came to live with me, a hand-me-down from my son. While a junior in college, the knucklehead had adopted a black Lab mixed with something huge. Son was living in an *Animal House*-style frat house, not the best environment to raise a puppy. No surprise the underaged furball had quickly developed a taste for beer. Specifically, the beer of choice for frat boys on a budget.

Fast forward a year and son fell in love with a sorority girl. She didn't like dogs (that should have been his first clue she wasn't the one for him.) Girl won the battle of loyalty. Son didn't have the heart to let Natti out of his life completely, so he asked if the mongrel could stay with me. *Temporarily.* That was two years ago, a year-and-a-half since said sorority girl had exited, stage left.

Having Natti in my life had been quite an adjustment for both of us. He'd come with no training, just a big, dumb, cuddly monster. Thanks to a few months (and loads of dollars), Doggie Boot Camp gave me a dog I was proud to call my fur baby. I now had him under voice control. Most of the time.

"Natti," I called again, this time while shaking his leash over my head. He associated that motion with a reward. No surprise, he came running and sat at my feet. I'm one of those crazy dog ladies who always has a pocketful of treats, so I made sure Natti was amply rewarded for his responsive behavior.

I said my goodbyes and headed for home, six driveways west from Kinney's. I live in a community of 160 townhomes that make a big frame around a beautiful park. Each one of the border roads was named Grant's Garden Way, but with its own appropriate cardinal direction. I know, not very imaginative. It gets worse.

Mr. Grant and his successive family members had owned the land since the Civil War. I guess back when there was a family home here, the formal gardens were somewhere in this vicinity, and they used it for play or relaxation. Some developer must have given it a lot of thought to come up with the name Grant's Garden for the space the Grants had called The Garden.

A recent modification to the greenspace was the fenced area in the northeast corner, now known as Grant's Garden Dog Park. (Trust me, I was not part of the naming committee.) It had not been an easy task to convince the non-dog owners that the rest of us wanted exclusive use of one-fourth of the park. But thanks to the tireless efforts of Ryleigh and Tilda, who had petitioned the condo association and pointed out that there would be no loose dogs, or, more importantly, no "forgotten" doggie droppings in the main park, their mission had been accomplished. It would have been more appropriate to name it Tilda-Ryleigh Park, or even Chewy-Hooch Park, but the humorless homeowner's association board had vetoed that. The fence had been installed last year. About a week later, Yappy Hours commenced.

I've lived here for more than twenty years. Our identical townhomes—boxy, three-story brick structures with forty units per street—had been built in the 1960s. They weren't the most fashionable, but they were certainly functional. We all had a 2-car garage and adequate storage space (some had converted to craft rooms or workout space) on the first floor. Second-floor offered an open floorplan living space. Third floor consisted of two bedrooms, each with a private bath. Most of the residents had lived here for more than a quarter of a century, but with all the stairs, not all are able to age in place, and we were starting to see some turnover.

We were a tightknit group, beyond neighborly yet a smidge shy of family. It made me sad that one of our "pack" was hurt or in trouble, especially in trouble with the law. Fingers crossed it was all a big misunderstanding.

But since when does a misunderstanding require an entire fleet of police vehicles? There had to be a logical explanation. *Had* to be.

Natti hit the sofa for his post-romp/pre-supper nap. I poured a Diet Coke over ice and hit the computer under the auspices of getting to work on the puppy shower.

But my thoughts soon turned to "Kinney" Copeland. I knew his nickname had come from his momma, who had a heavy southern accent, so Kenny had sounded like Kinney, and the pronunciation stuck. I knew little about else him, other than he'd moved into Grant's Garden four years ago. He didn't have a dog and lived a relatively solitary existence. Maybe half-a-dozen times he'd come down for the happy part of Yappy Hour. He worked from home as a web designer and marketing consultant. I knew him more professionally, as he was a recent addition to the board of our city business league, of which I was currently vice president.

We worked hard to promote local businesses, trying to keep local dollars in our community. If he was involved in anything unethical, it could affect our good name and our efforts to bring new business to our little corner of the world.

I needed to know more.

How much could a friendly guy who lived alone and seemed to work hard have to hide?

Answer: a lot!

Google returned 1.5 million results in a half a second. There was only one Kenneth Copeland in Brookville, North Carolina, so that narrowed things down to a couple thousand. I began clicking through. What I read knocked me for a loop. It seems I didn't know my neighbor six doors down at all.

He'd been married five times, three suspiciously ending in the death of his spouse. That's a lot of ceremonies for a guy still in his forties.

Another shocker—he'd written fifty-two romance novels published under the name Diamonique Davis. I clicked over and read a few blurbs. It was beyond romance. It was, plain and simple, Mommy Porn. Although not illegal, it was still kind of creepy to wonder what exactly went on behind his blue front door, all in the name of research, I'm sure.

On top of that, he was an outspoken vegetarian. Really outspoken. Obnoxiously so, at least online. Yet I've witnessed him eating roast beef sandwiches at the local deli. Again, not illegal, but methinks that Kinney wasn't at all what he appeared to be on social media. Oh, what to believe?

My cellphone vibrated against the table. I answered without glancing at the screen. Anyone who uses a cellphone for business answers every call, even though the odds of it being a robocall were astronomical. "Pruitt's Party Planning. Pilar speaking."

"Pilar, it's Ryleigh."

"What's up?" I settled back in my chair. Conversations with Ryleigh were never short.

"We're still watching what's going on at Kinney's house. Local news stations have shown up. This could be a scandal that puts little ol' Brookville on the map."

"And that's good how?"

"You know what they say, there's no such thing as bad press."

I didn't want to go into what I'd discovered about Kinney's background, but once that hit the social media scene, it wouldn't be good. For anyone.

"Anyway," Ryleigh continued. "Tilda said something that got my Spidey-sense zinging. Have you ever heard about Kinney's wife?"

"Which one?"

Ryleigh gasped. "You mean there was more than one?"

"I don't know for sure. Something I read on the Internet. I repeat, which one?"

"I didn't catch the name. All Tilda said was that Kinney once confessed to her that he'd killed his wife."

Well, well, well. It appeared the law had finally caught up with Kinney Copeland.

Chapter Three

Seven members of the Brookville Business League huddled around a table for four at Cuppa Joe's. The aroma of fresh brewed Arabica filled the air. Coffee-mug clatter and patron chatter echoed off the exposed pipes in the loft-style building. Business was good here. Not so much for the rest of the community, but not for lack of trying on our part.

The shop's owner, Joe Foster, was the league president. I held the position of vice president, which meant I covered all the responsibilities when another elected official was unavailable. Translation, I hadn't done anything other than show up to meetings for four years. That changed when Kinney Copeland got arrested yesterday. Today, I would be filling his shoes as secretary.

Joe made the motion of rapping an invisible gavel against the table. "I bring the meeting to order. Pilar will be serving as secretary until we can elect a replacement. Any objections?"

Not surprisingly, nobody objected. I glanced at my league-mates. Everyone smiled at me, those I'm-glad-it's-you-and-not-me smiles that bordered on pity.

I raised my cup in appreciation of their support, took a long sip of what some would consider cream with a splash of coffee, and then set my fingers to keyboard to record the business of the day.

It was a long agenda as we tried to develop a marketing plan that reminded our neighbors to think, shop, and spend local. The right tone was important as we didn't want to sound desperate, even though we were. It amazed me that the forty-mile roundtrip to the big metropolis of Franklin wasn't enough of a deterrent, but our residents seemed to like the drive, not to mention the prices offered at big-box stores. Shopping online was hurting us, too. Bigtime. I don't think anyone has devised a marketing gimmick to combat Amazon.

We had lots of energy in our group, and tons of new marketing and fundraising ideas that, sadly, had high costs in monetary and/or personal-time categories. We all agreed to try harder to bring in new members to help share the burden.

Joe drained his coffee and wiped up an imaginary spill with his napkin before speaking again. "I don't want to reinvent the wheel here. Kinney had drawn up a bang-up recruiting letter. Anyone have any idea how we can get access to his files while he is, ah, unavailable?"

Six people shook their heads. No need to expound upon Kinney's unavailability, small town that we were.

While we all knew Kinney on a professional level, not one of us was good enough friends with him to have a key to his property.

Jessica, our treasurer, spoke up. "He's also got all the bylaws and meeting notes and members' nametags." She tapped her lower lip, as if lost in thought over all the files that were in Kinney's possession. "God knows what else. We're going to have to get our hands on all of that." She sat back in her chair and sighed.

The other six members of the group echoed her sigh.

Wait! I had a Kinney connection! He had been a student of Tilda's back in the early 1980s, and they had formed a friendship upon his move into the neighborhood. Not real close, but close enough she might visit him in prison and ask permission to go into his house and grab the business league files. I told the group, and they agreed this was the best (really only) course of action.

With that issue resolved, Jessica motioned to adjourn, and we all went back to our own businesses.

I'd ridden my trusty, rusty Schwinn the five blocks between home and Cuppa Joe's this morning, it having been a pleasant seventy-four degrees at the time. But the temperatures were rising fast, as happens in mid-summer in the mid-south. Cruising along a stretch of a residential road, I dared take my hands off the handlebars long enough to lift my hair off my neck in hopes that a whisper of a breeze would cool me. My thoughts zipped between planning the puppy shower and getting the files from Tilda. Was there someone I could contact about adding a few more hours to the day? That was the only way I'd be able to accomplish everything.

I turned onto North Grant's Garden Way and slowed to a stop. My neighborhood looked so peaceful in the dappled summer sunshine. Grant's Garden was a place I was so proud to call home. No one would believe a criminal dwelled behind one of the stately brick facades. To my knowledge, Kinney is the first in over sixty years to hold that distinction.

My fervent hope is that he would be the last.

Chapter Four

"Hello, Tilda, period," I began my voice-to-text. "I need a favor, so if you could give me a shout back, I would appreciate it, period. You've got my number." After disconnecting the call, I tossed my phone on the kitchen counter.

I mentally ticked off that task . . . for now . . . and focused my attention on the puppy shower for Geoffrey Burnside. A police escort? That man was goofed on skunkweed. But I had to board the crazy train with him and get the job done. Who knows? This bash could rocket me to the status of Event Planner of the Stars. Or at least to the hoi polloi of Brookville. I grabbed my idea pad, slid onto my kitchen barstool, picked up a pen, and began brainstorming. Geoffrey had been very specific that he wanted a police escort to Grant's Garden Dog Park. Who should I call? The mayor? The chief of police, whose name I couldn't even remember? My local tequila supplier? He had a few connections with local authorities, or so I'd heard.

My phone chirped. Incoming text from Tilda.

HEY, GIRLFRIEND. GOT YOUR MESSAGE. WHAT'S UP? AT THE CANTINA WITH RYLEIGH. JUST ORDERED MIMOSAS. WE WORKED UP A POWERFUL THIRST ON OUR MORNING WALK AROUND THE BLOCK.

Heck, breathing worked up a powerful thirst for Tilda.

I tapped a reply on my phone. WONDERING IF YOU HAD ACCESS TO KINNEY'S HOUSE AND IF WE COULD GET

PERMISSION TO GO INSIDE AND GRAB FILES FOR THE BUSINESS LEAGUE.

I stared at my phone for a few minutes, expecting a quick response, but nothing. The mimosas must have arrived.

I could sit and stare at the wall and accomplish nothing, or I could kill two birds with one party blowout if I took Natti to the park and let him romp while I visualized the puppy shower set up.

"Natti," I called. No response. I got up and walked to the steps where his leash hung. I jangled it a bit and he came a running, tail wagging and tongue dragging. This dog loved the great outdoors. My outdoor space was a mere ten-by-twenty patch of hardscape, which calculated to three strides for Natti. Trips to the dog park to get his zoomies out were the highlight of his day. I'd thought about moving to the country so he could run free, but that would be at the expense of friendships with my neighbors. I wasn't ready to sacrifice that much for my dog . . . yet.

Cuddles, the Scotty dog, was there to great us, along with her owner, Mrs. Bruner.

"Hello, Pilar." The corporate-attorney-turned-real-estate-agent gave me a quick hug. "Is it true you're planning a puppy shower for Geoffrey, complete with a mini circus, pony rides, and petting zoo?"

Seemed the gossip train had hit full Mach One speed on this one. "Nothing that far-out," I said, laughing. "Well," I added, "unless you consider a police escort for the new arrival a little over the top."

"You are such a kidder, Pilar." Mrs. Bruner waved off my ridiculous idea.

I agreed. The idea was, indeed, ridiculous.

"Now seriously, what's the plan?" she asked.

My shoulders slumped of their own accord. "I'm still in the idea-development phase."

"When's the party?"

"Friday."

Her wide-eyed look mirrored my own deep-seated anxiety. "Well, then," she said. "We need to get crackin' on this."

More dogs and owners arrived. Mrs. Bruner huddled everyone around and led a brainstorming session. I grabbed my phone and took notes.

The theme: The Pitter-Patter of Puppy Paws.

The centerpiece: A diaper cake made out of piddle pads instead of baby diapers.

The ideas: Park decorated with Milk Bones (or the all-natural, locally-sourced, high-brow equivalent) hanging from the fence. Dog party hats with a paw-print theme. Frosty paws for all the canines. An old toilet bowl as the communal canine water trough.

The ideas kept coming. Some were great, like Scooby snacks. Others were bad, like bottles of toilet water for the people (it's a real thing . . . check it out.) A vote was taken. Dog-themed craft beer won, hands down.

While the group argued about the appropriateness of one of Brookville's finest dressing up in a Paw Patrol or McGruff the Crime Dog costume—even if we could find one on short notice—my phone chirped. Text from Tilda. I'VE GOT A KEY. I WATER KINNEY'S PLANTS WHEN HE TRAVELS. I'LL DO THE SAME UNTIL HE GETS SPRUNG FROM THE HOOSEGOW.

Problem solved.

I left Mrs. Bruner in charge of taking additional notes from the brainstorming session. My neighbors astonished me with their creativity. I might consider putting some of them on staff.

Right now, I needed to start actioning their ideas. Natti and I headed home. We passed Ryleigh and Chewy as they headed to the park. "Any word on why Kinney was arrested?" I asked.

Ryleigh grimaced and shook her head. "I consider myself a good judge of character, and Kinney was one of the kindest souls. He had a good aura. Or so I thought. Just goes to show . . ."

It really doesn't show anything at this point, I thought but didn't say. I was willing to wait until the facts came out before powering up the electric chair. It could be a case of mistaken identity. It happens all the time. At least on TV shows. I sincerely hoped that was the case here.

Geoffrey's dog walker, a Meghan Markle doppelganger, exited

his townhome. Holey and Moley tugged on the end of their Gucci leashes. (Ryleigh claimed they were knock-offs. She'd seen them on Etsy.) Dog walker Amber gave us a nod and headed away from the dog park.

"Wouldn't be surprised if she did more than walk his dog, if you get my drift." Ryleigh bumped me with her elbow twice.

"Eww. Can you imagine?"

"There's not enough money in the world." Ryleigh shook her body like a dog shaking off bath water.

"I saw him once without his shirt on. His flabby belly was fish-belly white. That's not something you can ever un-see."

"I can't believe you're planning a party for that pompous twit."

"His money is as good as anybody's. And there's plenty to enable me to hire an assistant." I slipped my arm around Ryleigh's shoulders in a conspiratorial way. "Any chance you're interested in making a few bucks? Party is six days away, and there is much to be done." I smiled my most beatific smile.

She scowled her most distasteful scowl.

"Great," I said before she could decline my offer. I recapped some of the ideas the group had come up with so far.

Chewy barked and whined, impatient to get to the dog park. Ryleigh and I made a date for breakfast tomorrow at Marla's Diner. Right now, I had a bit more planning and a lot more shopping to do. It looked to be an all-nighter for me. Such is the life of a sole proprietor. Gotta make hay while the sun shines—or as most often is the case for me, while the moon glows.

But maybe, just maybe, I'd find a few moments to Google Kinney Copeland again. Inquiring minds want to know why he'd been arrested.

My mother had often reminded me that curiosity killed the cat. Her sentiments echoed in my head now. It's never a good thing when you hear your Momma's cautionary voice. You'd think by age forty-five I'd have learned to listen.

Chapter Five

The shrill clanging of my phone woke me. No good news ever comes in the middle of the night. And 2:23 qualified as smack dab in the middle of prime sleep time. Gawd, please let all family members be all right. Adrenaline surged as I scrambled for my phone. With shaking hands and a thumping heart, I connected the call.

"What's wrong?" I questioned to whomever was on the other end of the line.

A raspy voice replied, "Do you hear that?"

"Hear what? Who is this?" I was marginally more awake now and scanned the rooms to get my bearings. Kitchen. Lights on. Computer screen filled with a series of Ps. So much for pulling an all-nighter. I hadn't made it past midnight.

"It's Ryleigh. Do you hear Hooch?"

"Hooch? As in Tilda's dog?" I was almost all the way awake now.

Ryleigh let out an exasperated sigh. "Yes, that Hooch. He's been howling that Beagle howl for over an hour. I called Tilda, but she didn't answer. I think something's wrong."

"Call the police. I'll meet you there."

Still dressed in my work-at-home clothes—yoga pants and a t-shirt—I slipped on the nearest pair of flip-flops and headed for the door. Natti thought we were going to the park and raced me. He won. I reached in the jar of dog bones I kept on the small table for such emergencies. "Can't go with me now, Natti." I tossed a bone upstairs into the den. Being food-driven, he fell for the ruse.

I escaped out the door and raced down the street. Hooch was indeed howling. Not the let-me-out-of-here howls we've heard when he's locked in the garage, but low, mournful wails that echoed in the quiet night. I kicked into a full-out run. Something was wrong, all right.

Ryleigh met me on the sidewalk. She was breathing hard, from physical exertion or all-out fear, I wasn't sure. "Police are on their way."

"We can't wait for them. Let's go." I trotted along the short front sidewalk to the door, which I found cracked open ever so slightly. A sliver of light glowed through the one-inch space. Could someone have broken into Tilda's house? And if so, was he still there?

The heavy oak door resisted my gentle push, so I pushed a little harder. It swung open with an ominous squeak. "Tilda," I called. I looked down the hallway leading to the garage. Pitch black. I looked upstairs leading to the living room. Pitch black. The fixture lighting the stairway was down to one bulb. It cast eerie shadows that had my skin crawling as if a swarm of ants were marching in formation. "Tilda," I called again, louder.

Ryleigh put a trembling hand on my back. "Try calling for Hooch," she whispered.

Come to think of it, the dog had stopped howling when I opened the door. "Hooch. Come see your favorite aunt." Silence. "I've got treats." Nails scratched on the wood floor above. He was moving around, albeit slowly. That was unusual behavior for him. He usually ran at the prospect of a treat. Could he be injured?

The nails-on-wood noise stopped. Silence.

Where in the heck was Tilda? "Tilda," I called again, this time in my loudest lifeguard voice. I had a bad feeling. A really bad feeling. The worst kind of feeling I'd ever had in my life.

I looked over my shoulder and down the street. Still no sign of the police, but there was no doubt in my mind that assistance was needed upstairs. Immediately.

Sensing trouble ahead, I picked up the heaviest object I could find, a thick book sitting on the side table by the door. I flipped the switch to turn on the family room lights and then made my way cautiously up the steps. Ryleigh, her trembling hand still on my back, followed.

As we made the turn at the top of the steps and flipped the light switch, I saw the mess that defined Tilda's lifestyle. She decorated in what she jokingly called "modern post-tornado." Truth be told, it looked messier than usual right now.

"Tilda," Ryleigh called. "Tilda?"

Hooch peeked his head up over the top of the sofa. I sensed—and smelled—his fear. He turned his head and glanced at the foot of the stairs leading to the third story.

I followed his gaze and saw Tilda. Lying in a pool of blood.

Chapter Six

I couldn't move. At first glance, the scene at the bottom of the stairs was something out of a film noir. A scantily-clad woman lay sprawled face down at the bottom of the steps, an empty bottle of Hendrick's Orbium gin near her hand, and a puddle of dark red goo leaking from the back of her head. On second glance, the movie details were all wrong. The body did not wear a suggestive outfit but a tattered yellow seersucker housedress, and the legs splayed at awkward angles were not shapely gams but pale, scrawny, wrinkly limbs, the likes of which would haunt my nightmares for decades to come.

One thing the movies protect the viewer from is the truly awful stench of death. My dinner of Stouffer's Mac and Cheese threatened to make a repeat appearance.

The police arrived and took control of the situation. One of the officers raced over and checked Tilda's vitals. Yeah, that should have been me checking to if she was still alive, and offering aid if necessary.

Another policeman on scene, Officer McNeely, escorted Ryleigh and me to the stairs. Hooch followed on our heels.

"Please wait outside," McNeely said. "We'll need a statement." A gently pressure on the small of my back let me know we weren't wanted.

I dared to glance over my shoulder and saw the officer who had raced to render assistance to Tilda was now arranging a multicolored afghan over Tilda's body. It was a blanket made by her daughter who had been killed in a horrible car crash a few years ago. Tilda kept it on her sofa to curl up with whenever she watched TV. It seemed fitting it provided comfort one last time.

Sadness washed over me, but I was too numb to cry.

Ryleigh leaned against me, her shoulders shaking as she began to deal with the loss of her best friend.

Hooch showed his grief with a head-hung, tail-down shuffle out of the house. My heart broke for him.

As we walked out the front door, the EMTs hurried in. I could have told them not to rush, but that's not how they're wired. Those underappreciated heroes race to render whatever medical assistance they can. Even if it's too late.

We joined a huddle of neighbors gathered across the street, a dozen of them dressed in various stages of middle-of-the-night fashion. Strobing lights from the emergency vehicles flashed over their faces, illuminating a shared attitude of curiosity and fear. They turned to me, hopeful for some good news.

I pursed my lips and shook my head. They got the message. Marilyn Matilda Young was no longer of this earth.

Ryleigh cried gut-wrenching sobs and was welcomed into the folds of Mrs. Bruner's waiting arms.

Neighbors turned to neighbors, and within minutes the scene turned into on big cry/hug fest.

I knelt down and wrapped my arms around Hooch's neck. He had lost the most important person in his life. I couldn't help heal his broken heart, but maybe Natti could. "Be right back," I said to no one in particular.

With Hooch's collar held tightly in my hand, I walked bent over and escorted him to my house. Natti greeted us at the door in his enthusiastic way, but sensed something was wrong. He calmed down to a state I hadn't seen him in since he'd had a horrible tummy ache after eating an entire family-sized bag of Cheetos. He looked at me, and then turned to Hooch and nudged him toward the sofa, one slow morose step at a time. Hooch hopped up on the La-Z-Boy. Natti joined him. The two cuddled up next to each other in yin-yang fashion. Natti gave me a look that said, "I've got this, Mom. You go on and do what you need to do."

I needed comfort, too, in the way of Grape Therapy. Grabbing a box of cabernet and a stack of red Solo cups, I headed to join my neighbors standing vigil in front of Tilda's house. The group had nearly tripled in size. A few people were crying, but nobody was talking. That added to the aberration that seemed to define tonight's events.

Babs Newsome passed around coffee and little powdered-sugar donuts. The box wine swung in my hand. Everyone had a different way of coping.

Under normal circumstances, I might have grabbed a donut to enjoy with a cabernet chaser. These were not normal circumstances. Wine was my coping mechanism of choice.

"Pilar," Babs asked. "Is what Ryleigh said true?"

I pressed the valve on the boxed wine and filled my cup to the rim. "What did Ryleigh say?" I took my first swig. And I don't mean a gentle sip, but a healthy glug.

"That Tilda fell down the stairs?"

"It looks that way."

"Was she drunk again?"

I thought about the gin bottle by her hand. "Probably."

"That's odd, because Tilda told me she never went upstairs when she was drinking because she'd had some sort of premonition that's how she would die. When she over indulged, she slept it off on the sofa."

Given Tilda's age and propensity for over-indulging, that was probably a good policy to have. What reason would have compelled her to break her rule tonight?

As if sensing my question, Babs said in such a low voice I had trouble hearing her, "Do you think it was suicide?"

I took another glug of wine. The idea of Tilda, the happiest person I knew, committing suicide was more than I could process.

Activity at the front door drew our collective attention. The EMTs emerged, rolling a sheet-draped gurney between them. The shape under the sheet was a mere bump that had once held the heart and soul of our neighborhood, the indomitable Tilda.

No longer able to hold the tears in, I let loose the waterworks. They didn't make me feel any better than they had the last time I cried, when my mother died. Of course, I'd only been ten years old at the time. I was older and wiser now. And still had so much to learn about life . . . and death.

Chapter Seven

Long about sunrise, Officer McNeely approached me and asked me for a statement. By that time, I was mentally, physically, emotionally, and spiritually exhausted, not to mention a wee bit tipsy. But I answered his questions to the best of my ability, which turned out to be a little ramble-y and very emotional.

"Ryleigh heard Hooch, that's Tilda's dog, howling. She tried to call Tilda's phone but nobody answered, so she called me to go with her to see if something was wrong. We met out front. The door was open. We went inside to see if she needed our help. She didn't." I swiped at the tears oozing out of the corners of my eyes. "She didn't need our help because she was already dead." I drew a deep breath and only marginally succeeded in calming myself. "You showed up, and we left." I closed my eyes and saw the gruesome scene all too vividly. "Babs thinks it might have been suicide. Do you think it might have been suicide? She didn't seem depressed to me at all but one never knows what's going on in another's life. Please tell me you don't think it was suicide, because I don't think I could handle the idea she killed herself right now." I finished what was left of my wine, a mere drip left in the bottom of the cup. "Does it look like suicide to you?" I whispered to my now empty Solo cup.

"No, not at all. It looks like an accident," Officer McNeely replied to my somewhat rhetorical question. "I've seen more cases of that than I care to count. Unless we have reason to suspect otherwise, which we don't, it will be officially recorded as accidental death caused by tripping and falling. Intoxication may be a factor. We won't know until the tox report comes back."

I cleared my throat against another onslaught of tears, gave him my name and contact information, and then pointed him in Ryleigh's direction.

I pointed myself in the direction of home and meandered my way along the sidewalk to my townhouse.

Natti and Hooch greeted me at the door.

I needed some doggie snuggles. Lots and lots of doggie snuggles. We all curled up on the sofa while I checked my phone. Over a hundred texts had come in over the past few hours, most from friends asking if I'd heard what had happened.

I scrolled back to the first unread text so I could work through them from the beginning.

Tilda's name popped up. She had texted me just before midnight, still very much alive.

Hey Sugar, wanted to let you know I snagged two boxes from Kinney's house. You can come get them sometime tomorrow. I've hidden them from the bad guy. Ha ha ha.

That Tilda. What a kidder. Bad guy. That's a good one. Oh boy, I sure was gonna miss that sense of humor.

The text being my last connection to a very much alive and upbeat-sounding Tilda, I held my phone tight to my chest, as if I could somehow keep her in my heart. There was no way she'd committed suicide, as Babs had suggested. Something else must have happened tonight to make her go upstairs in her condition. Maybe it was Hooch-related, as in the dog, not the liquor. Was it possible she went upstairs to get something for him and tripped over him on the way down? I sighed, a great big sigh as I thought of all the questions we would probably never have answered.

My phone rang. Ryleigh's name flashed across the screen. I swiped to answer. "You okay?"

"No, but I will be. What a shock, huh?"

I agreed.

"I'm at your front door. Can I come up?"

"Sure thing. Door's unlocked."

The dogs and I met her at the top of the stairs. She wasn't her usual smiling, bright-eyed, put-together self, not by a long shot. Her hair looked like it had been whipped by an egg beater, and her face was red and blotchy and swollen from crying. I don't imagine I looked any better.

We hugged, and then hugged some more.

"I think I'm out of tears," Ryleigh said, despite the droplets of water oozing out of the corners of her eyes.

"Me, too. And the last thing we want to deal with is dehydration. We need liquid and salt. A glass of ice-cold lemonade and a feast of Pringles should do the trick."

Ryleigh smiled. "Did Dr. Oz prescribe that?"

"Nope, but my dear sweet granny did. She always had the perfect cure for what ailed ya."

We settled on bar stools at my kitchen counter. Pushing the comfort-food envelope, I added a container of French onion dip to our breakfast of champions. I even pulled out the fancy napkins, the ones printed with my favorite saying: Handle every stressful situation like a dog. If you can't eat it or play with it, just pee on it and walk away.

Between Kinney's incarceration, the crazy puppy shower hosted by Geoffrey, and now Tilda's death, there were a lot of things that needed peeing on right now.

Chapter Eight

By the time we'd polished off the chips and dip, Ryleigh had talked me into fostering Hooch until a permanent situation could be found.

And by the time we'd polished off a fifteen-ounce bag of pretzel M&Ms, I had Ryleigh talked into being responsible for notifying friends and making funeral arrangements. After all, when someone is the last of the bloodline, it's up to the BFF to take care of the final arrangements.

Ryleigh schlumped back in her chair and rubbed her belly as if the unconventional breakfast wasn't sitting too well. "In order to notify all of her friends, I'm gonna need a list of contacts. I'll make the calls if you get me her phone."

"Me?" I squawked. "How is that my responsibility?"

"No way I'm going into a room where my dear friend passed away less than six hours ago. Her spirit is probably still hanging around." Ryleigh waved her arms in the air in her customary woo-woo motion. "Do you know what Tilda's spirit is gonna be like?"

"Drunk?" I asked.

"It's bad luck to speak ill of the dead."

She was right, of course. It was the chocolate talking.

"There's no question in my mind her spirit will take great delight in scaring the bejesus out of me. I'm not going. So, you get the phone, and I'll take on the role of contacting every damn one of the thousands of people in her contacts."

Surely, Ryleigh was exaggerating. "I'll go in, but I need you to come with me." I showed her the text from Tilda about the boxes. "I can't carry them myself."

"Can't that wait until her spirit has left the building?" Ryleigh asked. "Say, in about a year or so?"

"Nope. I'm on the hook for getting stuff to the business league next week. We'll do this together. Like ripping off a bandage, let's get this over with now."

Ryleigh remained silent for so long I thought she may have fallen asleep. "Okay," she finally said, "but can I get a shot of a little sumpin'-sumpin' in my lemonade first? No way can I go back to the room where Tilda died while I'm in a stone-cold sober state of being."

Two hours—and three-quarters of a bottle of tequila—later, Ryleigh and I marched outside into the pouring rain. Arms linked, we channeled our inner Laverne and Shirley, did our "Schlemiel! Schlimazel!" routine and headed down the sidewalk in the direction of Tilda's house.

I would have turned tail and run, were it not for Ryleigh pulling me across the threshold and into the front hall. I think she had more tequila in her than I did.

"So, Tilda," I called to the spirit world. "Where did you leave the boxes?"

Ryleigh looked at me, a devilish glint in her gypsy-green eyes. "Did you hear that?"

"Hear what?"

"Tilda said 'They're in the garage.'" Ryleigh imitated Tilda's teacher voice with inflections of ghostly spookiness.

Goosebumps the size of molehills popped up on my arms. I rubbed them away. "Cut that out. This is freaky enough."

Ryleigh laughed. "It's an educated guess. If I know Tilda like I think I know Tilda, she was too lazy to get them out of her car. Let's go." Ryleigh headed down the hallway toward the garage.

Sure enough, we found two cardboard storage boxes in the backseat of Tilda's old Buick. First mission accomplished!

We carried the boxes into the hallway and set them by the

front door.

"Now the phone, and then we're outta here," Ryleigh said. We headed upstairs in the opposite order of when we'd climbed the stairs in the middle of the night. This time Ryleigh led the way while I clung to her arm. My legs shook so bad it was like I was on the last mile of a marathon. Not that I'd ever run a marathon, or even a mile, for that matter. But I'd seen plenty of exhausted people cross the finish line on TV. I have no earthly explanation as to why I felt so jumpity. I'd seen them remove Tilda's body. I knew the house was empty.

"Ya know," Ryleigh said as we stood at the top of the stairs, "Tilda wasn't known for her housekeeping skills, but this place is a total mess."

I peered over her shoulder. Indeed, it was as if a Category 4 hurricane had blown through: sofa cushions scattered; drinking glasses knocked over; papers tossed hither and yon; one lamp on the floor, the lightbulb shattered. I took a few steps into the room in order to better see the kitchen. It was equally messy, with cabinet doors and drawers opened, and dishes scattered on the floor. If I didn't know better, I'd say Tilda had been searching for something important. But what?

Eventually my gaze landed on The Spot. The one at the bottom of the steps where we'd found Tilda. The bloodstain was about the size of a dinner plate, whereas in my mind's eye it had been the size of a kiddie swimming pool. I sank onto the arm of the sofa, willing my teeth to stop chattering. This had been a bad idea. The very worst of ideas. Returning to the scene of the crime, as they say. Only there hadn't been a crime. Or had there? My Spidey sense kicked in. Something was not right about the situation. But the reasons did not bear thinking about. Not now. Not when the emotions were still running off the charts, and I still had a goodly amount of Jose Cuervo coursing through my veins. "Is Tilda telling you where to look?" I asked, half sarcastically and half scared to death of the answer.

"Nope. She usually keeps it on the coffee table, but I don't see it."

"Guess we're out of luck, then." My legs were still shaky as I stood and headed for the steps to leave.

"Where do you think you're going, missy?" Ryleigh asked.

I glanced over my shoulder. Ryleigh stood in the middle of the mess, hands on her hips, a stern look on her face. "Um, home?"

"Um, this was your idea, remember? You bail on me now, and I won't invite you to any more Cork and Candle parties."

Her wine tasting parties were legendary. Plus, I made a lot of business connections when I attended one. She knew a LOT of party people. And, oh yeah, I was the one responsible for talking her into doing the dreaded task of contacting friends and acquaintances with the sad news, so it's kind of my fault we're in this predicament in the first place. I sighed, one of those sighs that left me feeling like a deflated balloon. "Let the search begin," I said with as much enthusiasm as I could muster, but I don't think I convinced Ryleigh, or even myself. "You take the family room; I'll take the kitchen."

We searched and searched, making a bigger mess than it already had been in our eagerness to find the phone. I was about to suggest we head upstairs to look when I pulled open the only drawer I hadn't looked in yet, the one under the oven. There it sat, tucked atop a broiler pan. "Got it," I called to Ryleigh, waving the antiquated iPhone 4 over my head. "Let's get the hell out of Dodge."

We battled each other to be the first down the stairs. I won. We each grabbed a box and tucked it on a hip. I swear to gawd that as I reached for the front doorknob, I heard Tilda's voice. "Y'all come back now, ya hear?"

Not bloody likely!

Chapter Nine

Once back in the safety of my home, I dragged myself up the steps and forced myself to put a mug of water in the microwave to heat for instant coffee. Heavy on the caffeine. Even then I wasn't sure how was going to get through the rest of this day.

With my energy level at negative ten, I used the thirty seconds of water-heating time to plop down on the sofa and rest.

I woke up five hours later feeling refreshed and energized. Natti had joined me on the sofa. His long body stretched out on top of me, his nose touching mine so that we exchanged breath. I scratched him behind his ears, rocketing him into doggie bliss. His tongue dangled from his mouth as he enjoyed the attention. A few bits of slobber dripped on my chin, which I swiped away. A little doggie drool never hurt anyone.

A second black nose appeared in my field of vision. Hooch. A tentative tongue reached out and licked my cheek. My feeling of happiness evaporated as memories of the early morning adventures came crashing back. I had custody of Hooch, which meant it hadn't all been a terrible nightmare. Tilda was well and truly dead.

I lifted my gaze beyond Hooch to the family room. Natti's basket of toys had been emptied and all manner of Nylabones and squeakies were scattered across the room. And somebody had gnawed on the corner of my antique wine rack that I had inherited from my grandparents. The two had been very busy boys while I'd been dead to the world. *Ouch.* Bad choice of words.

"Come on, you mischief makers." I extracted myself from Natti's full-body embrace and sat up. Things looked worse from this vantage point. They had gotten into the pantry and demolished a few bags of ranch Doritos, tore into a new bag of pearl barley, destroyed an undeterminable quantity of Rice-a-Roni boxes, and somehow still had the time and energy to play with a five-pound bag of flour. Sanity check: was fostering Hooch in my best interest?

My phone chirped with an incoming text from Ryleigh. YAPPY HOUR ANYONE? FOUND SOME INTERESTING STUFF ON TILDA'S PHONE. WE NEED TO TALK.

I responded immediately. MEET YOU AT THE DOG PARK IN FIFTEEN. I slipped on my flip flops and headed to the first floor where I stored all manner of party supplies.

An image popped into my head of Tilda lying at the bottom of the steps with an empty bottle of gin near her hand. How fitting to send-off our friend with gin and tonics. Although I didn't stock Hendrick's Orbium brand of gin (too many botanicals infused for it to have much versatility in drink concoctions), I did have a goodly supply of Tanqueray in my liquor inventory. I grabbed the liquid fixin's from my party supply cabinet, a bag of ice from my garage freezer, and a stack of red Solo cups from the party supplies cupboard. I shoved everything into my rolling cooler. With both dogs leashed and poop bags stuffed into my pockets, the dogs pulled me, and I pulled the cooler down the street to the dog park.

The park was crowded on this sunny, unseasonably cool afternoon. As soon as I'd released the hounds into the enclosed dog-play area, Ryleigh pulled me aside. "I've looked at Tilda's text and browsing history for the past three months. There are no indications that she was depressed or considering suicide."

Love it when I'm right!

"So," Ryleigh continued, "that begs the question, what exactly happened to our dear friend?"

"I'd call that the proverbial $640,000 question."

"I thought it was $64,000."

"Inflation," I told her. I opened the cooler and proceeded to prepare a dozen cups of G&Ts. I passed them around. "To Tilda," I said, offering my red Solo for a toast.

"To Tilda," chorused the small crowd.

"May she be enjoying a G&T wherever she is." I brought my cup to my lips, but before I could take a sip, Ryleigh stopped me.

"Wait." She held up her hand. "Small point of order. Tilda is not enjoying a G&T anywhere. She never touched the stuff."

"What?" That didn't make sense. She was drinking gin when she tumbled down the steps. I saw an empty bottle of gin by her body.

Ryleigh shook her head. "Tilda said some old guy got her really drunk on 'em when she was in high school, and swore off them the rest of her life. Wouldn't even touch gin."

Hmmm. That was a puzzler. Added to the other idiosyncrasies we'd discovered I was beginning to think there was more to Tilda's death than met the proverbial eye. I stared into my G&T as if it held the answers. It did not.

Babs shared Tilda's affinity for drink. No surprise after a few moments of silence she offered up a tribute of her own. "Tilda would have appreciated us enjoying any kind of adult beverage in her honor. I propose a toast to the woman who was the lifeblood of this neighborhood, who always had a good story, whether it was true or not."

We all chuckled, raised our glasses, and chorused, "Hear, hear!"

The G&T went down smoothly. Too smoothly. I listened with half an ear as the neighbors shared memories of Tilda. The other half an ear listened to a tiny little voice in my head that ran through the oddities of Tilda's death. The bottle of gin by her side. The fact she didn't go upstairs when she was drinking yet was found at the bottom of those steps. The browsing history that didn't hint at any depression or thoughts of suicide. Her house which had been tossed in search of something. But what secret could an 85-year-old retired schoolteacher have that was so important it led to murder?

A vital clue tap-tap-tapped inside my skull, but I was unable to decode the message. I was missing something critical that would connect the asterisks on the report on Tilda's death. The tapping wasn't Morse Code or anything helpful, just incessant tapping. *Tap. Tap. Tap.*

Ryleigh joined me by the fence, startling me out of my musings. "Thinking big thoughts?"

"Huh?" I looked at her. "Sorry, I made a quick mental trip to la-la land. What's up?"

Ryleigh took my hand and gave it a nice, strong, I'm-here-for-you-sister squeeze. "Tilda's death is so hard to process. I'm pushing it all away right now. Shoved it to the back corner of my mind and built a brick wall around it. I'll deal with it all later. Maybe never." She took a long draw on her G&T.

Everyone processed death differently. I wasn't sure Ryleigh's way was the healthiest, but it seemed to be working. She tilted her head skyward and smiled. I hadn't smiled all day. Couldn't imagine ever smiling again.

I turned around and mimicked Ryleigh's elbows-on-fence pose. "Something's bugging me about the events surrounding Tilda's death." I laid out the things I'd been thinking. "But I'm missing something. Help me walk through the early hours of the morning."

We started with Hooch howling and went through us entering the house, creeping up the steps, and discovering the body.

"Wait!" I replayed the scene again to be sure. "Tilda's front door was opened a crack when we got there, remember?"

Ryleigh nodded. "So, the wind pushed it open?" She didn't sound convinced, and failed miserably at convincing me.

"It was a windless night. She always locked her door. Even when taking out the trash."

We both chuckled at the memories of phone calls we'd get from Tilda to come unlock her door. Sometimes at two in the morning.

Ryleigh seemed to consider the unlikelihood Tilda had left her door not only unlocked, but open.

I blew out an impatient breath. "Don't you see? Someone else must have been in the house with her. Someone who wasn't as careful about locking doors."

"Who and why?"

"I don't know. Looking for something? Or maybe . . ." I couldn't finish the thought.

"Maybe what?"

"Maybe killing Tilda. The mystery person could have pushed Tilda down the stairs or something."

"Oh, dear gawd, Pilar. Are you saying Tilda was murdered? The cheese has done slipped off your cracker, girlfriend. No more G&T's for you." She reached to remove the Solo cup from my hands.

I turned away before she grabbed it and took another sip while another little tidbit clicked into place. My hands shook as I pulled out my phone for confirmation. I scrolled through Tilda's last text about the business league boxes. I'VE HIDDEN THEM FROM THE BAD GUY. HA HA HA.

I'd thought she was joking, but maybe she had been serious and there really was a bad guy. And maybe, just maybe, he had been responsible for Tilda's untimely demise.

So now the $640,000 question was: What had the bad guy been looking for? Maybe more importantly, was the information hiding in the boxes I'd collected from Tilda's? Inquiring minds wanted to know. Sort of.

"Come on," I said to Ryleigh, grabbing her by the elbow and pulling her toward the gate. "Time to channel your inner Nancy Drew. We've got us a mystery to solve."

CHAPTER TEN

"Good god, what happened in here?" Ryleigh walked across the Natti/Hooch playtime disaster area that had once been my so-clean-you-could-eat-off-it kitchen floor. No matter how tippy-toed she tried to walk, her Birkenstocks crunched something with every step.

"The dogs had some fun while I took a siesta." It looked worse standing in the middle of the mess than it had while assessing it from my perch on the sofa. It would take great effort and energy to properly clean up. Beyond my ability to deal with right now.

It's like Ryleigh could read my mind. "I'll sweep," she offered. "You grab the boxes we swiped from Tilda who took them from Kinney."

In all the chaos of the past few hours, I had completely forgotten about Kinney. Poor guy, sitting in a jail cell. I hoped we'd hear the details soon.

The two boxes were on the floor by the sofa, currently under the guardianship of two snoozing pups.

I lifted and placed the first box on the counter that separated the kitchen area from the family-room space. With my hands resting on opposite sides of the lid, I hesitated. "Did you study Pandora's box in Greek mythology?"

"Of course. A source of great and unexpected trouble. Where did that come from?"

"I have a bad feeling."

"Open it already," Ryleigh snapped. "Let's get this over with, 'cuz as soon as I'm done sweeping here, I'm going straight home to crash. It's been a long, emotional day."

That was the understatement of the century.

A tremor of fear coursed through me as I lifted the lid. I waited for a swirl of evil spirits to be released into the air, but nothing happened. A peek inside the box revealed a treasure-trove of files.

Kinney got props for his organizational skills. Folders were clearly identified, in alphabetical order, and pages inside coincided with the labels. Most, but not all, were related to the Brookville Business League. The ones that weren't seemed to relate to his web design business. A quick flip through the printouts of the designed pages looked pretty benign. Author websites seemed to be his moneymaker.

Ryleigh had finished sweeping and now stood over my shoulder. "Find something interesting?"

"Not unless you find website design interesting."

"Nope." Ryleigh hauled out box two and began pawing through the well-organized files inside.

"I'm gonna need a shower after this," she said, holding up an 8 x 10 glossy by the corner for me to see.

A glance was all it took before I turned my head away. Like any red-blooded girl, I'd sneaked a peak at *Playgirl* back in the day, so it's not like I'd never seen pornographic images. But still, with it a few inches from my face, it made me feel icky.

"The whole box is full of pornographic images. Along with what appears to be a manuscript." She flipped through the coil-bound stack of papers, the scowl on her face deepening with every flip. She tossed it my way. "Ewww. I double-dawg dare you to read it."

"Yeah, so not my thing." I tossed it back. "But you could be holding on to the next *Fifty Shades* or something. Didn't I tell you about Kinney's career as a writer of mommy-porn?"

"What? Back that truck up." Ryleigh rocked back on her heels, arms akimbo, and gave me the look. "You been holding out on me?"

"No, it just wasn't anything that came up in polite conversation. His pen name was Diamonique Davis."

"Get out of town." Ryleigh laughed like I'd never heard her laugh. She even woke up the dogs. Not that they got up, merely lifted an eyebrow in her direction before going back to sleep. "I never would have guessed it from mild-mannered Kinney. Paws-itively scandalous, as Tilda would say."

"*Woof, woof, woof,*" I said. We bumped fists.

Ah, Tilda. It hurt to think I'd never see her again.

Tilda, who was friends with Kinney. Kinney, who had been arrested for something, but nobody knew what crime he had committed. Could there be a connection? Or simply a coincidence that an arrest and a possible murder occurred within forty-eight hours of each other? In a neighborhood that hadn't had a whisper of a felony for as long as I'd lived here?

"Let's go back to Tilda's. I want to take a look around, with a different perspective in mind."

Ryleigh hesitated. "You sure about that?"

"I think Hooch deserves closure." I ran my fingers through my short hair. "Honestly, I do, too."

Ryleigh's shoulders slumped. "Yeah, me too."

We left the dogs sleeping, after a firm admonishment from me not to get into any more trouble.

We walked west until we reached Tilda's home. As we'd done in the wee hours of the morning, we paused on the sidewalk and looked at the townhome. It looked exactly the same, to include the front door cracked open.

"Didn't you lock it after we left a little bit ago?" I asked.

"Of course I did."

We looked at each other. "Time to call the police," we said in unison.

Chapter Eleven

Saying you should do something is one thing, but actually doing it is quite another. We didn't call the police. I didn't want the police involved until I'd had another look around. I had no earthly idea what I expected to find that would connect Tilda and Kinney, but I hoped I'd know it when I saw it. Ryleigh agreed, reluctantly.

Once again, we crept up the stairs to the main living level of Tilda's home.

"Holy crap," Ryleigh said as we crested the top step.

"You took the words right out of my mouth." If possible, the room was in even worse shape than when we'd been there getting the boxes and cellphone a few short hours ago. So, either Tilda's ghost or somebody every much alive had returned to look for something. My gut told me it was the latter.

"We need to call the police," Ryleigh said in her brook-no-argument tone.

"Give me a minute." I walked to the bottom of the stairs leading to the third floor. It took every ounce of mind control I possessed not to stare at the blood stain. The only thing I needed to see was the gin bottle. The question that had been bugging me all day was if Tilda never ever drank gin, then why had there been a bottle on the floor next to her? I hadn't noticed it earlier, but I hadn't been looking.

So, where was the bottle now?

I scanned the area, expecting to find it in a corner or under a piece of furniture where it had been kicked when the medics tended to Tilda. Nope. No gin bottle anywhere.

Had it been there when we were looking for her cellphone? I tried to recreate our last visit in my mind's eye. I even scrunched my eyes, as if that would help, but I couldn't remember seeing it. But I couldn't remember *not* seeing it, either.

"I'm going upstairs," I told Ryleigh.

"Wait! What if the person who broke in is still up there hiding or something? It could be dangerous."

"If you hear me scream, call 9-1-1. And then save yourself."

Ryleigh pulled her cellphone out of her pocket and held it up, her thumb poised to hit the emergency call button. She positioned herself by the top step, one hand on the handrail, one foot pointing down the stairs. Yeah, she was gonna save herself before she called emergency. I'd do the same thing if I were in her Birkenstocks.

I climbed the stairs, one slow step at a time. My flip-flops didn't make a sound on the carpet, and I kind of wanted the bad guy to know I was coming, so I tapped my fist against the wall as I went. There were no sounds of an intruder scurrying for cover. That was a good thing, right?

The only sound I heard was my blood rushing past my eardrums. Good to know my heart could still pump in a stressful situation. I wish it would stop so I could hear a crazed killer's raspy breathing. Or maybe not.

While the hardwood floors downstairs were fairly new, the upstairs still had the carpet from the day Tilda moved in. The edges held onto the original beige, but the high-traffic area was now more of a dingy gray. What struck me as odd were the tiny little indentations, like pockmarks, that meandered around the upstairs like a *Family Circus* map. If I were a detective, which I am not, I'd deduce that someone wearing stilettos had trampled down the hallways and through the bedrooms. Hmm. Curious that, considering I'd never seen Tilda wear anything other than flat, sensible footwear.

Not wanting to contaminate the potential crime scene—for with every step I became more and more convinced that something really bad had happened here—I stayed to the edges as I skulked down the hall to the master bedroom.

It, too, had been tossed.

I pushed the bathroom door open and peaked in. What a flippin' mess. But it wasn't the disarray that made me scream. It was the words written in cherry red lipstick on the mirror.

GIVE IT TO ME, BITCH!

CHAPTER TWELVE

We really had called the police and explained to the very patient detective what we knew—and didn't know—about the events surrounding Tilda's demise. Since we'd been in the house so many times, they'd scanned our fingerprints right then and there with some amazing new technology, in order to eliminate us from the suspects list. Theoretically, that is. I suspected the detective had us pretty high on their list, considering we'd not only found the body, but also had phoned in the break-in.

That was five days ago. Not a peep from them, no updates on the case or more questions for us.

I wasn't sure we were ever going to have closure on this. Or see Kinney again, for that matter. He was still in jail and refused my request to speak with him. I'm sure he was too embarrassed. Rumor had it he'd been busted for possession of significant amounts of methamphetamine. He didn't have a meth lab in his house or anything, but law-abiding citizens didn't stockpile it in their homes unless they intended to sell it. Kinney didn't seem like the drug-dealer type, but as I've said before, there was a lot about Kinney I didn't know.

I'd kept my mind off the Grants Garden crime sprees by getting ready for Penelope's Puppy Shower scheduled for two o'clock. Everything was on track, granting me a few blissful moments to relax—but not sleep—for fear I'd sleep through the entire party. Yeah, I was that tired. So were the dogs, judging by the snores coming from the family room. The two were getting along great, wearing each other out. I should have adopted a playmate for Natti in the beginning. Hindsight's twenty-twenty.

The two boxes we'd retrieved from Tilda's still sat on my counter. They'd been there almost a week. Since the detectives assured me Tilda's death had been an accident, they weren't the least bit interested in the boxes. Frankly, once I saw the pornographic contents, neither was I. Now was as good a time as any to move them. I reached for the first box. Tilda's text ran through my mind, for about the ten-millionth time. What had she hidden and from whom?

I completely emptied the boxes again, thinking maybe there was a zip drive tucked under the bottom flap or some secret note that would explain everything. But there was nothing there we hadn't seen the first time.

After restocking the boxes, one item remained on the counter. Kinney's latest manuscript, titled *Ruff Day*. Maybe I was missing something. The title sounded like a pet-friendly cozy, quite a contradiction to whatever had elicited Ryleigh's disgusted reaction.

I opened to page one to judge for myself.

Nope, not a cozy. It took thirteen pages for me to realize the book was about the sexual escapades of a man on the dog agility circuit that detailed intimacies that made my skin crawl. In my sheltered life I had no idea such things even happened. Perhaps in an effort to make the story all-inclusive, the main character was a cross-dresser, one who had a penchant for stiletto shoes. Up until that last detail dropped, I'd cast Geoffrey Burnside in the starring role in the movie running in my mind. The physical description fit. The life's work matched. The character even owned two Australian shepherds. But stiletto-wearing cross-dresser?

Okay, maybe.

Could this be Geoffrey's biography?

Once I opened my mind to that, puzzle pieces started clicking into place. Could Kinney have written Geoffrey's biography without his permission? Maybe Kinney was blackmailing Geoffrey to keep it from being published? I imagined Geoffrey wanted that manuscript in order to preserve his reputation. Kinney must have told Tilda about it and asked her to keep it safe while he dealt with his legal issues. But did Geoffrey know that Tilda had some boxes? I may never know the answer to that, but it seems Geoffrey must have found out somehow and gone to Tilda's to retrieve the incriminating manuscript. If he had wanted to be incognito, say, dressed as a woman, that would explain the stiletto heel marks in the carpet. And his weight would certainly poke the high-heels into the old carpet. Heck, in heels, hefty Geoffrey would indent a solid wood floor.

But I couldn't imagine he went to Tilda's with murder on his mind. Perhaps he had tripped—I know from personal experience those shoes are a bitch to walk in—and knocked Tilda down the stairs. Or perhaps Tilda had tripped trying to escape and fallen down the stairs. Or maybe Geoffrey had pushed her out of his way, resulting in her fatal tumble. A horrible accident, but not murder.

Bottom line, Geoffrey had killed Tilda.

It all seemed crystal clear now.

If I went to the police with this crazy theory, would they haul me away in a straightjacket? Possibly, but then the puppy shower would be without a party planner.

If I accused Geoffrey of murder, would the police arrest him before the party? Probably, but then the puppy shower would be without a host. And a puppy. And I would be without the thousands of dollars I was fixin' to bill him.

And really, it wasn't very neighborly to accuse a neighbor—one who had engaged my professional event planning services—of being a killer without a shred of evidence. Everything I had so far was merely wild and crazy supposition.

Once the party was over, I'd enlist Ryleigh and maybe Babs to help me get some hard evidence to either convince myself he was a killer, or convince myself my whacky suppositions were nothing more than the result of an overactive, sleep-deprived mind.

I turned my focus to the party, the whole party, and nothing but the party, so help me gawd.

The next few hours passed by in a blur.

Thirty minutes before the guests were due to arrive, Ryleigh and I dragged a sanitized toilet bowl to the corner of Grant's Garden Dog Park, where it would serve as the water station for the dogs. I hoped to talk the homeowner's board into letting it stay, but I didn't get my hopes up. That group had zero sense of humor.

"Heard anything from the police about Tilda's murder?" Ryleigh asked.

"No," I said. "But Officer McNeely will be escorting the new pup from the county line to the party." That had been a major coup to my party preps. It had been as easy as asking . . . and making a sizeable donation to the Police Benevolent Fund, which would be added to Geoffrey's bill.

I certainly hoped the police had the case wrapped up, and I could stay out of it. As the day wore on, I doubted my conclusions about Geoffrey killing Tilda. It was but one of many, many possibilities for Tilda's death. I tried my very best to keep an opened mind.

"Oh, shoot," I said as the first dog and owner arrived. "I forgot to grab a trash can. A party for forty-five dogs and fifty people is going to produce way more trash than that tiny park bin can handle."

"Geoffrey's is sitting by his garage," Ryleigh, ever the quick problem solver, said. "I'll run and get it."

"Thanks."

I greeted each of the guests, gave them dog tags with their names, and pointed out the food and drink.

While the guests mingled, I ran the first bag of trash to Geoffrey's bin. When I lifted the lid and prepared to heft the garbage in, something gave me pause. Were my eyes playing tricks on me? I held my breath—the bin reeked of eau de doggie waste—and pushed my head in further to make sure I'd seen what I thought I saw. Yup. One lonely bottle lay amidst the discarded poop bags and other household detritus. An empty bottle of Orbium Gin. Identical to the one that had been lying by Tilda's dead body. The one that had disappeared. Really, what were the odds?

A moment of panic set in. I had wanted proof, and there it was in Geoffrey's trash can. Hiding in plain sight. Sort of.

Should I grab it and turn it over to the police?

NO! I'd already contaminated one crime scene, and I'd learned my lesson. Do not touch anything.

I didn't. But it would have to wait. The photographers from the national dog magazines had arrived. This could be my big business break.

I hauled Geoffrey's bin back to his driveway. I then trotted to my house, grabbed my rolling trash bin, and hauled it to the party just as Penelope arrived with her police escort. Everyone cheered, and every dog barked. People drank and ate. Dogs played and pooped. At least that was my perception of things, because my mind was a million miles away. I paid more attention to Geoffrey's trash can across the street than I did to the party. I didn't want the evidence disappearing without a trace.

"What's up with you?" Ryleigh tipped a bottle of Downward Dog Brew into her mouth.

"What do you mean?"

"You keep looking towards Geoffrey's house. Is there some big surprise waiting? I know, you arranged for a Paw Patrol after all!" She grinned.

"If you only knew," I replied.

Geoffrey joined us at the food table. He sported the dog-agility-circuit attire of plaid shirt, blue blazer, Dockers, and black athletic trainers. He had some big feet, like size thirteen, at least. He could definitely leave some holes in carpets if he were wearing stilettos.

"Good afternoon, Pilar," he said in that pompous way he had.

"Hello, Geoffrey." Should I be worried that I was carrying on a polite conversation with a deranged killer? Had it not been for all the people around, including one police officer with a gun on his hip, I would be so scared they would officially declare me witless. As it was, I was only majorly discomfited.

"Isn't she cute?" Geoffrey nodded his head toward a sleeping Penelope cradled in his arms.

"Adorable." I reached out and stroked her silky nose.

Amber sidled over, dressed way to sexy for a puppy shower, in my opinion. She was here in the role of dog walker, yet her apple-green knit dress was so short that if she bent over to scoop the poop, her lady parts would be on display for all the world to see. But maybe that was the point.

"This is a great party," Geoffrey said. "I admit, I had my doubts you could pull it off."

Well, that was a slap-slap backhanded comment. Yet it's still nice when a client is happy with the results. Even if the client is a killer.

A pack of dogs ran past, chasing a frisbee. Hooch stopped, sniffed the air, and then looked right at us. The hairs on the back of his neck rose, and he dropped on his belly in hunter-ready-to-attack mode. That was odd behavior for Hooch.

His rage seemed pointed at Geoffrey.

"Get that mangy mutt away from me," Geoffrey ordered, clearly frightened.

"What, is he rabid or something?" Amber asked, from where she'd taken shelter behind Geoffrey.

"Hooch," Ryleigh called. "I've got a treat." She led the dog back to the pack, bless her heart.

The animosity Hooch had showed Geoffrey scared the beejezus out of me. But if he had witnessed the man killing his owner, it would be justified. That was the last bit of evidence I needed.

If we could use Hooch in the police line-up, he'd identify Geoffrey as the killer. But is that admissible in court?

"Question for you," Geoffrey said, once calm had returned. "I've been so busy working with this little sweetheart I haven't heard what's going on around here. Any word on why Kinney was arrested?"

"All kinds of rumors but nothing concrete. Why?"

"Just curious." Geoffrey rocked gently side to side, the way a mother does when trying to calm a fussy baby. "He was my neighbor, and I miss having him next door. Plus, he's got some things of mine I need to get back."

Things like a manuscript that tells the true tale of your depraved lifestyle? I was feeling brave and decided to try to prove my theory. "Yeah, I had the same problem," I said. "He had our business league files. But I've got them back now. Or I should say, Tilda got them back for me."

The look Geoffrey gave me made my skin more than crawl. It made me want to run, screaming, for the hills.

My mind processed the ramifications at a slower pace.

He knows I have the manuscript.

He's killed once for the manuscript.

He's gonna kill me next.

I could not let that happen.

"Excuse me," I said, my voice not quite as steady as I would have liked. "I see someone I need to speak with."

I took off running. All forty-five dogs thought it was a game and gave chase, yipping and nipping at my heels.

When I reached the gate, my adrenaline surged like it had never surged in my life, enabling me to leap over the four-foot fence in a single bound.

Picking up speed, I raced after the police car easing out of a parking spot. I jumped on the trunk, did a belly flop on the cruiser's roof, and then slid until my head hung over the windshield. From my upside-down vantage point, I could see Officer McNeely's startled face through the glass.

I banged on the glass and yelled in one of those the-zombies-are-after-me screeches. "Geoffrey killed Tilda. And he's gonna kill me, too!"

CHAPTER THIRTEEN

Adrenaline surges are funny things. They activate in the blink of an eye and give you Super Woman capabilities, but can take their own sweet time melting away. Three hours later I still buzzed like my hands were touching an electric fence. Geoffrey was safely behind bars with no possibility of parole, so nothing to worry about, right?

Time for a Netflix and vino break. A binge session of *The Great British Baking Show*, accompanied by a glass of my favorite pinot grigio, would surely settle my nerves.

Natti and Hooch had taken themselves upstairs to stretch out on my luxury foam mattress, totally pooped after the party. That left the entire sofa for me. Stretching out the entire length, I relaxed against the pillows to enjoy a nice long nap. I would wake up covered in pet hair, but like I've always said, you're never fully dressed without some dog fur. I firmly believed that.

I closed my eyes.

Then I heard a noise. Soft footsteps on the stairs. Not dog nails clicking against the hardwood, but more of a tapping, like high-heeled shoes against the tread.

I muted the TV and sat still as a statuette, listening, my ears straining for the slightest noise.

Silence.

I looked at my wine glass. Half full. It's not like I was blitzed off my butt. Could exhaustion cause auditory hallucinations? They must.

I settled back against the cushions and unmuted the show.

"You've got a bit of a soggy bottom," Paul Hollywood told the amateur baker.

Tap.

I sat up straighter.

"It's a shame," Prue Leith said. "You left too much moisture in the fruit."

Tap.

That was not my imagination. Someone was creeping up my steps. "Ryleigh?" I called. I'd given her a key a few months ago when I went out of town, but she would text me or ring the doorbell to see if I was home.

Ryleigh did not respond.

I looked over my shoulder towards the stairs.

Tap.

The top of a head emerged above the top step. Blond. Bangs.

I tried to scream, but my vocal cords failed me. All that came out was a strangled gurgle.

Tap.

A face emerged.

"Amber?" I called. "How'd you get in?"

Tap.

She climbed another step, revealing her torso. Her arm bent in an unusual angle to accommodate something she was holding in her hand. It looked like a tiny gun, a harmless toy. But looks, especially when it came to guns, could be deceiving.

She pointed the barrel right at me. "Give it to me, bitch." Her raspy voice was straight out of a horror movie.

If her goal was to scare the beejezus out of me, she'd succeeded.

"I . . . I . . . I don't understand." But suddenly I did. Amber had trashed Tilda's home. Amber had left the message on Tilda's bathroom mirror. Amber had left the stiletto pock marks in Tilda's carpet. Amber had tossed the empty gin bottle in Geoffrey's trash can. Amber was who Hooch had growled at during the puppy shower. Amber had killed Tilda. "Why?"

A sinister smile crept across her face as she planted both feet on the floor. "I wanted my manuscript back. Kinney said it was crap and wouldn't help me publish it. But I figured I could make more money if I blackmailed Geoffrey, only that rat bastard Kinney wouldn't give it back to me. It was my only copy after my laptop mysteriously disappeared."

The gun was vibrating a bit. Or was it my head vibrating? One of us was shaking nervously. Maybe both of us.

She raised her arm holding the gun and took direct aim at my head, and then took a wobbly step in my direction. "At the risk of repeating myself, give it to me, bitch."

A guttural growl sounded, but it didn't come from Amber.

It came from Natti as he lunged, the full force of his 120 pounds hitting her right between her shoulders.

She went down. Hard.

The gun went off. Loud.

Natti grabbed Amber by the hair and held on tight.

Hooch sunk his teeth into Amber's leg as if it were a tasty rawhide treat

The two tugged on Amber like it was a game of tug-tug-tug.

She dropped the gun to use both hands to wrestle the dogs. Neither was gonna give up.

If I didn't step in, they were gonna kill her. Which she probably deserved, but it wasn't something I wanted to witness.

I picked up the gun and pointed it at her. "Natti, heel," I ordered.

He complied, and came and sat calmly at my side, but his eyes didn't leave his prey.

"Hooch, come here, honey."

He skulked to my side, baring his teeth as he walked past Amber's head.

She started to stand up. The dogs growled in perfect harmony, deep, guttural, make-a-move-and-I'll-be-on-you-like-you-are-a-juicy-porkchop growls. She glanced between the dogs, looked at the gun in my hand, and then dropped to the ground. She cradled

her head in her hands and wept.
It was then I realized I was bleeding. A lot. And it hurt. A lot. Who'd have guessed Amber was such a crack shot?

Chapter Fourteen

It was my first Yappy Hour since being shot. I went down early to enjoy the beautiful summer day and use the quiet time to contemplate life, and other things.

Kinney walked through the gates. "Okay if I join you?"

I slid over on the bench, making room for him.

We sat in companionable silence.

Kinney had been released from jail after Amber confessed to planting the drugs and snitching to the cops. She needed him out of his house so she could search for the manuscript.

"How are you feeling?" he asked. The concern in his voice was real.

I placed my hand on the bandage wrapped around my middle. It still hurt. A lot. But the docs had promised me a full recovery. The bullet had miraculously missed any vital organs on its path through my left side. A clean exit wound is a good thing, I'm told. It had embedded itself in my wine rack (again, miraculously missing any vital bottles of my private wine collection). The police kept the bullet as evidence, but the hole left behind was gonna make a great story for anyone who asked. "I'll be fine, thanks."

Amber was in jail, hopefully for a long, long time. The police told me Amber's prints were all over the gin bottle, which she had used to beat Tilda about the head. She'd also confessed to beating Hooch with it, too. For that alone, she deserves the electric chair. Tilda's cause of death was officially a tumble down the stairs, which

Amber claims was accidental. It would be up to the courts to figure that out.

Still, what a tragic ending to Tilda's wonderfully carefree life.

Hooch came over and sat by Kinney. He rubbed the dog under the chin. "You probably thought me rude when I refused your jail visit, but I didn't want to drag anyone else into this drama. I had warned Tilda someone was after the manuscript, but I wasn't in a position to give her the details. I never imagined Amber was capable of killing. I still haven't processed what happened."

He turned away, but not before I saw tears in his eyes.

I waited while he calmed himself down. "That *Ruff Day* was pretty, ah, rough reading, huh?"

Kinney smiled, a weak smile, but a smile none-the-less. "Yeah, you probably figured out whose life it was based on."

I nodded. "Geoffrey Burnside's. Paws-itively scandalous," I said. "*Woof, woof, woof.*"

He smiled again. We bumped fists.

"As long as we're telling all here, can I ask you something personal?"

He nodded.

"I read on the Internet about you. Some things concern me. Like you had five wives, some dying under suspicious circumstances. And you write mommy-porn under the name Diamonique. And you're a vegetarian, and yet I've seen you eat meat down at the deli."

Kinney laughed. "You have done your homework, my friend. I'm impressed. But you know you can't believe everything you read on the Internet. I'm a publisher, not an author. I farm out story ideas to my stable of writers and publish them under Diamonique's name. I have ten writers, and we push out twelve titles a year. Lots of money to be made in mommy porn, if you market it properly. Selling books is about likes and followers and retweets. My life here isn't exactly exciting, so I sometimes throw out some, ah, misinformation. Stir the pot, if you will. For the record, my one and only wife, died of breast cancer five years ago. You can Google that if you want. Her name was Helena J. Copeland." His voice cracked as he spoke her name.

"I'm sorry for your loss, and I'm happy to know you didn't kill anyone. And that you're not a vegetarian."

We both laughed.

Ryleigh, Chewy, and Babs entered the dog park. Ryleigh carried two of the biggest rawhide bones I'd ever seen, each tied with a big red bow. "These are for my furry heroes," she said, offering one each to Natti and Hooch." If you hadn't barked your heads off alarming the neighbors, your mommy would have bled out on the floor."

It's true, my dogs had saved my life. I don't remember the specifics, but I'd been told that one of my neighbors had come to see what the commotion was about and found me laying on the floor in a pool of blood. It wasn't until I regained consciousness the next day that I could tell them who'd shot me. Amber had been captured at her brother's cabin in the mountains where she'd gone to "clear her head," as she'd told her family. Yeah, I'd like to clear *more* than her head, but I'm trying to forgive. I doubt I'll ever forget. Amber is in jail, now, hopefully for a long, long time.

More people arrived and Yappy Hour officially commenced.

"What's in your Yeti today?" Ryleigh asked.

I held up the gallon jug containing a fresh batch of icy basil-lime martinis and poured the beverage into red Solo cups. When everyone had a drink in their hand, I held mine high in the air. "Today I'm serving a little something I like to call Paws-itively Scandalous."

The assembled group chorused, "*Woof, woof, woof.*"

THE END

RUFF GOODBYE

By Rosemary Shomaker

Bar owner Len Hayes' frenemy Perry Lambert brings misery to all. Len finds himself strong-armed into shady business dealing by Winks family human attack dog Rocco Moretti, compliments of Perry. Len's grief over his best friend Curt's cancer death imbalances him, and everything unravels at Curt's funeral home visitation. The bar's stoic black Lab and Curt's miniature poodle have Len's back and resolve the mayhem.

ROSEMARY SHOMAKER *writes about the unexpected in everyday life. She's the woman you don't notice in the grocery store or at church but whom you do notice at estate sales and wandering vacant lots. In all these places she's collecting story ideas. Rosemary writes mystery, women's fiction, and paranormal short stories. Stay tuned as she takes her first steps toward longer fiction. She's an urban planner by education, a government policy analyst by trade, and a fiction writer at heart. Rosemary credits Sisters in Crime with developing her craft and applauds the organization's mission of promoting the ongoing advancement, recognition, and professional development of women crime writers.*

Chapter One

Len Hayes planned this would be the club's last meeting. Now to tell the others. He slowly rapped his knuckles on the oaken bar three times as he often did to cut through the din of the establishment, although at eleven o'clock this Wednesday evening The Beacon was mostly empty. Four men sat on barstools and two tables held late diners.

Len spoke softly to the two men at the end of the bar. "Gentlemen, please retire to the P&P Club, and we'll toast our fallen member." Perry Lambert and Charlie McFadden pushed off their stools and headed for Len's office in one of the bar's back rooms. Len stopped The Beacon's young waitress Marsha, once she cleared the men's glasses from the bar and before her circuit into the fresh blue and white dining area.

"Marsha, please let Joyce know the P&P Club members are gathering."

"Yes, I'll let her know. I was about to hand her today's mail anyway. And Len," Marsha continued, "You might want to check on Clarion. Perry may have knocked him over. I saw him handling the statue earlier. He said his jacket got hung up on it."

Len nodded. The black Labrador retriever replica, in its alert guard position, was The Beacon's sentinel. Leave it to Perry to knock over the bar's mascot. He'd check the statue for damage later. He didn't want to add defilement of The Beacon's faithful friend to his list of grievances against Perry.

He turned away before Marsha listed all her observations of the day. That woman could talk and talk. Before he took one step in the direction of his office, George Yeonas blew in. A low-pressure system colliding with a cold front worsened the fickle April weather, and swales of diagonal rain followed George in The Beacon's front door.

"Safe port in a storm, eh, Len?" George said.

Len chuckled. George's comment and dramatic entrance, along with the rainsquall, complemented the bar's nautical theme and decor.

George hung his dripping windbreaker on a hook along the entry wall. He let his hand drop to stroke the head of the twenty-seven-inch dog statue beside the hostess podium. Clarion, the stoic black Labrador retriever, looked on. Beacon regulars formed emotional bonds with the hand-cast stone sculpture of a seated Labrador, especially George, who had won the name-the-mascot contest nine years ago, soon after The Beacon opened. After one last pat on the statue's head, he joined Len in the aisle.

"I'm not late, am I?" George asked.

"No. We'll have a short meeting tonight, though," Len said. "We should have done this earlier. Maybe gone to Curt's house and had a meeting there."

George shrugged. "There's no good way, Len, when someone is dying. And no easy way to know what's best."

As Len and George bypassed the ocean-hued kitchen door, Len glanced at the red-topped tempest within—Joyce—in chef garb, clattering dishes and clanging pots. His view through the porthole window distorted his wife's image. Escaping locks of her lustrous coppery hair, barely subdued with a headband, waved and floated as if underwater. He'd found the right partner in Joyce. She was crucial to The Beacon. From her insistence on an ocean blue and sea foam white paint scheme and use of blond wood, to her maritime-meal-of-the-day menu.

Len and George descended three steps and entered a door on the right. Inside, the tile-floored office gave way to a thick-carpeted seating area where three caramel-colored club chairs flanked a mahogany coffee table. To the side, five dark wooden captain's chairs ringed a large circular table. A sizeable flat screen TV on the far wall completed the man cave, its ambiance markedly different from that of The Beacon's public areas.

Charlie sat in a club chair. Perry hovered near the round table.

"You've got jazz playing in this room, Len. How about piping it into the bar?" Perry suggested in his thin, reedy voice.

"And displace 'Yellow Bird,' 'Sloop John B,' and 'Haul Away Joe?'" George asked, grinning.

"Yeah. Marsha read the latest restaurant review to us," Charlie said. "'The Beacon's unique seafaring appeal, in a city with tavern choice limited to dark and old, austere minimalist, or characterless sports bars, guarantees its continued popularity.' The review cited 'the inspired sea shanty and maritime soundtrack as critical to the bar's charm.'"

George added, "Joyce does a nice job of including fishing and sailing music from Canada, the UK, and the Caribbean, along with American-sourced music. In my opinion."

"Thanks for your unsolicited business advice," Len said to everyone, but he glared at Perry. Perry's suggestions had led to trouble too many times. "Don't mess with my brand, friends. As long as I have this oasis," Len motioned to the expanse of his office, "I can live with sun-and-ocean overload."

Len's glower did nothing to censure Perry. Indeed, Len was startled when Perry called the P&P Club to order. "Gather by the table, gentlemen. Tonight's meeting is in memory of Curtis Blankenship Powell, our friend and P&P brother."

Len sniped in a low voice, "Oh, geez. Who made you Master of Ceremonies, Perry? I was his best friend."

"What's that, Len? Hold our commemorations until later," Perry said, questioning, yet at once dismissive.

George put his hand on Len's back, in support or in restraint, Len wasn't sure.

The 1994 Fonseca vintage port breathed in a round-bottomed crystal carafe on the circular table. Perry had stopped at The Beacon in the afternoon to decant the fortified wine.

"George, Perry may have dinged Clarion," Len said under his breath. "Marsha found him righting a toppled Clarion earlier today. He said his coat snagged on it. I'm not responsible if I go off on him."

"Clarion looked okay when I came in. Relax, Len," George said.

Len couldn't relax. Since Curt's death, his equilibrium was shattered. His head spun, thinking about the club and its repercussions. Last year when Perry suggested they form a once-a-month port club, the regulars at the bar laughed, yet here they were. The club had met on the third Wednesday of the month for the past fourteen months. That Curt would miss this serving of the club's best port further soured Len's mood.

Perry's pretentious tales of worldwide vintage port soirees and the accompanying traditions and rituals were legendary. And considered bluster. "Put up or shut up," Perry had challenged, and he offered to provide the first three months' starter ports and to school them in proper port imbibing etiquette.

Against better judgment, and curiously led by Curt, they had formed a five-man club. Perry pushed Len to open his backroom office for meetings and to allow members to invite other Wednesday night regulars at The Beacon to occasionally join them. Charlie made small, wooden P&P Club shields for each of them in his woodshop.

The club's run had its blissful moments of "oenophilic" epiphanies. Perry's lessons to the club included haughty terminology. "The Greek *oinos* means wine. You'll be oenophiles, wine connoisseurs specializing in port, when I'm done with you," Perry boasted.

Sadly, Perry's largesse was coupled with his aberrance, and two of those bombs had exploded. Perry's lust for the ladies, and his nefarious business connections, had hurt both Curt and Len. The name change from the Port & Porn Club to the Port & Poker Club occurred after the first crisis. Charlie altered the club's shield insignia, a token and meaningless action, in Len's opinion.

The second of Perry's transgressions necessitated, in Len's

mind, club dissolution.

George nudged Len to get his attention as Perry said, "Curtis Powell. One heck of a guy."

The four men raised their copitas. "Hear! Hear!" Charlie, George, and Len chorused as they toasted the empty chair and lone, table-bound glass of port. Each lowered his glass, and before sipping, swirled the opaque purple-colored liquid and drew the tulip-shaped glass to his face.

As Len savored the pungent aroma concentrated by the glass' narrow taper—an inviting nose of spice, violets, and berries—he lost track of what the others did. Len sipped in Curt's memory, satisfied with the black cherry, smoke, and currant layers of flavor, the well-integrated brandy and tannins, and the sweet finish.

The four imbibed in silence. Perry set his glass on the table. Shifting his jaw and mumbling something about a loose crown, Perry excused himself and left the room. To the men's room, Len surmised. The four sat in silence, each lost in his thoughts.

Perry returned quickly. "Any words?" he asked, motioning with his glass to Len.

George once again put his hand on Len's back, and to Len's relief, no one spoke.

Len couldn't bring himself to announce the final dismissal of the club, not when they had so solemnly bid their friend Curt goodbye. Len knocked three times on the round table and jerked his chin to the door, signaling the end of the meeting. These four men still had a bond, one that Len was loath to sever so soon after Curt's passing. But, in time, sever it he would.

The P&P Club regulars walked single-file out of The Beacon's backroom led by Charlie, and then George. Perry held back a step before he and Len followed, allowing space for Curt—a missing man formation. They climbed the three steps into the bar proper and proceeded toward the front door.

George grabbed his jacket and patted the mascot's head. "Good dog, Clarion. Work as hard for Len as your ancestors did for the fishermen of Newfoundland—"

Perry interrupted, "Yeah, yeah. His noble breed's fifteenth

century origins in Newfoundland, not in Labrador, yada, yada. You won the mascot-naming contest, already. Clarion, for the Lab's loud, clear, attention-getting howl. We get it." He and Charlie collected their coats, tapped Clarion's head, and trailed George out the door, masking Perry's derisive comment with smiles and chuckles.

Len felt it, though. Perry's loutish ways didn't win him friends, they invited trouble. Perry's quasi-retirement life, however, didn't suffer. His word-of-mouth housesitting assignments kept him busy, and Len saw cars and trucks dropping by and taking Perry places or working with him on some garage projects. Perry had a social life and was never at a loss to share a story about a short trip he took or event he attended.

Len poked his head into the night air. The blowing rain had calmed to a permeating mist. As he held the blue and white color-blocked door open, Len called to the group on the sidewalk, "See you at the funeral home at seven o'clock, Perry. George, you and Charlie are covering the three o'clock to five o'clock visitation, right? I know Curt's wife could use the support."

Charlie called, "George and I will be at the funeral home at two o'clock." Stopping to face Len, Charlie added, "Merle Overby is the manager at Last Respects. I'll make sure they treat Sharon—and Curt—well."

Perry shouted over his shoulder, "Len, yes. I'll see you at seven o'clock tomorrow." As Perry hurried to catch Charlie, he called out, "So that investment opportunity in the Sincere Serenity line of funeral homes is working out for you, Charlie?"

Len scanned the parking lot and his heart stung. He'd subconsciously been looking for Curt's silver Toyota Tacoma, expecting to see the truck with Curt's most valued truck accessory, his bright-eyed miniature poodle, Cloud, at an open window. The shy gray and black little thundercloud always waited for Curt in the truck.

Len shook off the melancholy. Remembering Curt's defense

of poodles in the face of "sissy dog" insults from Beacon clientele, his heart warmed. Curt's recitations of poodle qualifications reduced George's Labrador retriever breed history to a footnote. The inclusion of poodles in Albrecht Durer's fifteenth- and sixteenth-century drawings and prints, and in Francisco Goya's eighteenth-century paintings, was of particular interest to Curt, as was the breed origin disagreement among international kennel clubs. The European kennel club cited the poodle's French origin. The British, American, and Canadian kennel clubs favored the German origin theory. "The German word *prudel* means 'to splash in water.' Need I say more?" was one of Curt's favorite lines. He delighted that the breed name of the waterfowl-retrieving poodle shared the same etymology as the English word puddle.

When challenged by Curt why The Beacon's mascot wasn't a poodle, Len cited Joyce's random find of the Labrador statue at an estate sale. Part of Len wished Clarion was a poodle, in Curt's honor. "Huh. I don't need a poodle to remind me of Curt. Not when I think of him every day," Len said to the stillness of the now vacant sidewalk.

Len closed and locked The Beacon's front door. What had Perry said about Charlie? That he'd invested in the Sincere Serenity funeral homes? Charlie and Sandra lived in Pekoe Acres, the same modest neighborhood where he and Joyce lived. Charlie was in middle management with Monacan Foods. Something about logistics. That Charlie had extra cash to invest in anything was a surprise, yet Charlie lately drove a new car, and he and his wife had enjoyed upscale vacations in the past two years. Family inheritance? Sandra's job success? Len was mystified but tossed the matter into the "not my business" file in his brain.

Len extinguished the neon "open" sign and cut power to the exterior high-mounted sconce, a commercial version of an old-fashioned lighthouse beacon, his establishment's symbol.

Joyce and Marsha had covered duties while Len met with the P&P members, and the bar had emptied. Official closing time was in twenty minutes, at midnight, but Len was done for the day. If patrons drove up, they'd see the beacon light turned off, and if they knocked on the door, well, he'd decide what to do then.

Len retraced his steps along the twenty-foot length of the white oak bar. He'd heard Joyce in the kitchen when the club members filed past on their way out. At his effortless tug, the kitchen door swung outward on the well-oiled hinges of an entry loosed by constant use, and he stepped through.

Joyce wiped her hands on a dishcloth. "You ready to go, honey? I let Marsha go home ten minutes ago. She cleaned and mopped the dining area and bar, and I've finished up here."

Len glanced left to right. Finding everything in order, he said, "Yes. Thanks for closing up, my love. Enough with the P&P Club. Enough with The Beacon. Let's go home."

"Wait. I didn't open the mail until Marsha left, and I want her to see this first thing in the morning." Joyce reached in a storage cupboard near the pantry shelves and lifted an oversized purse onto a stainless-steel worktable. She fished out a folded piece of paper.

Joyce was known for her purses, and this one was new—and worse—than the last. Len couldn't tear his eyes from the giant pansy print. The enormous purple and yellow flowers, easily ten times normal size, and their green leaves and stems, bright on a black background, screamed for attention.

Joyce noticed his interest and said, "Do you like it? I nabbed it on sale at The Gift Fairy while on my break. I love it!"

"It's colorful," he said. With her red hair, big jewelry, and Bohemian clothing, no one could accuse Joyce of being understated. Her love of all that was big and bright was genuine. Her eye-popping style matched her huge smile and huge heart.

"If Marsha gets here in the morning before we do, I want her to see this," Joyce said. She unfolded the paper and again dipped into her commodious handbag. Out came silver duct tape. She tore a piece from the roll and affixed the paper to the door of the commercial refrigerator.

"There. Marsha will see that. It's a notice from the health department. We're due for a food safety inspection."

Before Joyce slung her purse over her shoulder, she withdrew another item. "Is it still raining outside?" she asked as she held a cache of plastic rain bonnets.

Len knew better than to challenge Joyce on her one point of self-consciousness. Joyce said her hair was both the gift and the bane of her existence. Humidity in any form morphed her hair from manageable to wild, or in Len's opinion, from beautiful to sensuous. He thus departed The Beacon with his wife donning a granny's cheap plastic rain bonnet.

Chapter Two

After a full afternoon at The Beacon, including an employee meeting about the upcoming health department inspection, Len and Joyce put the bar in the capable hands of Marsha, chef Joey Hall, and two new waitresses. They then set off in a light rain for Curt's visitation.

The Last Respects funeral home sat on a slight rise at the corner of two heavily traveled streets, surrounded by Bradford pear, ginkgo, Japanese maple, and crepe myrtle trees. Medians of ornamental grasses, and cotoneaster and yew bushes, adorned the generous parking lot. Wide walkways guided visitors from parking spaces on three sides of the building, leading them past azalea, shrub roses, and annual flowerbeds to the building's main entrance.

Last Respects' other clients—the dead—arrived and departed via the drive-through carport on the building's west side. The rear alley served as a lane for emergency vehicles and as garbage truck access to dumpsters.

"No calls yet," Joyce said.

"Joyce, they are fine at The Beacon. Marsha will make sure they close properly tonight, and they'll open the bar for us tomorrow, so we can go to Curt's funeral. It's all under control."

"I know, I know. I just wanted to hear customer feedback on my Maritime Meal Mussels Special," Joyce offered as an excuse as she kneaded her hands. "This funeral home looks fancy. How is it we've never come here before? Hmm. Maybe I was here years ago for a funeral."

"We're getting to the age, I'm sorry to say, when we'll no doubt become familiar with all the city's funeral homes," Len said. "Whoa. Full house tonight. Look at all these cars." Selecting a promising parking area, Len veered the car into a row on his left.

Joyce smiled as she craned her neck in awe at the crowd. "Not many open spaces left."

The car that had driven in behind them trolled for a parking space in an adjacent aisle. It was no one they knew.

Joyce's face sagged. "Oh. I forgot. These big funeral homes usually host more than one visitation at a time. These people are not here for Curt."

Len scanned the cars. He saw Curt's Takoma, and his heart leaped only to descend in despair. "That's a jolt to see Curt's truck. You know, I looked for the truck last night when the P&P Club dismissed."

"I'm sorry, hon," Joyce said. "I bet you expected Curt drove it here."

"Yeah. For a minute, I did."

As they neared the truck, flashes of red between the Takoma and the SUV next to it drew their attention. Len braked. Three forms beside the truck resolved to Curt's widow Sharon, Perry Lambert, and a dog springing off its back legs, repeatedly raking its forepaws down a suited pant leg. Cloud's pawing was not done in play, but in attack.

Sharon slapped Perry's face.

Joyce bolted from the passenger door, her purse airborne but tethered by its shoulder strap.

"Okay, okay!" Perry said as he backed away from the truck.

Joyce dashed to Sharon's side, passing the slap-marked Perry as he turned and beelined to the funeral home entrance without a backward glance.

Len put the car in park.

Joyce hugged Sharon. "What happened?" she asked, her attention unwavering as she detached from the hug to pull on a hairdo-saving rain bonnet.

Len exited the car, walked to the Tacoma, and picked up the scampering poodle to set in Sharon's arms.

Sharon took Cloud in her arms and nuzzled him. "Oh, you are my protector, sweet Cloud."

"Are you okay, Sharon?" Joyce asked. "Were you leaving?"

"No. Of course not," Sharon said. She released Cloud into the truck and rearranged a towel to absorb any rain. With a ruffle to the poodle's neck scruff, Sharon said, "Cloud, stay. I'll check on you soon." She reset the window ventilation screen the dog had knocked out to defend Sharon. Once satisfied her canine charge was secure, Sharon turned to face Joyce.

She shook the burgundy garment she'd had folded over her arm. "It's cold in the funeral home, so I came out here to get my sweater." Sharon straightened, squared her shoulders, and began walking. "I'll tell you later what that was about. Come with me. I need to get back to the visitation. A crowd of Curt's coworkers from the VoTech Center has arrived, and I'm expecting Julie."

Joyce kept pace with Sharon, her plastic-ensconced head and jaunty pansy purse bobbing along a walkway as she dodged raindrops.

Len got back in the car to find a parking space.

He fumed that Perry would cause any trouble for Sharon today. He was also leery of Sharon's rebellious daughter Julie's role at the visitation. Would Julie be a balm or an irritant to Sharon?

Len pulled into a spot next to a panel truck with a full advertising wrap for DogFun Doggie Daycare. He exited his car and flinched. The vehicle's six-foot tall image of dogs jumping amid colorful balls was a bit terrifying, the garish vehicle ill-placed in a funeral home parking lot.

As he shut his car door, four people marched from the side garden to the main entrance. Only the middle-aged woman used an umbrella to deter the rain. Len recognized her as Lucy Powell, Curt's ex-wife. She carried a purse the size of a gym bag that rivaled Joyce's in bulk, but its smooth brown leather surface subdued its gargantuan quality. Joyce's purse may win flash and color awards, but this woman's gets the class—and expense—award.

The three men looked of an age to be Curt's sons. Len's brain connected the woman to the advertising-emblazoned van. Curt had mentioned his ex-wife Lucy had approached him about investing in her new business, DogFun, citing the profit possibilities from the buckets of money people spend on their dogs. "Len, I turned her down. You know, she doesn't even like dogs," Curt had said.

The sidewalk to the Last Respects front door sloped slightly uphill. The glass sliding doors, darkened with ultraviolet light protectant, seem staid and gave no hint as to what lay within. The landscaping of the grounds was flawless, but not showy. The eight graceful twelve-foot crepe myrtles standing guard along the semicircular drop-off drive were a nice touch, their smooth tan bark-and-branch arrangement exuding serenity.

Len trailed Lucy and her sons into the funeral home and stepped to the side of the doors to smooth his hair. Joyce, doffed rain bonnet dangling from her hand, was in the foyer, head tilted up and mouth agape. Curt's ex-wife, sons, and Sharon were nowhere in sight.

Once past the funeral home's tidy exterior and the simple doors, one had access to higher spirituality. That's the effect Len felt, and he reached for Joyce's hand in confirmation. They beheld a hanging sculpture of reflective vertical rods that reached toward the sparkling windows of the peaked roof.

Len hadn't thought to look up when he drove onto the property. He saw now how the high angled roof beams at the front over the lobby supported clear glass. Other skylights accented the ceilings of the two main corridors off the lobby.

The gently swaying prismatic rods drew the eye skyward in a most uplifting way. Len moved his eyes from the sky, visible above the sculpture, to the earthly view at his level. A modernist plant and fountain lobby centerpiece graced the space. Marble blocks and granite stones both protected the fountain and allowed seating.

Joyce had dropped his hand and her purse to do just that—sit on a boulder and gaze upward.

Beyond the lobby's astounding floor-to-ceiling art, Len made out a central welcome and office area. Suited staff greeted visitors, and discreet signage posted the events in progress. Len was close enough to hear when a female staff member greeted Joyce. She gestured in opposite directions and asked if Joyce wished to join the Winks or the Powell reception. Joyce replied, nodded her thanks, and returned to his side, her serenity broken.

"The fancy people are here for the Winks viewing," she said in a voice between a cry and a snarl. Lionel Winks was a city mover and shaker—and one Joyce did not like. "You're lucky to not have grown up in this city, Len. Lionel Winks pulled all the strings and caused pain to many. He's dead. But is he really, if his son fills his shoes?" She tilted her head to one broad passage. "Curt's visitation is on the other side of the lobby."

Len moved no closer to that landmine. He'd earlier asked Joyce her opinion of the Winks family, and she refused to answer, except to say that she and Sharon Powell knew of Winks' manipulations. He and Joyce had heard of Winks' death, and it was his bad luck that Last Respects scheduled Winks' and Curt's visitations at the same time.

Len stood sweating in the minefield of duplicity. He had hidden from Joyce that Perry had dragged him into questionable business dealings with Winks' son, Lionel junior.

Chapter Three

Len and Joyce found the Bluebell Salon along the funeral home's wide eastern corridor. They agreed to mingle and to check that all was running smoothly, so Sharon wasn't overburdened by guests or funeral home details.

"I'm going to stand with Sharon in the receiving line to help her remember names and move people along," Joyce said to Len before they separated.

The receiving line wound double in the reception room and trailed into the corridor. Len left the Bluebell Salon and sat in an upholstered chair in a furniture grouping offset from the funeral home's wide east hallway. As he was sideways to the hall's overflow receiving line queue, Len avoided greeting acquaintances, secure in their respect for his solitude. This was his best friend who had died.

This didn't mean Len didn't do a bit of scoping of his own. The owner of the No Frills barbershop stood in line with his staff. Two of Len's neighbors chatted with the barbers while shepherding Mr. and Mrs. Oldham, octogenarians the kindly neighbors likely piloted here from the Pekoe Acres.

Curt had helped the Oldhams with handyman tasks. He'd recruited Len to help him on Len's rare days off from The Beacon. George would also help, and Len wondered if Curt guaranteed the Oldham's upkeep by specifically bequeathing their care to George.

"Len," a high voice murmured, and he felt a hand pressing his shoulder. Len hated when men used this gesture. What demonstrated connection and comfort from a woman conveyed control and dominance from most men, especially when the hand's pressure was excessive.

The voice, elevated in pitch as well as spoken from above, was Perry's. He wore an expensive dark suit, the pants a little worse for wear due to Cloud's pawing. Len cringed at Perry's inappropriate scarlet shirt and black tie. He'd seen red in the parking lot earlier, but he'd thought his vision clouded with anger or attributed it to Sharon's sweater. No. The red he'd seen was part of Perry's indecorous ensemble.

From Perry's perch on the sofa, he leaned into Len's personal space. "Sorry you had to see that incident in the parking lot. A simple misunderstanding. I'll explain later."

Len battled his tight shoulder muscles, trying to relax. He fought his dislike of the man. Clearly Perry had upset Sharon in the parking lot. Had he, Curt, George, Charlie, and others from The Beacon been hoodwinked into accepting Perry as a regular?

Perry leaned back and crossed his legs, revealing red, black, and white rooster print dress socks. "We all feel the loss, Len. But we can honor Curt in many ways. I have an idea for a P&P Club activity in his name."

Before Len could stand and deliver a nose-punch to Perry, a hulking form eclipsed his field of vision. Len and Perry canted their heads to see what had absorbed the light, and they rose in unison, as if meeting a challenge.

A large man had blocked the light from the ceiling's recessed chandelier. Rocco Moretti's 5'11" wasn't quite as threatening to Len's 6'2" frame, but Perry's slim and fashion-curated 5'10" size was disproportionally disparaged by Moretti's 240-pound football player's bulk.

"You're in trouble. Each of you," Moretti said, shaking a finger at them.

A pressure detonator clicked under Len's feet. His discomfort with receiving bargain liquor matured into sweat-drenching fear. His forehead moistened. Perspiration coursed down his back, even while his throat dried to where he had to cough. He felt decidedly ill.

Moretti's hand moved in front of his muted, optically discordant Glen plaid jacket. The bulk of Moretti's shifting shoulder and arm unbalanced the jacket's fit so it hung unevenly. Moretti's charcoal button-down shirt, front placket separating and straining at the neck, added a nauseating backdrop to the crisscrossing patterns of the jacket's irregular checks.

Len switched his focus to Moretti's broad face. The close-up of Moretti's ruddy, stubbled face did little to retard Len's sick feeling.

Moretti glared at Len, his fists bunched. At the murmur of women's voices, Moretti swung his head to the sounds. They had an audience.

Forcing a swallow, Len put his hands up, palms outward. "Let's take this outside, gentlemen."

"Yeah. Follow me." Moretti stomped around an inconspicuous corner.

An emergency exit sign suspended from the ceiling indicated an exit door, and Perry and Len followed.

The drizzle hit Len's face like he'd misdirected the air freshener can in the bathroom after a sit-down. With unfocused technique, he usually sprayed himself. In the grassy side lot of the funeral home, a scent akin to "fresh rain" misted his face.

Len propped a shoe-sized rock in the doorframe, so they'd not be locked out. Flagstones set in a path of white gravel led from the building to three benches around a sundial. Moretti's bulk blocked the meager footlight illumination as if he was a human black hole absorbing the universe's energy. Len had arrived late to Moretti and Perry's discussion. Well, their argument.

"I will not take it easy on your buddy," Moretti said as Perry made urgent, palms-down, pumping motions with his hands. "Here he is now," Moretti continued. "I'm gonna deliver the Boss' message."

Len walked closer to them. "It's okay, Perry. Let him talk, and then we can all get back to our obligations."

Moretti jutted his chest and balled his hands into fists. He scowled over Len's left shoulder at the funeral home door they'd exited.

Len turned. A ten-inch gap narrowed, and the door bounced against the rock prop. He faced Moretti again and raised his eyebrows.

Moretti said, "Some lady in a ridiculous rain hat. I scared her off." He thrust his chin forward. "Back to business. Mr. Winks is having your order delivered Monday. Four cases of mixed spirits. Next month it'll be six cases."

"I didn't place any orders with your group," Len said through clenched teeth.

Perry said, "Len, I told you an ongoing arrangement would be profitable. My delivery to you was only the beginning. Winks does business with half the bars in town."

With slow deliberateness, feeling one long neck muscle stretch and another contract, Len turned his head to face Perry. Len's hands bunched and his lower arm muscles tightened. "Yeah. Thanks, 'buddy.' You keep bringing the joy, don't you?"

Perry stepped back.

Moretti grinned. "Nice, Ace," he said to Len. "If you ever want collections work, I'll vouch for you to Mr. Winks." His grin faded, and he added, "I'll personally accompany that Monday delivery and pick up Mr. Winks' money." Moretti stepped closer to Len. "In case you are considering defaulting on the deal, know that the police would be very interested in your Port, Porn, & Poker Club." He turned, trudged to the exit door, and reentered the funeral home, leaving Len and Perry in the mist.

"How does he know about that?" Len huffed.

"It's not rocket science, Len. Liquor. Girls. Gambling. All are within the Winks sphere of influence."

"I've told you, Perry. I want out. I'm not paying on Monday."

Looking down, Perry scuffed his shoes in the loose white rocks.

Stabbing his finger into the scarlet of Perry's shirt, Len said, "You straighten this out. I'll pay a fine to the city if I have to for housing your P&P Club, just get me out of this. Let's go in. I won't

let Winks or you poison any more of this day. Curt's day."
  Perry, eyes still downcast, shuffled to the door ahead of Len, and they both went in.

Chapter Four

Len peeked into the Bluebell Salon, past the waiting mourners. Joyce and Sharon sat on high stools positioned near the windows receiving condolences. Even as it lay on the floor propped against a stool, Joyce's flashy print handbag flagged their location, as if the giant pansies called, "Here we are!" Eighteen or so people waited to speak to Sharon. Len expected Joyce had commandeered the stools so Sharon could sit in comfort and chat with the advancing line of standing guests.

Joyce loved this friend, as Len had cared for Curt. Her empathy was evident when Joyce took the burgundy sweater from Sharon's lap and placed it around her shoulders, a soft, dark red hug to comfort Sharon as she faced Curt's death again and again with each person's expression of grief and concern.

Joyce left Sharon's side when she saw Len, came to the door, and drew him into the salon. "Len, thank goodness you are here. I don't know how Sharon is holding it together."

"Looks like you got her seated, at least. That should help some," Len commented. With a pang he spied Curt's simple variegated walnut closed casket on a bier draped in forest green in the front left quadrant of the salon. He couldn't yet face the reality that his best friend was in a box.

"She did share that the afternoon visitation went okay," Joyce said. "Except when Lucy appeared and rearranged items on Curt's Celebration of Life tables, moving some of Sharon's items into an empty box and stashing them under a table." Joyce motioned to a flurry of activity in the room. "Just look at Lucy. When we were young, she had the nice clothes, new car, and rich father. She lorded that over us. Reduced us all with her derisive sneer."

The ex-wife contingent, Lucy and her three grown sons and their families, had decamped to comfortable couches and chairs near the fireplace, abandoning Sharon and slighting those remaining in the receiving line. The children, Curt's grandchildren, had removed the wooden P&P plaque from the memorial display. One was holding it like a shield while another pelted it with Jordan almonds.

"That can't all be her hair," Joyce said. "I wonder who her stylist is. She must have those volumizing hair inserts." Joyce gathered and hefted her thick untamable hair and then let it fall from her fingers. "Imagine needing to add volume with those hair puff doodads! She's bound to have anchored that style with scores of hair fasteners. Look. You can see them. All those gold bobby pins."

Len nodded, although he'd not listened to half of what Joyce had said. He'd been captivated by the woman. As the most fashionable person in the room, Lucy commanded attention. Her tailored charcoal suit complemented her hairstyle, her lightly graying brown hair in a sweeping swirl and roll that evoked 1940s film stars. Small gold wire clips with gray pearls sprinkled throughout Lucy's hair tied together its sun highlights and graying.

The *tick-ticking* of nuts against wood hypnotized him as he watched almonds bounce off the shield. He recalled Curt's enthusiasm for the Port & Porn idea. Curt had commended Charlie's woodcraft of the club's insignia, proclaiming the P&P Club was official, with its own coat of arms. Len regarded the design tacky, its port bottle and female silhouette fairly debauched. The lighthouse beacon was nicely done, though. The overall shield design was stylized, yet the tractor-trailer nude woman mud flap icon was not disguised.

Perry brought expensive port and pricey porn recordings, the likes of which Curt, Charlie, and Len had never seen. Then Perry brought the girls. The exotic dancers. The untaxed booze. Curt's cancer and death, and now Moretti's threats, deepened Len's turmoil.

"Honey? You look miles away," Joyce commented.

"I'm fine, sweetheart," he lied.

"One more thing, Len. Some of Curt's old coworkers from Leader Industries told Sharon that Matt DeLong was in the building. He and Curt were enemies, apparently. A bad work accident killed one of Curt's friends, and Curt blamed DeLong. I'm hoping DeLong is here for the Winks viewing. Sharon doesn't know what to do if DeLong comes through Curt's receiving line."

Len stared at Joyce, wheels turning in his mind to recall Curt's issue with DeLong. "I'll see what I can find out," Len said.

"Julie is here," Joyce prattled on, referring to Sharon's daughter from a previous marriage. "She just got off work, so she's changing her clothes and freshening up. Heavens! I forgot about that bad situation with Perry last summer."

Oh, yes. The situation when Perry brought exotic dancers to the P&P Club. Julie's roommate Sierra was one of them. Through Sierra, Curt learned of Julie's sordid performance career.

"I hope Julie doesn't run into Perry. That reminds me, Len. Have you seen Perry? I don't know what went on with Perry and Sharon, but keep an eye on him. Maybe encourage him to leave?" Joyce requested before she left to rejoin Sharon.

"I'll do what I can," Len said.

Len didn't see Perry in the salon, and he didn't want to face the crowd sharing platitudes about Curt. He meandered the hallways, his thoughts far away. He looked in the Artemisia Salon where the Winks gathering was being held. Scores of people milled around a space twice the size of the Bluebell Salon. Attendance included a United States senator, a police department captain, two city council members, and several corporate leaders familiar to Len only from their photos in the newspaper's society pages. This was not Beacon clientele.

A confusing mix of sadness and elation emanated from the room, and another glance from Len cracked the code. The average

age on the left side of the cream and purple-accoutered room was perhaps seventy-eight years. Solemn faced men and women murmured quietly, stepping up in pairs to take the hand of a veiled older woman in front of a black Rolls Royce of a casket. With ornamented corners and silver hardware, the ebony casket was striking. Corner embellishments depicting the urban skyline looked a lot like the city seal.

Len blanched, realizing the casket was half-opened. The body of Lionel Winks senior, in a dark bespoke suit, rested on tufted black leather. Ah, a viewing. Len silently thanked Sharon for choosing a closed-casket visitation for Curt. The veiled woman, supported by older men, cried into a lace handkerchief. Mrs. Winks? Perhaps the men were her brothers or Winks' own brothers. Or confidantes. *Consiglieri.*

A younger set—the next generation—populated the right side of the room. Lionel Winks junior held court, his mouth open, no doubt entrancing his hangers-on with his wit. Flashes of color adorned these mourners, from a few bright dresses on the women, muted by dark sweaters and blazers, to garish men's ties and pocket squares. Len saw Perry's tasteless scarlet shirt in the festive panorama. Len wanted to believe Perry's presence in the Artemisia Salon signaled Perry's intent to make things right, but what happened next seemed the opposite.

Perry approached Lionel junior, a Gould Campbell gift box in his hands. He said a few words, presented the gift to Winks junior, and shook his hand.

Winks held the box aloft. "Ah, friends, take note. This man knows what he's about. Here's a fine bottle of 1977 Gould Campbell vintage port—awarded a ninety-seven on the *Wine Spectator*'s one-hundred-point scale."

The onlookers clapped and cheered until looks from the other side of the room reminded them of the occasion and the venue.

"Lambert, thank you. You remembered the spice-mocha-licorice palate I enjoy. Hey, everyone, the label says this port is big, rich, and powerful—like me!" He enveloped Perry in a semi-embrace with his free arm.

Perry's globetrotting stories of drinking port with royalty could be true. He had bestowed a bottle on Prince Winks, and Len was furious at their camaraderie.

As if sensing Len's glare, Perry looked his way. He flicked his eyes to the room's back wall.

Len followed the glance to the unmistakable form of Moretti, in serious conversation with two similar body types. Len flinched and back-stepped from the Artemisia Salon's entrance. He sought refuge in an out-of-the-way grouping of Morris chairs that echoed the design of the lobby planters.

Had Perry reacted as if caught out in the Winks reception, or had Perry's darting eyes meant to warn Len? To threaten Len with Moretti?

Len edged to the salon's entrance to intercept Perry when he exited and to get a better read on Moretti. Lionel Winks junior's coterie of hangers-on had dissolved into smaller groups. Moretti and his two heavies ringed Mrs. Winks near the casket, giving the older men previously attending the widow a break. Len thought he saw Perry talking to two women. Although middle-aged, Perry's height, and wearing a dark suit and red shirt, the man's ponytail marked him an imposter. Perry's slicked back undercut left no hair to gather.

Len shifted to the hallway shadows on the other side of the door to start another scan of the room. Perry and the junior Winks were near the bank of standing flower displays emblazoned with husband, father, uncle, and friend sashes.

Winks and Perry talked, each employing expressive arm gestures. Winks waved his hand as if dismissing Perry, but Perry's insistent posture and delivery persisted. Nearby, the ponytailed man turned from his conversation partners, taking note of the exchange. Perry's kowtowing, imploring, and pleading evaporated, and his body language switched from insistent to impervious. Winks folded his arms as Perry drove at him. Perry ended his assail with a smug headshake. Len wasn't sure what he'd witnessed, but he knew he'd seen enough. He made his way back to the Bluebell Salon.

Chapter Five

Len shared stories about Curt with guests in the salon, feeling lightened as he did so.

Perry swaggered into the room like he'd beaten a foe. Within a few minutes, Len and Perry were side by side, viewing mementos of Curt's life displayed on tables along the far-right wall of the salon. Len wasn't going to ask about the encounter with Winks. He'd let Perry bring it up. But Perry didn't. He instead focused on Curt . . . and on himself.

"Len, the P&P Club shield made it to the 'Curt's Life' tables. I've made a difference."

"Perry, this evening is not about you." Ugh. The shield. Why hadn't Charlie removed the reclining woman icon, or overlapped it with the added poker hand, when the club changed from Port & Porn to Port & Poker?

"Look at those photos of a young Curt," Perry commented.

The ponytailed man from the Artemisia Salon stood ahead of them at the tables. He picked up a loving cup trophy. Len could see the script engraving on the shiny silver surface: Curtis Powell – Team Leader Safety Commendation – Zero Safety Violations – 2008.

Perry put his hand on the man's shoulder and spun him around. The man started at Perry's manhandling, much as Len himself would have. No one likes an intrusive hand on his shoulder, especially not one grabbing from behind.

"Matt DeLong," Perry said. "You have nerve coming to Curt's reception."

"Perry Lambert." Matt stepped up to Perry's face, almost spitting the words. "Talk about a bad penny."

Perry didn't back down. "Curt wanted you to go to prison." He whispered, "You killed Randy Gage."

DeLong swung the shiny, foot-tall cup in Perry's direction.

Len pulled Perry back, and the cup missed its mark.

As if his swing of the trophy was an intentional flourish, DeLong held the cup in both hands and said to onlookers. "Curt received a load of awards. He was that kind of guy. His leaving Leader Industries was the city's VoTech Center's gain."

Only Len and Perry knew Curt's award had almost been a weapon. The trophy, no mere silver-colored gewgaw, was pewter and easily weighed five pounds.

Len sidled to the end of the display tables, giving DeLong a wide berth.

Perry, showing uncharacteristic sense, followed.

"Perry, Curt mentioned his buddy's death to me a time or two, but I didn't know who was responsible. How did you know?"

"Curt and I, we talked, you know. We were tight."

Len stared at Perry, fighting to comprehend the statement.

"What? You think you had a monopoly on the guy?" Perry challenged. "Randy Gage's death was the subject of one of Curt's afternoon obsessions a week before he died. Sharon apologized for Curt's mania once she realized. She'd left us alone, happy to have me visit with Curt and give her a break. Sharon said the hospice meds affected Curt that way sometimes."

Len had seen that himself with Curt when he visited. "So, Curt was troubled about Randy's death, even as Curt approached his own."

Perry nodded. "The Occupational Health and Safety Administration and the police cleared DeLong. That never sat well with Curt, and it's the reason Curt changed jobs"

Lucy Powell greeted DeLong and talked with him for several minutes, catching up like old friends. Others grouped around them, all people Len did not know.

"Curt's ex-wife seems chummy with that group. Must be Curt's old coworkers from Leader Industries," Perry said.

"The visitation is open to the public. If Sharon can withstand Lucy's involvement and that of these people from Curt's past, so can we," Len said.

Perry smiled. "Maybe Curt will smite DeLong from the great beyond," he said as he excused himself to the men's room.

A disturbance in the hallway cut short Len's chat with the barbers about American Legion baseball. Len and others from the Bluebell Salon investigated the hallway noise. A startled Matt DeLong jumped from his seat on one of the lobby's granite stones.

A young woman walked away from, who else? Perry Lambert. She stopped near Len. "You're Curt's friend Len, right?" At his nod, she continued, "Do us all a favor and get this guy out of here. He made a pass at my mom at Curt's truck earlier when she just wanted to get her sweater and check on Cloud."

This was Curt's stepdaughter, Julie Echols. She'd been a teenager six years ago when she decided to live full time with her biological father, breaking Sharon's heart. She'd be twenty-two now. All Len could think to say was, "Cloud's in the building?" as he grasped for a redeeming aspect to the evening.

"Yes, Mr. Hayes. He's in the client kitchen. I brought him in from the truck when I arrived, but that's not the point. Mr. Lambert's conduct is the issue. Oh, and your wife is looking for you." With that she traipsed into the salon.

As she walked away, she gathered her brunette locks in her hands and rearranged her hair, twisting and securing strands with flashy green leaf-shaped barrettes Len thought would look terrific in Joyce's hair.

Len didn't see Joyce in the salon. Perry was on hands and knees looking for something on the carpet. Len went to help Perry stand.

"Oh, man. I lost that loose crown," Perry said. Then he told

Len about his encounter with Julie. Len listened with one ear and then tried to persuade Perry to leave. An offended Perry refused and stomped off.

Next on Len's list was to look for Joyce, although he was wary of what she wanted. He'd guessed it was Joyce who witnessed his meeting with Perry and Moretti, probably as she sought an outside spot for a cigarette break. Moretti's comment, "Some lady in a ridiculous rain hat," said it all. He peeked at his cell phone. Eight-twenty? Would this night never end?

As Len considered a trip to the client kitchen to see Cloud instead of looking for Joyce, Matt DeLong approached from near the sculpture. "I saw Lambert and that chick fight. What's gotten into him? He came at me, and he even challenged Winks today."

"I'm not his handler." Len snorted as yet another person charged him with corralling Perry. He'd had it with Perry's escapades. Before he could formulate another reply to DeLong, Joyce stumbled in the front door, sodden and disheveled. He jogged to her and caught her elbow, supporting her. She ripped off her rain bonnet, crumpled the dripping plastic, and jammed it into a nearby wastebasket.

"Honey, are you okay?" he asked.

"Yes. Well, no. I'm worried and upset. Misdeeds from my younger days are catching up with me. I've got to see Sharon right away. The Winks organization is out to cause trouble. I overheard some damning information. Plus, I learned some damaging information about The Beacon. Len, you've got some explaining to do."

"What did you hear? Are people outside talking?"

"No. No. I heard this in the hall outside the chapel."

"You were in the chapel?"

"Yes, Len, but that's not the point."

He'd heard that complaint from Julie moments ago. Was he really that clueless? He chalked up his befuddlement to his upset about Curt's passing.

Joyce said, "I was in the chapel thinking. Avoiding the crowd. People do take time to meditate and pray, you know." She brushed rain droplets off her blouse and looked around. "And in my discombobulation, I've mislaid my purse," she huffed.

Len led her to sit in one of the lobby seating alcoves.

Sharp barks echoed through the foyer and ricocheted up the hanging sculpture. Julie dashed from the Bluebell Salon down a narrow hallway near the funeral home office. A startled Len and Joyce stared at the retreating figure. Then Len remembered. "Julie has Cloud in the client kitchen. He must be stir-crazy to bark like that. He's not one to bark."

"Len, let me tell you who I heard talking. It was Lionel Winks junior, a tough-looking brawny man, and Lucy Powell."

"They said something about The Beacon?"

She began again, and Len tried to distract her another time. A third time he tried a preemptive strategy. He did not want to have this conversation. "You said you needed to find Sharon right away. You should do that. We'll talk about this later."

"No, Len—"

A flurry of activity by the funeral home office interrupted them. Funeral home staff, typically trained for composure, scurried and spoke in strained voices. Len watched one person separate from the clump of dark suits surrounding Merle Overby. This female staff member entered the Artemisia Salon and closed the double doors. Another black suit entered the Bluebell Salon and shut those doors. A lockdown, Len thought.

They heard approaching sirens. Two police cars skidded to a stop and disgorged officers near the crepe myrtles. A rescue squad truck braked in the drop-off crescent. EMTs with gearboxes sprinted for the funeral home door.

Len hustled Joyce through the doors to the Bluebell Salon and into the arms of the Last Respect's staff member on the other side, derailing the man's attempt to calm salon guests and explain the emergency. He exited the salon doors, closed them firmly, and ran behind the EMTs into a back hallway.

Charlie McFadden materialized out of nowhere. "Merle called me. 'Trouble at Last Respects,' he told me, so I got here right away. I knew you were here—what happened?" he asked as they kept pace with the EMTs.

"I'm not sure," Len said. "You must have been right around the corner to get here so fast."

An agitated Merle Overby sprinted from behind them and grabbed Charlie's arm. "Charlie, you've got to help me with the police—"

"Police? What are you talking about?"

"The showroom. Perry Lambert—he's in the Selection Salon. I think he's dead."

Chapter Six

Charlie and Merle barreled into the Selection Salon behind the EMTs. From the doorway Len saw them gawk at the scene and then step to an aisle for a hushed conversation between caskets prominently labeled Pembroke Cherry and Universal Colonnade. A minute later, they exited the frosted glass double doors into the hallway near the funeral home office.

Police held Len at the room's entrance, but he continued to mentally log details of the scene. As his gaze shifted to the floor, he saw Perry's hands and feet bound with duct tape and one of Joyce's rain hats partially taped over Perry's face. EMTs ripped away the last of the plastic and began lifesaving measures by checking for airway blockage, pulse, and heartbeat, and by beginning chest compressions, hands pressing against Perry's horrid scarlet shirt.

Perry's skin pallor and motionlessness suggested that reviving Perry was unlikely. Bile rose in Len's throat at the sight of Joyce's garish handbag spilled next to Perry's body, three-packs of cheap rain bonnets and duct tape jumbled amid the purple and yellow flower print, along with other items including an orange, a trowel, and a garlic press.

The CPR continued while another EMT felt around Perry's head and body. He said to his team, "Here's a contusion behind his left ear." A nearby police officer visually scrutinized the scene, regarding one stone urn in particular.

Len backed through the rear door, confusion and fear coursing through his body. Someone had knocked Perry out and strangled him. A black menace squeezed his lungs, making his breathing fast and shallow. Joyce's face swam in his vision. He'd left her minutes before. She was in the Bluebell Salon. He'd been in the foyer when she entered Last Respects, wet and dripping, from outside. She'd been upset, but why were her belongings next to Perry?

He stumbled down the hall a few steps and caught himself against a doorframe. Soft crying made him look into the room. Julie Echols sat weeping in a chair, Cloud clutched to her chest. The little poodle's black eyes gazed at Julie, and his pink tongue licked the tears from her cheeks. A police officer was also in the room, a solid and silent presence.

Julie's eyes met Len's, and he felt her fear. She sensed the same evil that gripped him. He petted Cloud and felt drawn to hug Julie. The officer watched and listened but didn't intervene. Cloud's leash was anchored to one table leg. Len noted the room's sink, stove, and refrigerator. The client kitchen.

Len sat next to Julie and put an arm around her shoulders.

"I found him," Julie wept.

Len stayed with Julie and Cloud in the kitchen for a few minutes, witnessing the departure of rescue personnel, sans body. Terse conversation in the hallway led Len to stand and peer into the corridor. A police sergeant pleaded with the captain he'd seen in the Winks reception. The captain marched away, dismissing the sergeant's entreaties. The officer in the kitchen suggested Len move away from the door and sit. Len did, but not before he heard the sergeant make a phone call and ask for Major Barnes.

"Officer," Julie said. "We need to take this dog outside for a minute. Please stand with us beyond the door at the end of the hallway so Cloud can relieve himself in the grass."

The officer acted at Julie's direction and led them out the door. Len looked into the funeral home products room as he passed. It was awash with people. The medical examiner and forensics people, he surmised.

Once out-of-doors, Len was surprised to see several cars lined up to leave the parking lot. This outer door was near the hearse drive-through, and Last Respects staff was loading boxes and supplies into a black funereal-looking Lincoln Town Car, Charlie's Buick LaCrosse, a Sincere Serenity van, and a DogFun van. If Last Respects was to be closed for an investigation, the funeral home would need to transfer equipment and products to the other Sincere Serenity locations. Good of Lucy Powell to volunteer the use of the van.

Cloud left Julie's side for less than a minute, accomplishing his outdoor task with efficiency. Len and Julie spoke low and casually, hoping the officer would ignore them.

"Julie, how are you feeling?" Len asked. "This must be quite a shock. When you are up to it, I'd like to hear how you found him."

She replied, "You saw Perry, right? Perry Lambert was a real jerk, but who'd want to do that to him? But I have to ask, why was your wife's purse in there?"

Why, indeed? Joyce hadn't been the only one with an issue with Perry. Len had a few thoughts on that subject as he reviewed Perry's missteps of the day. He, himself, had threatened Perry. Moretti wasn't fond of Perry. He'd angered Sharon, had an argument with Matt DeLong. What else? Hadn't DeLong said that Perry and Julie had fought? And Winks junior? Perry had feted junior Winks, but then challenged him on something later in the Artemisia room. Had any of these altercations risen to the level of a murderous attack?

The police officer listened to his radio and then said, "We need to go back inside, folks. We'll be collecting statements from everyone soon."

Late on Thursday evening, Last Respects housed stunned mourners and staff, along with an extraordinary number of police. The funeral home was closed to new entrants. Current occupants were required to stay. Merle Overby called other funeral homes in the Sincere Serenity system to plan early Friday transfer of bodies and equipment and reschedule Friday funeral home events. Last Respects would be off-limits to the public all of Friday.

Len had learned from the officer in the kitchen that the captain Len had seen in Winks' reception was Eugene Wilson, and that it was Wilson who had immediately taken charge of the crime scene once the body was discovered. Yet Len counted more than thirty minutes before the funeral home and property were secured, allowing no one to leave the building or the parking lot.

Len's hands scrubbed his face as he leaned back in the chair next to Joyce at a folding table. The funeral home occupants were divided into the two large salons.

Captain Wilson was nowhere to be seen. It was Major Barnes who addressed those in the Bluebell Salon. "I'm sorry to detain you, but the gravity of the situation demands we collect information while your recall is fresh. We'll be taking statements from you tonight and allowing you to leave, but we will contact each of you again tomorrow.

"The medical examiner has found the manner of Perry Lambert's death to be homicide. She's taken custody of the body and is having it transported to the Office of the Chief Medical Examiner for cause of death determination. Please remain quiet and follow the directions of Detective Collins and the other police officers."

Officers handed each person a form to fill out with his/her name and asked to list every person he or she remember seeing at the funeral home, including contact information, if known, for those persons.

Detective Collins said, "This will help us, since we need to contact guests who left before the police arrived. One of those people could have vital information." He short-circuited the murmur in the room by speaking more loudly, stating clear instructions. "This is a voluntary witness statement. Please indicate if you are Last Respects staff, an event visitor, or family of the deceased honored here tonight. Then, include the order of occurrences from your arrival to now, to the best you can recall.

Especially note the occasions and times you went into the smaller areas of the funeral home, like the hallways, bathrooms, chapel, or other rooms.

"If you entered the Selection Salon or noted any activity in or around that room, or if you knew or recognized Perry Lambert and saw him at any point tonight, please sit in this area and bring that information immediately to the attention of Detective Garcia's team." Collins indicated the plainclothes female police officer at the head of an empty row of tables.

"The rest of you, please fill out your forms quietly and keep conversation to a minimum. When you have completed your form, bring it to this table to have one of these officers review it. Once your form is reviewed and accepted, you will be free to leave, and officers will escort you in groups to the parking lot.

"Sincere Serenity counselors and our Community Support officers will staff this table. If you feel you need help processing this situation or help completing your form, please line up here."

Len, Joyce, Julie, and Sharon moved from their seats to the row of tables headed by Detective Garcia and began work on their forms. Len was surprised when Charlie's wife Sandra entered the room, nodded to Julie, and sat by Sharon.

"Charlie drove home to get me. He thought you could use the support, so I came back," she said.

"Oh, Sandra! How kind of you. And after staying for the earlier visitation, too. Thank you for coming."

Len shrugged, amazed at the sisterly support network and more amazed that Charlie initiated the favor. He concentrated on his witness account, and listed his arrival behind Joyce and Sharon, his hallway time with Perry and Moretti and their foray outside, Len's viewing from the hall of the Winks reception and his notice of Mrs. Winks and her entourage, Winks junior, Perry, Moretti, the man he'd come to know as Matt DeLong, and the community notables he'd recognized, including Captain Wilson.

He went on to list his return to the Bluebell Salon, his chatting with neighbors, his table viewing with Perry, their encounter with DeLong, and his notice of Lucy Powell in the room. His final observations included mention of Julie and Perry near the restrooms, Julie's return to the Bluebell Salon, Matt DeLong in the lobby, Joyce's entrance from outside via the front sliding doors, the dog barking, Julie's dash from the salon to the client kitchen, the arrival of the police and EMTs, his ushering of Joyce into the Bluebell Salon, and his and Charlie's following the first responders to the rear hallway and the back entrance to the Selection Salon.

Len heard Sharon whisper to Sandra, "Should I start by listing my arrival at two-thirty for Curt's three o'clock to five o'clock visitation?"

"Oh, yes. That's good to note. Mention you have the guest book record for each visitation. That could help the police," Sandra said. A uniformed officer walked closer to Sharon's seat, so she and Sandra stopped whispering. Sharon focused on her form. Sandra also began a form.

Detective Garcia took great interest in Len's account and in those of Joyce, Sharon, and Julie. She reviewed the forms and spoke with each of them separately underscoring their need to be available for interviews on Friday. After Len pointedly advised the detective of their unavailability for part of the day due to Curt's funeral, her compassion training kicked in, and she had a few sentences of condolence for Sharon and Julie but reiterated that police would contact them tomorrow.

CHAPTER SEVEN

Once at home, Len and Joyce debriefed a bit. They sat together on the living room sofa. With her face in her hands, Joyce rubbed her fingertips across her closed eyes. "This is all so horrible. Perry is—was—an ass, but I'd never want to see him killed. He was rude to Sharon and upset her, but he was offensive and inappropriate often. It's unfortunate he didn't clean up his act for Curt's reception, but what happened that led to this?"

Len stared at the landscape on the opposite wall above the bookcase. "Yeah. Perry was his usual self. I've seen him push people's buttons before, but I've never seen anyone strike him. Why was today different?" Len said.

Joyce turned and put her hand on his cheek, swinging his gaze to her face. "Now's the time to tell me what dealings you and Perry had with that man at the funeral home. The beefy guy you two talked with in the side garden."

"What?" Len said, his heart in his throat now that the jig was up.

"Before we heard the sirens and police and rescue arrived, I told you I'd heard some alarming information. About The Beacon."

"Yeah. About that," Len began. His eyes grew huge; his mind cycled furiously. Recalling the adage that the best defense is a good offense, he said, "You start by telling me where you were and what you heard. And, think about who might have found or taken your purse."

"My purse? What's that got to do with anything?"

"Joyce, your purse was next to Perry when he was found."

"That's ridiculous. I think I left it in the Bluebell Salon."

"Duct tape bound his hands and feet, and one of your rain hats was taped across his face."

A frozen look of horror took hold on Joyce's face one moment and melted the next, her sobs dripping onto Len's shirt as he held her.

Her sobs turned to anger. She fisted her hands and pounded them against his chest. "Damn, damn, damn!" she cursed. "It all comes back to Winks! It has to. He ruins everyone's life. He blackmails everyone with the excesses of their past. If he wasn't already dead, I'd kill him myself," she said. She pushed away from him and put her hands on her hips. "Now his son Lionel junior will take his place. You know something about that, don't you?"

Plead insanity was the next defense that came to mind. Len said, "I wasn't thinking straight. While Perry was droning on and on about port wine one day in The Beacon, he mentioned he could get some cut-rate liquor for the bar. I must have okayed the idea because the next Monday he arrived with a mixed case each of whiskey, vodka, and gin. Some of the good stuff, like a twelve-year old Aberfeldy single malt scotch, Beluga Gold Line vodka, and Bols Genever gin—"

Her stony look cut him off.

"And what happened to those cases?" she asked, her eyes emitting a leveled laser of anger straight into his reintegrating brain.

"I gave him some money. He wouldn't take much of it. Then, I put the cases in the storeroom. I thought we could run some specials. Grow some goodwill with the customers."

She jumped from the couch and stood with arms raised. "Arrggghh. Len! This is an alcohol control state. You know that. You violated at least ten Alcoholic Beverage Control Act laws."

Len slumped to the side, landing on one pillow. He gripped a second pillow to his chest. "I know," he moaned. "But that's not the worst of it. Now, apparently I'm due to receive four more cases on Monday."

Joyce took four deep breaths. "Let me outline to you the danger we are in," Joyce said. "Listen to this and tell me what you make of it. I heard Winks, a rough-sounding guy, and Lucy Powell talking." Joyce paced and gestured as she recapped what she'd overheard near the chapel. She set a compelling scene, and Len experienced it as if told a story.

Joyce began, "The chapel was dark, serene. A golden spotlight shown on the altar, and the focal window included stained glass in greens, browns, and pale yellow in a forest-inspired theme. I saw a simple cross in the window's design, but it was subdued and not readily recognized. No overt religious symbols were in the room. An older man was using the kneeler in the far front pew, hands clasped.

"I remained in the back of the chapel, moving to the corner to sit in its deepest shadow for a few moments of peace and invisibility. I was drained by all the people and by the heavy energy of their expressions of grief.

"The older man crossed himself, rose from his knees, and left the chapel. The total peace and isolation was not to last, though. I heard people approaching in the corridor. A heavy, wide-shouldered man stepped into the chapel and scanned the seats. He glanced past me and then returned to the hall. Maybe I'm invisible? I thought. The group's low-toned conversation near the chapel door was hard to ignore. Once I realized who was conversing, I was interested.

"It was Lionel Winks junior I heard first. He said, 'That fool Lambert dared to threaten me! First he appealed to me to let his friend off the hook, and then he menaced me. I'm Mr. Menace, himself! He thought that would work?'

"Then another man spoke. 'Boss, he told you he had insurance? I'll toss his house. I'll go now.' I assumed this was the big guy.

"Winks said, 'No. Stay, Rocco. Lambert said the insurance was not on him or at his house but in a safe place. If I let The Beacon off the hook, he wouldn't use whatever information he had to damage me.'"

From his sideways position on the couch, Len saw Joyce's body wilt, and he feared she'd collapse. She didn't, but her recitation lost energy. Her gesturing and pacing ceased.

"Len, when they named The Beacon, I about jumped out of my skin. I'd had a sense something was wrong with the business. When I saw you outside with Perry and this Rocco thug, red flags waved and my unease deepened.

"What Rocco said next crumbled my insides. He said, 'But we've got leverage on Hayes we haven't even used. Recordings of his wife in her dancer days.' I've fought my whole life to live that down. I was crushed." Joyce heaved a sigh and sat cross-legged on the floor, her face in front of his.

Len lifted his arm, placed his hand behind her neck, drew her towards him, and angled his head so their foreheads touched. "Joyce. I love you. The incredible woman you are is the sum of all the experiences of your life."

Her eyes gazed into his, and Len did all he could to project to Joyce his unconditional love.

After a minute, she leaned back, gently pushing his chest so he'd not topple to the floor. A few deep breaths later, she resumed her story.

"A woman spoke next. When she said, 'Joyce and her friends have always been low-class. Let's not forget the health inspection we can influence,' I knew it was Lucy Powell.

"Winks said, 'When Lambert mentioned this insurance, he mumbled a place or name, but I didn't catch what he said. It sounded like two names—Clare? Clara? And maybe Ian or Leon? Moretti, look into that.' I connected the last name Moretti to Rocco at this point. Winks then asked, 'Lucy, what's Matt DeLong been doing?'

"Lucy told him, 'He's nervous because of Curt's death. He's worried Curt gave information on Randy Gage's death at Leader Industries to Perry.'

"Winks said, "I thought you took care of that years ago when you divorced Powell. You went through all his belongings then, right, when you divided the house?'

"Lucy assured Winks, 'I did. Curt had none of Randy's stuff. Or any papers about the investigation. No one knows Leader Industries was actually a Winks warehouse. You saw to it that Randy was silenced.'

"By now Len, my heart was in my throat. Lucy was accusing Winks of killing a man, but Winks didn't let that accusation stand. He said, 'Oh, for God's sake, Lucy. I told you we only wanted to scare him, maybe rough him up. His death really was an accident.'

"Lucy's response confused me. She said, 'I was forced to choose between my father and my husband then. Curt wouldn't let the matter alone. I chose my father, to keep the family name out of the mud.'

"Rocco chimed in, 'And to protect all that money. Your dad was in it up to his eyeballs, to favor his own business interests,' he said, adding a laugh. Winks laughed, too.

"Lucy said, 'Have some respect. My father is deceased. And your father recently died.'

"Len, her frosty words made me shiver. She's no fan of Winks.

"He replied, 'Yes. That's why I have to secure my interests. This is no time to go soft. All have to see that it's business as usual but with a younger Winks at the helm. You understand that. Right, Lucy?'

"Lucy answered, 'Yes. I sided with Papa ten years ago, at the expense of my marriage. My younger sons are not involved. Ted, my oldest, will protect our stake in this. He's most like my father anyway. He loved his grandfather and seems to have inherited the gift to keep us in the money.'

"My mind was reeling. These were puzzle pieces, but I couldn't guess the overall picture. Rocco Moretti doesn't know when to shut up. He said, 'Your son Ted, he's not like Curt? I'm hearing from people here today how your ex was a saint. Squeaky clean.'

"That fired Lucy up. She said, 'You didn't go into the Bluebell Salon, did you? You have no right—'

"Moretti countered, 'Settle yourself, Mrs. Powell. I didn't

desecrate your dear ex's gathering. I only sent my ears around to pick up information.'

"'You rotten thug! Keep Curt's memory out of this!' she hissed.

"Winks said, 'Lucy, Rocco didn't mean anything by that.'

"Lucy screeched, 'Lionel, keep your attack dog on a tighter leash!'

"Winks tried to soothe Lucy. He said, 'Lucy, Lucy. I, for one, honor your ex's memory. He was a good man.'"

Len was disgusted these people would drag Curt into their discussion. That Winks offered any opinion on Curt's character was ludicrous. Lucy Powell defense of Curt was unnerving.

Joyce said, "The three moved away from the chapel. Winks junior, from his tone of voice, giving Moretti orders."

Joyce lay back so she was fully supine, as if fatigued by her recounting. "Len, I was stunned. I was scared you were mixed up in drugs or stolen goods. I snuck out of the chapel, left the funeral home, and cried in the alley. And smoked a few cigarettes."

Len had no words. Joyce's information raised questions. She'd have to tell the police.

They retired for the night, but neither slept well.

Chapter Eight

Friday morning, an early call caught Len on his way to the shower. Detective Collins requested that Len and Joyce meet him at police headquarters as soon as possible. Len protested, reiterating their commitment to Curt's funeral. Len was irritated Detective Garcia hadn't communicated to Collins that important detail.

"As soon as the funeral is over, you can stop by." Collins added, "You'll pass headquarters on your way home from Holy Cross Church anyway."

"Can't it wait? This is an emotional day," Len appealed.

"I insist. I'd like you and your wife to identify property found at the funeral home," Collins said.

Not the contents of the dreaded purse, Len prayed. Giving up, he answered, "We will come to headquarters. But I'll have to call you with a specific time, and that depends on the duration of the funeral and burial."

Curt's funeral began at ten o'clock. His remains and casket were transferred to another funeral home in the Sincere Serenity system once they'd been examined as part of the crime scene investigation. No complications ensued, and Curt was properly delivered to Holy Cross Church as planned. The burial on church grounds followed the funeral. Instead of the customary post-funeral lunch provided by the church ladies guild, a short reception in the fellowship hall allowed mourners to pay respects to the family.

Sharon and Julie accepted condolences on one side of the room, and Lucy and her sons spoke with people on the other side. Neither family group spoke to the other.

"After last night, I cancelled the luncheon. Perry's demise has everyone upset, so I thought public events in Curt's honor today should be basic," Sharon said.

"Tasteful and respectful," Joyce agreed.

Len was distracted and solemn. With this final ceremony, he felt his disquiet about Curt's sickness and death begin to dissipate. However, questions about last night filled that void, and Len feared he and Joyce were not in the clear.

He ventured to the other side of the room. He wanted to say something to Curt's sons. He spoke first to Lucy Powell, expressing his sympathy. She responded woodenly, passing Len off to her eldest, Ted, who stood at her right hand. Len shook hands with the man who bore no resemblance to Curt. Len mentioned how proud Curt was of Ted's baseball accomplishments in college. Ted was terse and unemotional in his reply.

The two younger sons, Drew and Kent, looked like Curt, and Len found speaking with them very healing. Drew's voice sounded like Curt's, too, and Len reveled in hearing it. These sons were both handy, like their father, and worked in skilled jobs. Brother Ted ran the canine daycare business with his mother.

The crowd had thinned and the remaining mourners were packing up. Julie sat alone near a window.

"How are you holding up?" Len asked.

"Mom is amazing. I don't know how she can field endless small talk with people tangential to Curt's life.

"Well, Curt was kind of amazing," Len said.

"While their repetitive comments grated on me, she was gracious to people, relished in the comments about Curt, and embraced their support."

"Well, Sharon is also kind of amazing," Len said.

Julie stood, turned to look out the window, and was silent for a moment. "I owe Mom and Curt a lot," she said. "They straightened me out and helped Marsha and Sierra, too. It sickens me to think we could be working Winks' red-light entertainment clubs. I appreciate your hiring Marsha, Mr. Hayes."

The depth of Julie's distain for Winks was an echo of Joyce's. It dawned on Len the longevity and extent of the Winks organization's immoral and pernicious activities. Winks' dominion had ensnared Joyce and Sharon decades ago, reached for Julie recently, and baited and hooked him.

Through the window Len saw a woman in the church burial ground standing at an ornate monument of stacked rectangular granite blocks. Her hand rested atop the monument-capping polished marble slab that shone with an unearthly gleam at odds with the sunshine-inhibiting heavy cloud layer. The woman's dignified posture emanated reverence.

Len looked at Julie from the corner of his eye. Her gaze out the window looked contemplative but unfocused. She hadn't commented on the woman.

"Let's go ahead and leave, Julie," Sharon called, and Julie joined her mother.

Joyce motioned Len to head to the door, and he moved that way at first but changed his mind.

"I'll be there in a minute," Len called to Joyce. He exited a side door into an empty graveyard. The woman had left, but he strode to the grave marker that Lucy Powell venerated and read the inscription.

When Len joined Joyce, Sharon, and Julie in the parking lot, they were not actually ready to leave. Len waited at the car while Joyce made last minute plans with Sharon. He called Detective Collins and estimated he and Joyce could meet Collins in twenty minutes in the lobby of the police building. An appointment with destiny to add to the dire day.

Curt's son Ted lingered by a new model gray Nissan Infiniti. The dog daycare business must be good, Len thought. To Len's surprise, Ted sauntered over.

"Mr. Hayes, that was quite a hub-bub at the funeral home last night," he said. "Perry Lambert was a friend of yours and of my dad's, right?"

"Yes, I guess he was. Perry had his good traits and his peculiar ones."

"Too bad about his death. Did he have a girlfriend or ex-wife or brother or anything? We're talking about sending his family some flowers."

"He didn't talk about anyone specific, although, from the comings and goings at his house and stories he told, he had an active social life."

"So, you don't remember him mentioning a Clare or a Clara, then? Or an Ian or Leon?"

Alarm bells sounded in Len's head. Joyce had heard those very names from the mouth of junior Winks. He nonchalantly answered, "No. Where'd you come up with those names?"

"Oh, just people my mother thought Perry had talked about." With that, Ted ambled toward to his car. "Have a nice day, Mr. Hayes."

CHAPTER NINE

Len and Joyce stopped at police headquarters on their way home. The exercise Detective Collins led them through was simple. He took each of them separately into a room. Collins began with Joyce. Len waited in a gray stackable chair in the reception room. After five minutes, Collins exited the room with Joyce.

It was her turn to wait in a gray chair. "See you soon," Joyce said to him as Len followed Collins into the room. Evidence bags lay on several counters, and the detective asked Len to identify items belonging to him. Collins added, "If you recognized other objects, let me know that, also, and tell me who may own those."

Len easily identified things from Curt's memorabilia tables. When he saw Joyce's purse, he froze. Quietly he told Collins how Joyce had bought the new purse on Wednesday. Len had seen what he thought were spilled items from the purse in the Selection Salon near Perry's body. He admitted the packs of rain bonnets resembled those Joyce routinely had at hand, but he couldn't say if the trowel or garlic press was Joyce's.

At another counter, Len asked if he could lift a bag to examine the items more closely. Collins allowed this. Len identified the shiny green leaf design barrettes as those Julie had in her hair on Thursday, the ones he thought suited to Joyce's hair.

He'd never considered himself a hair man, but he guessed he was because when he saw the pearl decorated bobby pins, he associated those immediately with Lucy. "Thursday night Curt's ex-wife had hair fasteners like those in her hair. My wife and I noticed her complicated hairstyle." He looked more closely at the contents of the bag. "What in the world are those?" Len said, indicating two small brown pillow-like objects with rough, hairy surfaces.

Collins said, "Your wife informs me those are volumizing hair inserts."

"So, not dead hamsters, then?" Len cracked. The detective's face showed no amusement. Len didn't care. He needed the humor to buoy his own mood.

After their appointment with Detective Collins, Len dropped Joyce off at Sharon's and went to The Beacon. It was such a relief to walk into his bar that Len hummed along as "Blow the Man Down" played in the background.

He found Julie there, talking to Marsha.

"Good to see you, Roomie," Marsha said to Julie. "We miss you, but stay with your mom as long as she needs you."

"Yeah, Marsha. Thanks. I'll bring around a check for my portion of the rent, though. Okay?"

Catching sight of Len, Marsha said, "Welcome back, Len. Hey, I'm so sorry. Curt's cancer was bad enough, and now Perry's dead."

Len accepted a hug from Marsha. She left to wait on customers.

Julie said, "Mr. Hayes, can we talk?"

"Sure. Call me Len. Let's sit at this back table."

Once settled in their seats, Len asked, "Did your mom get any sleep last night? Yesterday was harder than expected for us all. Your mom must have been running on empty. And today is hard, too. The finality of Curt's ceremony. The shock of Perry's death."

Julie said, "Last night the police were kind when they questioned us. Mr. McFadden drove home to get his wife and brought her to Last Respects to help Mom. Mom was so happy to see her. Mr. McFadden was busy with the funeral home manager and the people in the other reception." She looked sideways at Len. "Do you know those Winks people?"

"No," Len said. "I'm surprised Charlie McFadden does."

"Mr. McFadden got Mr. Overby moving to coordinate with other homes in their system. Last Respects will be tied up with the police investigation until Sunday. Services, equipment, and—well, bodies—had to be transferred to other funeral homes. Curt was transported to the DeVere Avenue Sincere Serenity location. But he arrived at Holy Cross just fine."

My, she was talkative. When she stopped for a breath, Len said, "Remember when I first saw you yesterday at Last Respects? What happened between you and Perry?"

Julie stilled.

"Someone told me you and Perry fought. Did you tell the police?"

"I said I hit him."

"What? I figured you and Perry had an argument, not a physical fight."

"I was sipping from the water fountain near the restrooms when a whoosh of air messed up my hair. A guy had left the men's room and walked past me. I juggled my shoes from one hand to the other as I drank a few more gulps of water." She took a deep breath. "I remember flexing my knees and wriggled my toes, relieved to have removed my ankle strap heels.

"The departing man turned and stopped. I recognized him before he opened his mouth. He said, 'Julie. How's your roommate Selena—no, Sierra? I'd sure like to see her again. Sierra made a big splash at our August Port & Porn party.' I said, 'Perry Lambert. You sick bag of dung.'"

Julie was on a roll. Len didn't interrupt.

"Perry didn't shut up, though. He went on, 'It's a shame Curt recognized Sierra as your roommate. And then it all had to come out about your side job. Escort. Dancer. We all know what that means.'"

"Julie, you don't have to tell me more. I can imagine," Len said.

"I want to tell you. I stepped close to Perry and hissed, 'You know I got out of that. Curt and Mom came to my rescue. And to Sierra's and Marsha's rescues.' He kept baiting me. 'I'd say you broke your mom's heart, but she'd done her own stint on Winks' payroll. The apple doesn't fall far from the tree.' When his arm encircled my waist. I tensed. I really lost it when he said, 'How about some friendliness for your Uncle Perry?' He was oblivious to my seething," she said. She shredded a paper napkin with jerky rips.

Len shook his head, commiserating with Julie and marveling Perry's cluelessness.

Julie punched her palm forward stopping short of Len's face. "I dropped my shoes and slammed the heel of my hand into Perry's chin. I was too close to exert much force, but it stunned him long enough for my *coup de grace*."

Len scooted his chair back to stay out of range, in case she demonstrated her next strike.

Julie continued impassively, avoiding eye contact. "Perry's forearms flipped up, palms out, in what my jiu-jitsu teacher calls a startle response. When I danced back two steps, Perry's eyes widened. I bent to the left, unhinged my hip, and let loose a roundhouse kick to his mouth. Spittle and something else shot from his mouth as he staggered back."

Len gaped at Julie.

Julie looked directly at Len and said, "I hoped I'd knocked out a tooth, I was that angry. 'Maybe that will shut you up,' I said to him, and then I walked away. That's when I spoke to you."

Julie stared unblinking at Len, holding her breath. She exhaled. "I didn't kill him."

Len thought carefully about what to say. "No, you didn't. It's unlikely your kick caused his death," he said. "I went to Perry once you walked away and tried to talk sense into him. He was not hurt then. You didn't knock out a tooth, but you did dislodge his loose crown."

They shared a smile.

Len said, "Julie, at least one person saw the fight. Maybe more.

Be ready to answer police questions. Joyce and I plan to contact our lawyer. So should you and your mother. I saw your mother slap Perry in the parking lot. That won't look good."

"I saw your wife's purse next to Perry and one of her crazy rain hats taped over his face. That doesn't look good, either."

"I guess we all have actions to explain."

After a trip to the ladies' room, Julie's hardened, bitter mood further dissipated. She was alert and composed. Must have been a relief to get that off her chest.

"That's some fight story," Len said. Capitalizing on her improved disposition, he asked, "Are you up to telling me how you found Perry?" He was a heel to ask, but Julie may be able to shed light on why Joyce's purse was at the scene. Julie was a big girl. She could always say she didn't want to talk anymore. "It could help you remember for when you recount it to the police," Len persisted.

"Yeah. I'd like to go through what happened," Julie said. "Cloud was barking, so I ran to the client kitchen from the reception room. Cloud was straining on the leash I'd secured to a table.

"As I lifted Cloud to hush him, I saw a blur pass the doorway. I couldn't even tell you from which direction. Cloud wouldn't calm. Nothing in the kitchen spooked him, but his hackles stayed raised and his snarling seemed directed at the hallway. It all felt so creepy." She said this all in a rush, and now she panted, out of breath. "Wow. I guess I am more freaked out than I thought."

Len quickly got her a bottle of water from the bar. "Do you want to stop?"

"No. I can do this." After a few sips, she continued, "I commanded Cloud to stay and quiet down, and I investigated. The door down the hall from the kitchen was ajar. I slipped inside the room. The lights were low, and I jumped when I realized the waist high, body-sized rectangular objects were caskets. The vases on shelves were urns.

"The room was quiet as death and empty of humans, I thought. I used my phone for light and saw Perry on the floor. It felt like he was empty, too. I ripped the plastic from his face in case he could still breathe and stumbled into the hall for help. A staff person was in the kitchen consoling Cloud. She helped me sit, and once I told her what I'd seen, she texted her boss, raising the alarm."

"My God, Julie. I am so sorry you went through that," Len said.

"I think I'll go home to Mom's now," Julie said. "A short ride in the fresh air is good medicine. Taking Cloud for a long walk will be even better medicine."

CHAPTER TEN

Julie passed Detective Garcia at the door. Len sagged at the arrival. Marsha intercepted the detective and offered her a seat.

"Len, that woman is with the police, and she wants to talk to you. What should I do?"

"Give her an ice water and lead her back to my office," Len said. He walked away, taking two minutes to drink some water himself and clear off the round table.

Once they'd greeted and settled in seats at the table, Garcia started asking questions about the P&P Club, Len's business, and Rocco Moretti.

Len started sweating. This was another conversation he did not want to have.

Garcia turned up the heat. "Is your wife protecting you? You were angry with Perry Lambert at the funeral home. Three witnesses heard you ask him to leave."

Len stifled his answer.

"Maybe your wife and Mr. Lambert were involved romantically, and you attacked him?"

"That is NOT what happened. If I did hurt Perry, why would I implicate my wife by suffocating him with a rain bonnet?"

"How do you know about the rain bonnet?"

"I followed the EMTs and entered the casket showroom," Len said.

"How did your wife's purse end up next to Mr. Lambert?"

Not the blasted purse. Len vowed to burn the handbag. "I don't know." He truly was mystified. "My wife and I are contacting an attorney. Please coordinate further contact with him. I'll leave his contact information with your office."

Garcia left The Beacon.

Len finally had the chance for an Internet search. He Googled the name he'd read on the churchyard gravestone after Curt's service. He had spent less than ten minutes reading articles, checking dates, and collecting information before George Yeonas called with an odd request.

"Len, I think Charlie is on his way to The Beacon. I tried to talk with him in his driveway, but he didn't stop. He waved and called out he was on his way to see you. Get him to stick around. I'm on my way, and I think you and I need to talk to him. It's about Perry," George said.

"Yeah. Okay, George. I'll look for him. What's your concern?"

"I saw Charlie's Buick LaCrosse and a Sincere Serenity van at Perry's around nine o'clock last night. Charlie and one other guy were taking boxes from Perry's garage. That was thirty minutes before police arrived at Perry's house."

Hadn't Len seen Last Respects staff loading Charlie's car last night with funerary stuff? This didn't make sense. "Hmm. I have some questions for Charlie, too. Come on over, and we'll talk to him."

Len left the office and manned the bar. Charlie arrived within minutes, sat on the center barstool, and ordered a beer.

"Len. The Perry situation is a fiasco. I need your help," Charlie said.

Irritated by Charlie's tone, Len sniped, "Perry is not a situation. He was a man and an associate. One that was murdered."

Charlie looked left and right. Lowering his voice, he said, "You got the associate part right, Len. His death necessitated some fancy footwork to move some untaxed liquor before police found it. You're familiar with contraband liquor, aren't you, Len?"

Len shot Charlie a sharp glance. "Let's go to my office to

talk."

The front door opened, and George entered.

"George. You are just in time to join Charlie and me in my office. Come on back."

Once they were seated at the dark round table in Len's office, George was the first to talk. "You and I attended Curt's three o'clock to five o'clock funeral home visitation yesterday, Charlie, right?"

Charlie nodded.

"Ralph, the barber from the No Frills barbershop, called me last night to tell me the bad news about Perry. He saw you at Last Respects when the police were called in around 8:45 p.m."

"I was there. I went to help Merle Overby," Charlie said.

"I talked with Sharon this morning. She said you and your wife were so helpful last night. She's thankful you brought Sandra back to the funeral home to be with her."

Charlie admitted he'd left the funeral home to retrieve his wife.

"Charlie, I saw you at Perry's house last night after nine o'clock when I got off the phone with Ralph. What were you doing at Perry's?"

"I stopped at Perry's before I picked Sandra up to take her to Last Respects. Big deal."

"You have a key?" Len asked. "You were taking boxes from Perry's garage."

Charlie looked at Len. "Do you really want this conversation to continue, Len?"

Len was silent.

Charlie shrugged and then responded to George's challenge. "Yes. Okay. This is about low-price liquor from our neighboring state. We're talking small potatoes. No one gets hurt."

"Charlie, Perry got hurt. The police came to inspect Perry's home, and you had removed evidence."

Charlie shot back, "Yeah, and I didn't have much time to do it."

George looked at Len. "Can you help me out here?"

Charlie laughed. "Len's part of this, George."

George's brow furrowed, but he prodded. "I also saw a panel truck with Sincere Serenity markings at Perry's house around 9:15 p.m."

"It was one of their vans. Merle from Last Respects emptied his liquor cache and sent his guy with me to Perry's. We collected cases from Perry's garage, he offloaded boxes from my car so I could get Sandra and drive back to Last Respects, and he took the liquor elsewhere."

"Charlie, tell the police," Len said.

"What? And end up like Perry? Besides, you'll go down with this, too, you know."

"Enough," George said. "What does Charlie mean by that, Len?"

"I bought some of the contraband booze," Len said.

"It's okay, Len," Charlie consoled. "Winks has someone in the police department who will protect him. A captain."

Captain Eugene Wilson came to mind. Len was getting closer to danger or to criminal charges, but he was also getting closer to the truth.

Len and Charlie could not untangle the complexity of their involvement with Winks. It was possible the untaxed liquor would not be an issue if undiscovered. George pointed out that Len and Charlie had both violated liquor laws and that Charlie had tampered with evidence. George agreed to let them sort their affairs and culpability and encouraged them to secure legal representation.

"If the liquor operation is not discovered in three days, I'm going to tell the police what was said here," George vowed.

Charlie banged his fists on the table. "You'd do that to your friends, George?" he groaned.

George responded with a slight nod. Charlie launched from the chair and hustled out of The Beacon, a stream of curses in his wake until the closing of the bar door ended the tirade. George left the office and sat quietly at the bar drinking iced tea.

Len's office phone rang, and Len left the table to sit at his desk. Caller ID indicated it was his wife. With the danger of his situation on his mind, he answered with his heart in his throat, "Are you okay?"

"I'm fine. I called to let you know that Karen Hackett has left. She and her colleague Henry Birch will represent us."

"Good. No talking to police without an attorney." He didn't mention he'd done just that with Detective Garcia. Whew. He was glad his conversation with Charlie and George occurred after Garcia questioned him.

"Len, Sharon told me more about Matt DeLong."

Len said, "I met DeLong at Curt's reception. Perry accused him of killing his friend."

"Randy Gage, right? Sharon told me. Maybe this DeLong guy killed Perry?"

"Yeah, but why now? Quite a few people knew about the Leader Industries death and investigations."

"In the conversation I overheard, Winks wondered if Perry had new information. Do you suppose he did?"

"It's possible, but I saw DeLong in the Last Respects lobby before you stepped in from your crying, I mean your cigarette break. I saw him again when police and rescue arrived. I guess he could have attacked Perry before that. We'll tell the police about DeLong." He carried the wireless handset into the bar area. "How are you holding up, honey?"

"Okay, I guess. This is all so over-the-top. I want to come to The Beacon and cook my Maritime Meal of the Day, as usual. But I'm worried and exhausted. I also want to help Sharon process all of this."

Len scanned the bar. "Goodbye Fare You Well" was playing. He liked this setting-sail-for-home shanty. He thought of Curt, and of Perry, when he heard these lines, "We're home'ard bound" and "Good-bye, fare-you-well." He silently wished them a safe journey home.

"Are you still there, Len?" Joyce asked.

"Yep. I'm just wandering The Beacon." He spied Clarion. He hadn't had a chance to take a look at Clarion since Marsha mentioned Perry knocked him over.

"Len, what insurance do you suppose Perry had? Could it have been so incriminating he died because of it? And what about those names Winks is checking on? Clara. Clare. Leon. Ian."

Len hummed the names to the music in the background. When he stooped to lift Clarion, he almost knocked the statue over.

"Joyce! Joyce! Do you hear it? That's it!" Len crowed, lifting and hugging Clarion and dancing in circles.

"What's it? Len? What's going on?"

Marsha rushed to Len. "Are you okay, boss?"

Laughing, he called into the phone, "CLARA-LEON! CLARE-IAN! It's CLARION!"

"Oh! You're brilliant, Len!" Joyce yelled.

He handed the phone to Marsha. "Describe to Joyce what I do next."

"Joyce, Len is getting food service gloves from behind the bar. Now he's laying the statue on its side. Oh. There's a hole in the bottom. He's reaching inside the hole. His expression tells me he feels something inside."

Len said, "Yeah. I was hoping someone hid something here. I found something. Several somethings. Whatever's in here—each is stuck to the inside." Len pulled out two flash drives. He showed Marsha the adhesive side of one of the flash drives. "This globby substance is poster putty, I bet." He took the phone from Marsha. "Joyce, I think this is Perry's insurance! I'm taking the flash drives to my office and calling Detective Garcia right now!"

She wished him luck and asked him to call her back.

Fifteen minutes later, Detective Garcia arrived at Len's urgent request. Again they sat at the round table in the office.

"Joyce overheard people at Last Respects discussing trouble Perry was causing them. They wanted to find records Perry kept as insurance against them. Perry had muttered about where he kept the insurance. They thought it was someone's name he voiced.

"It wasn't!" Len pointed to the black Lab statue on the coffee table. "He hid the damaging information in this statue—Clarion, our bar mascot! I found two flash drives stuck in the statue."

He waved a Ziplock bag containing the flash drives. "These may include information connected to Perry's death."

Marsha tapped on the office door. "Sorry to interrupt, but something odd just happened."

"Is this important?" Len asked.

"Yeah. A guy came in and asked about the statue. I mean, that's too much of a coincidence, with you, Clarion, and the detective back here, and all," Marsha said.

"Marsha, what are you talking about?" Len asked.

Garcia jumped in. "Is this guy here now?"

"No. He left," Marsha said.

"Wait. This just happened?" Len asked.

"Start at the beginning," Garcia encouraged. "We've been in the office for twenty minutes. When did this man enter the bar?"

"Not long ago. Maybe ten minutes ago. This big guy came in and looked around the hostess stand and coat hooks before sitting at the bar. He ordered a beer, and then he said, 'I remember a dog statue here. Your bar mascot, right? What do you call him?'

"I said, 'His name is Clarion.' I could tell he was straining to be pleasant. I felt pressured, so I lied. I told him the bar owners took the statue home to clean him. He drank up, paid, and left."

"What did he look like?" Garcia asked.

Marsha's description of a 5'11" muscled, dark-haired, and swarthy man sent chills through Len. "What?" Len yelled. "You said we took the statue home? Detective Garcia, that man sounds like Rocco Moretti, and Joyce is at home, alone!"

"Call her now," Garcia ordered.

Detective Garcia also made a call.

Joyce answered Len's call. She was at Sharon's house. "You and Sharon stay put," Len said. "I'll call you back in a few minutes."

Len and Garcia got in Garcia's car. Peeling out of the parking lot, Garcia engaged her unmarked car's integrated flashing blue lights, and they sped to Len's house.

Several marked police cars met Garcia and Len at the entrance to Pekoe Acres. They proceeded quietly and stopped half a block from Len's house, on a side street, near an unoccupied sporty white Lexus LC Len did not recognize.

Police approached the house with stealth. Using Len's key to quietly enter, they surprised Rocco Moretti in the utility room as he was opening cabinets. Moretti was arrested without incident.

CHAPTER ELEVEN

Joyce didn't answer his call, and this unsettled Len. He had big news about the Moretti apprehension, and he wanted her to know.

Police needed some time at the house to collect evidence, so Len told Detective Garcia he and his wife could be reached at Sharon Powell's, a block and a half away. Garcia said she'd call when the police were finished.

Len walked to Sharon's, trying her cell number. Sharon didn't answer. No one was on the street. All was calm. Len didn't recognize the gray Infiniti parked half a block from Sharon's. His knock on Sharon's door was answered by Lucy Powell, and she had a pistol aimed at his chest.

He immediately looked past her for signs of Sharon and Joyce. And Julie? She said she was headed to her mother's after their talk at The Beacon.

"Well, well. Mr. Hayes. Come on in," Lucy said.

Len did as she directed, calculating his odds of overpowering her before she pulled the trigger.

"Go to the kitchen," Lucy said, and she stayed well out of his reach.

The kitchen. That's good. I can find a weapon there, Len thought.

He heard muffled grunts and was relieved to find Sharon and Joyce. They were back-to-back in kitchen chairs with duct tape looping around each chair and each of them multiple times. Strips of silver tape bound their wrists and ankles. Tape covered their mouths.

Their panicked eyes darted from Len to the gun. Sharon's eyes showed even more desperation than did Joyce's. When he locked eyes with Sharon, she shifted her attention to the back door and back to him three times in quick succession.

That hadn't escaped Lucy's attention. "It's lights out for you, Mrs. Powell, if Hayes springs for that door," Lucy warned.

Joyce flailed in her seat, distracting Lucy from Sharon's slight headshake that told Len bolting for the back door was not her message. She then stared at Cloud's food and water bowls in the alcove near the back door.

"Mrs. Hayes, stop moving or your husband gets the first bullet."

Lucy aimed at Len.

Joyce froze.

"I came here for Sharon, and now look at this mess. Hayes, keep your hands flat on the table where I can see them."

Len complied.

She lowered the gun. "It was easy restraining those two. I had Sharon tape up Joyce, and then I taped Sharon to the second chair. Joyce, I want to thank you for your purse. My granddaughter saw it propped against the stool in the Bluebell Salon and couldn't resist it. I found her with your purse in the corner of the salon. You carry around some odd stuff. The garlic press fascinated her. Carrying around duct tape and an orange makes some sense, but I laughed when Elise showed me the trowel.

"I scooped the contents back into it and hid it in my own bag. You being Sharon's friend, I thought I'd upend it in the parking lot or something. The duct tape and rain bonnets came in handy later. The tape continues to be of use. I ran out of tape tonight, but I knew I'd find more in the kitchen's utility drawer. Where Curt would store it. This is his house." A roll of silver duct tape lay on the counter.

Len coughed and sputtered to break Lucy's focus on Joyce. Surprisingly, Lucy got a bottled water from the refrigerator and handed it to him. He opened it and sipped. Then he capped it and carefully returned his hands to their palms down position on the tabletop.

Lucy paced from the refrigerator to the back door. Sharon's eyes widened and her eyebrows rose each time Lucy neared the exit.

"Lucy, what's this all about?" was Len's opening gambit. It sounded lame, even to him. Joyce's nod and bright eyes conveyed approval. Keep Lucy talking.

"It's about Curt . . . and my father . . . and my sons," Lucy said, stiltedly. "And about HER," she roared. She waved her hand toward Sharon. Her pistol hand. "I am the original Mrs. Powell! She isn't!"

Thankfully, Lucy didn't aim the gun at Sharon.

Lucy's chest heaved. Her pacing continued. She was far away in her thoughts until Len brought her attention back to the kitchen.

"I saw you visit your father's grave this morning. Theodore Pierce." He tried for a look of compassion.

Lucy said, "I gave up my marriage to protect the Pierce name and legacy. Curtis Powell was the finest man I ever knew, except for my father. It tore me up ten years ago to make that choice."

This was getting interesting.

Lucy shook her head as she paced and spoke, her hair loosening from its twist, her fashionable hairstyle flopping. The golden hairpins hitting the kitchen floor matched those shown to him at the police station. The ones with brown Tahitian pearls.

"And that Curtis took up with her, a stripper, was an insult!" This time she pointed the gun at Sharon.

"You and Curt had three fine sons. I'm sure he cared for you," Len placated.

Her face softened. Brown and grey stray locks framed her face and lent her a look of innocence. "Yes. Even after the divorce, he was a fine father."

Her rage returned. "Damn that Perry Lambert! I meant only to reason with him. Maybe scare him. I needed to make sure he didn't use his 'insurance.' Especially if it marred the Pierce name."

Len ventured, "Yes. I read how your father was an important man. A businessman. One of the Alcoholic Beverage Control Authority's most respected commissioners."

"He had a head for business," Lucy said. "He and Lionel Winks senior devised a system where everyone benefited. The state got its tax profits and oversight of alcohol, except for the private activity that allowed some fairness and profit in distribution."

So, that's how Lucy saw it. Interesting take on graft and corruption.

Len heard Sharon and Joyce scuffling as they strained against their bonds.

Lucy paced, absorbed in her story. Len heard a bark in the distance, or the soft bark of a quiet dog closer by. Len noticed Sharon concentrating her attention on the back door. He thought he understood. Julie wasn't here because she took Cloud for a long walk. Sharon was agitated because Julie had no idea what was happening in her mother's house.

"So, you saw Perry as a threat?" Len said.

"Me? No. He was weak. We could have bought him off. Little Winks is a sad substitute for his father, but he wanted something done to put Lambert back in line. He was furious Lambert went to bat for you and shocked Lambert threatened him." Her steps quickened as she walked back and forth.

"Did you reason with Perry?"

"He was so malleable. I had my granddaughter give him a note at the visitation. I knew he couldn't resist. It said, 'You're looking good tonight, you stud. Meet me in the product showroom in ten minutes.' Elise held her hand out once he'd read the note. I saw Lambert give her a dollar, thinking she was waiting for a tip. She said to him, 'Thanks, Mister, but the lady wants the note back.' He tried to ask her 'What lady?' but she'd grabbed the note and ran, like I instructed her. She gave the note back to me in the bathroom. She's four years old. It was all a fun game for her."

Lucy laughed at her own retelling. She spoke with her hands, and the waving of the pistol both relieved and worried Len. Lucy wasn't in a firing position, but the gun could go off accidentally.

He resolved to charge Lucy when she was next distracted. It was a risk, but he didn't have a better plan. Julie could return any moment. In Lucy's emotional state, his deliberate action could overwhelm her response.

"Perry showed up for the meeting, right?" Len asked.

"Yes, the egotistical fool! He turned a simple negotiation into a muddle. You know what he said when he entered the room? He called, 'Sharon?'" Lucy's breath came faster, and she stopped pacing.

"Sharon!" Lucy leveled the gun at Sharon. "Really? You? First you snare Curt. Then, even Perry hopes it is you who wants to meet him in a dark room for romance?"

She laughed and lowered the pistol as she doubled over in hysterics. A brown oval clump fell to the floor like Lucy's head was disintegrating along with her sanity. Len belatedly recognized the clump for what it was, not a dead hamster, but a hair puff.

She stood, wiping tears from her eyes with the back of her hand. "Rats," Lucy said. "That's the end of that hairstyle." She gathered her hair with both hands, bent to retrieve a dropped hairclip, and twisted and pinned her hair off her neck, all while holding the handgun. With such cavalier firearm handling, Lucy could have discharged a bullet at any of them, or through her own skull.

Len became her focus. "But the joke's on you, Hayes. You know what name Perry called next as he searched for his paramour?" She mimicked Perry's high, thin voice. "'Joyce?' He called for Joyce."

She switched her gaze to Sharon. Gleefully, or Len thought maniacally, Lucy said "And then he whispered, 'Julie?' No surprise there, the little tramp!"

Lucy looked around anxiously and said to Sharon, "Hey! Where is your daughter?" She relaxed in the next moment. "Ha. That's right. She doesn't live here. She can't stand to be around you. I heard how she didn't want you raising her."

Sharon breathed deeply through her nose. She looked in Lucy's direction but kept her line of sight above the woman.

Len exaggerated his gulping of water to get Lucy's attention and shield Sharon from further abuse. He said, "What did Perry do when he saw it was you in the room with him?"

"He didn't see me in the dark behind him. I hit him with an urn, and he went down. I remembered the duct tape in your wife's purse, so I dug in my handbag and burrowed into hers. A rain bonnet fell into my hand as I dug for the tape," Lucy said. "It was like a sign. I resolved to punish Perry, I was so angry. Taping the rain bonnet over his face and leaving the purse were nice touches that would point to your wife."

A bark outside the back door drew everyone's attention. The back door opened and Cloud bounded toward Lucy.

Julie screamed.

Len's phone rang.

Lucy shrieked, "I HATE DOGS," and she turned the gun on Cloud.

Len yelled, "NO!" as he leaped from his seat and launched himself at Lucy, a gunshot ringing in his ears.

Len tackled Lucy, shoving her arm skyward. The shot went wild, penetrating the ceiling. Len and Lucy hit the floor. He took the gun from her hand and kept her pinned. He hesitated, not wanting to hit a woman, but unsure what to do next.

Julie solved his problem. She slapped a strip of duct tape across Lucy's mouth and jerked Lucy's arms above her head to tape her wrists together. Julie handed Len the tape, and he secured Lucy's ankles. Julie guarded Lucy while Len found scissors and cut sections of tape to free Joyce and Sharon. He carefully removed the strips from their faces. Cloud sat at attention at Sharon's feet.

"Oh, Len," Joyce sighed. "Thank you, thank you, thank you for saving us from that horrible woman." Her wide brown eyes misted with relief, and then her head drooped in exhaustion.

"Len, can you call the police?" Julie asked as she snipped her mother's bindings while still keeping an eye on Lucy.

Len found his phone on the floor near Cloud's bowl where it had flown in the melee. Cloud yipped and left Sharon's side. He rushed to Len, placing his front legs on Len's knee as Len squatted to retrieve the phone. Cloud covered Len's face with dog kisses, and Len snuggled and hugged Cloud. He whispered in Cloud's ear, "No way I was going to let anyone hurt my best friend's pet." Len continued, "You did good, boy, coming to our rescue, ready to sacrifice yourself. I'm so glad you are okay." As he released Cloud and stood with his phone, he was surprised to find tears running down his cheeks.

He turned from the others, passed his hand over his face, and inhaled and exhaled deeply. Then he punched in Detective Garcia's number. When the call connected, he calmly said, "Hello, Detective Garcia. You may have heard a gunshot. Please come to Sharon Powell's house. No, no one is hurt. I'm here with Joyce, Sharon, Julie, and Cloud. Lucy Powell held us at gunpoint, and she fired the shot, but with the help of a miniature poodle, the shot went wild. We have Lucy Powell immobilized with duct tape." Len relaxed when he heard sirens. "We hear you coming, Detective Garcia. Goodbye." Len put his phone on the table and returned to freeing Joyce and Sharon.

Minutes later Detective Garcia arrived with backup. Lucy, still bound, was completely disheveled.

Garcia said, "I don't know if this helps, but we were closing in on the killer." Her serious tone intrigued Len. "We linked hair items from the crime scene to Julie Echols and Lucy Powell. I see hair items near Mrs. Powell here identical to those from the crime scene. Our theory was that the hair clips fell or flew from a woman while in close contact with Mr. Lambert. Miss Echols recorded her tussle with Mr. Lambert on her witness form, but Mrs. Powell never mentioned seeing or talking to Mr. Lambert, and she couldn't explain why her hair accessories were on or near the deceased."

Garcia's formal delivery ceased, and she chuckled. "Lucy Powell's confession tonight certainly streamlines the case."

Chapter Twelve

Although the next week involved meetings with police and prosecutors to build cases against the Winks organization and Lucy Powell, Joyce and Len worked every day at The Beacon, throwing themselves into cooking and reconnecting with patrons. Sharon and Julie left town for a two-day getaway to the mountains.

The four reunited on Wednesday at a memorial service for Perry. Perry's brother came from Portugal to honor his brother and sort Perry's affairs. Before the service, Len greeted the brother and learned of Perry's European upbringing and early career in the hospitality industry. After the service, a few people stayed to share a cup of church punch in a room set aside where family and friends could gather.

"Our ancestors were French wine merchants who relocated to Portugal two hundred years ago," the brother said. "They purposefully settled in northern Portugal's Douro Valley, east of Porto, where wine was first fortified into port in the eighteenth century."

Len spilled his punch. George choked on his. Charlie busted out laughing. He slapped Perry's brother on the back. "You've validated for us many of Perry's outlandish stories."

On Saturday, Sharon invited Len and Joyce to her house for mid-morning coffee. As they enjoyed fruit and coffee cake accompanied by fresh drip coffee, a sleepy Julie ambled into the kitchen and greeted everyone.

"Julie's moving in for a while," Sharon said. "She'll start community college in two weeks and be here as company for Cloud for some daytime hours when I go back to work."

Julie smiled at the dog and with a tender look at her mother said, "I can help sort Curt's belongings, too. When Mom is ready."

They sat at the table in the sunny breakfast nook and sipped silently, Len waited to see who would mention the elephant in the room: Perry's death and their harrowing experience with Lucy.

Joyce choked out the first words. "I knew someway Winks was responsible."

"Maybe ultimately, but there are layers of misdeeds," Sharon said.

"Looks like Charlie's caught up in this," Len said.

"Hmm," Joyce said. "I wondered how Charlie and Sandra could afford new cars and high-end vacations."

Sharon said, "Poor Sandra. I don't think Charlie would hurt anyone, though."

"I hope Lucy's sons weren't part of the violence. They are Curt's sons, too," Sharon said.

"Good thing Cloud was around," Len said. "For an abnormally quiet dog, he gets his point across."

Julie said, "He's super dog! First he protects Mom from Perry, then he signals Perry's death, and then he provided the distraction that pushed Lucy over the edge." She scratched Cloud's chest in appreciation.

A knock at the door drew everyone's attention. Julie rose from the table and answered the door. "It's Mr. Yeonas," she called as she led him to the kitchen.

Cloud left his guard position on the floor at Sharon's side and scurried to greet the newcomer. George knelt to take the dog's head in both his hands and ruffle his face and ears. "I saw the cars here and wanted to stop by. Sharon, may I join the coffee party, or am I intruding? I'm coming home from cutting back the Oldham's monster pyracantha bushes. They send their regards."

Julie quipped, "Who sends their regards? The Oldhams or the bushes?"

"Very funny, Julie," Sharon said. "It's good to see you, George. Please join us." She filled a mug for him at the counter, and he took it from her before sitting at the table with the others.

Joyce said, "Good news from The Beacon. Our Health Department inspection is postponed. That's a relief. It was inappropriately scheduled, and the Health Department is investigation Winks' interference."

"I've got news, myself," George said. "Word has it that Rocco Moretti is out of jail on bond, compliments of Winks' lawyers, for the breaking and entering of Joyce and Len's house."

"And who are you getting your information from?" Len teased.

"Come on, Len. You know. From the No Frills barbers. Want to know what's happening? Get the low-down from a barbershop," George said. "Ralph says things look bad for Winks. State Police, federal Alcohol, Tobacco, and Firearms agents, and the FBI are coordinating with the US Attorney's Office to cement charges against Winks, Moretti, and Lucy and Ted Powell. Oh, and the state police are reopening the investigation of Randy Gage. If I were Matt DeLong, I'd be sweating bullets."

"Whew," Len said. "Whatever charges Charlie, Merle Overby, and I face may be modest in comparison." He hung his head, feeling the weight of his own irresponsibility. A tentative look at George, however, consoled Len. His friend's face bore no expression of condemnation. "In fact, the Alcoholic Beverage Control Authority agent assessing The Beacon's violations updated me. The Authority is reviewing Theodore Pierce's history as commissioner. His legacy may turn from that of respected leader to scandal king."

Sharon suggested they bring their coffee mugs to the screened porch to enjoy the fresh air. They eased into various glider sofas and rocking chairs and savored the coffee and the woodland view.

"Speaking of Lucy's family," Julie began, "Kent and Drew visited Mom this week."

Sharon said, "Kent called ahead. Julie was here when they arrived." She gazed past them, her eyes misting. "They are so much like Curt. Their mannerisms. Drew's voice . . ."

"They apologized for their mother's actions and told us Lucy is in the security wing of Tall Oaks sanitarium," Julie said. "Curt's death destabilized her."

"Apparently, she never got over him," Sharon said. She shook her head.

Julie stopped rocking and leaned forward. "Drew had a bad feeling Thursday night. Before police allowed his family to leave the funeral home, his daughter Elise came to him with a fantastical tale of a 'secrets and silence' game she was playing with her grandmother. Elise said, 'Daddy, Grammy and I played a trick on a man in a pretty red shirt.' Drew got more anxious the more questions he asked his daughter."

Joyce weighed in. "They must be anxious about what will happen to Lucy."

Sharon said, "They are shocked she confessed to killing Perry. They hope treatment can rebalance her mind, but they agree that psychosis is no defense for murder."

Len lifted a brown paper bag he'd placed at his feet and set it on the table. "Sharon, Joyce and I want to visit the Holy Cross graveyard. Especially since Curt's funeral was abbreviated. I'd like to add a 'celebration of life' element. Would you like to go with us?"

Sharon looked around the living room. "Shall we all go?"

Everyone nodded.

"What's in the bag?" George asked.

"The rest of the 1994 Fonseca vintage port from Wednesday night," Len said. He removed a bottle from the bag. "I'd like to leave it for Curt, after pouring a few drops on his final resting place."

Joyce said, "Sharon? Julie? What do you think of the idea?"

Julie took Sharon's hand. Their eyes met and searched for agreement.

"I think Curt would like that. I know he'd like us all to be together, thinking of him," Sharon said.

Joyce took Len's hand as he continued, "The sprinkling of this fine port as a way to recognize Perry seems appropriate, given all that has happened. In the end, Perry may have tried to do the right thing, so I'll also sprinkle port in his name."

The End

A DOGGONE SCANDAL

By Teresa Inge

Catt Ramsey, owner of the Woof-Pack Dog Walkers, is back on the case when she receives a mysterious note in her pet supply order. Convinced the sender's motive is scandalous, Catt packs up her SUV and heads to the Outer Banks with her sister Em, family friend Jonathan Ray, and pups Cagney and Lacey to solve the mystery.

TERESA INGE grew up reading Nancy Drew mysteries. Today, she doesn't carry a rod like her idol, but she hotrods. She is president of Sisters in Crime Mystery by the Sea Chapter and author of short mysteries in Virginia is for Mysteries *and* 50 Shades of Cabernet.

Website: www.TeresaInge.com
You can also connect with Teresa on Facebook, Twitter and Instagram

CHAPTER ONE

Catt Ramsey slid her desk chair toward the window of the small apartment she rented over her sister's cottage in Virginia Beach. The space served a dual role for both home and business.

A man in a blue uniform shirt and shorts approached, carrying a small blue box. He took the outdoor stairs two at a time.

Her Yorkshire Terriers, Cagney and Lacey, stood on their hind legs, barking at him through the bay window.

After a few quick taps, he pushed the screen door open and entered. "Delivery," he said.

Cagney and Lacey jumped from the window seat to the floor and made their way toward the man, sniffing his shoes and socks.

Catt recognized the dog and cat graphics on the side of the blue box from her pet supplier, but not the man carrying it.

"Where do you want it?" he asked.

"I don't recall ordering any supplies."

"It's addressed to the Woof-Pack Dog Walkers." The man wiped his forehead with his shirt sleeve.

"Well, that's us." Catt pointed toward a table near her desk then reached into the mini-fridge on a shelf. She grabbed two bottles. "Care for some water?" She extended one toward him.

He set the box down and reached for the proffered water. He twisted the top and gulped. When the bottle was nearly empty, he recapped it. "Thanks. I needed that."

"You're not the usual delivery driver," Catt said.

"No ma'am. I'm Shane. Charlie retired last month."

"Oh. I didn't realize he retired."

"Yes, ma'am. I'll be your driver going forward." He reached down and petted Cagney and Lacey. "Well, if there isn't anything else. Have a nice day." He made his way out the door and down the stairs.

Catt grabbed a pair of scissors from her desk. She slid the pointed end across the top of the box, opened it, and yanked out the packing material. After pulling out the last piece, she grabbed a small red ball from the box and squeezed it in her hand. She pulled out the company information card included with every order. Catt turned it over and found a hand-written note. *You solved a model's murder and theft . . . Now come to Pet Products in OBX to solve the rest.* The OBX was the local vernacular referring to the Outer Banks of North Carolina, a spit of land between the Atlantic Ocean and the Pamlico Sound, and a mecca for beach vacationers.

Catt's eyebrows knitted together. Who would send her this cryptic message about the Outer Banks?

The door swung open and her sister, Emma Ramsey, entered. After taking an early retirement from a financial firm last year, Em now helped Catt walk dogs. Her blond, unkempt hair hung loosely around her neck. "I need coffeeeee." She made her way to the pot and poured a cup.

Catt sat at her desk holding the ball and insert, still trying to decipher its meaning.

Em leaned against the counter and sipped her coffee.

"You look like crap, Em. Where've you been?" Catt asked.

"Helping Jonathan Ray metal detect on the beach."

"All night?" Catt cast a curious glance toward her sis. Em and Jonathan Ray, who had dated as teenagers, had rekindled their relationship after they bumped into each other during last year's murder investigation.

"Mostly." Em shrugged.

"Did you find anything?"

"A few coins, but nothing of value."

"Is this a new hobby for Jonathan Ray? I thought he liked to dabble in chemistry?"

"Yes. Jonathan Ray said there's lots of metal to be found near water. Actually, we're heading to OBX to go metal detecting since I'm not scheduled to walk the dogs this weekend."

"Is that legal to hunt relics in protected areas?"

Em took another sip of coffee and faced Catt. "Look. I know you care about me, sis, but I've got this. Plus, we'll be among tourists and beach patrol, not in illegal areas. It should be exciting. Hey, why don't you come with us?"

"I would love to go, but I have to walk the dogs."

"Get a backup."

"When are you leaving?"

"Thursday morning. That gives you two days to find a substitute. There's a cute cottage in Nags Head by the beach. We're booked to stay there. It has an extra bedroom, so you wouldn't have to bunk with me. And you could use a weekend off from walking the dogs."

"I *could* use a break. It's been a long time since I've had time off. Now that the business is up and running, it would be a good get away." Catt leaned back in her chair. She was grateful that Em invited her. They didn't always get along but when Catt's world fell apart two years ago after losing her corporate event planning job in a downsize, and then finding her cheating husband with a neighbor, Em let Catt stay above her garage and start her dog walking service.

"Promise you'll try. It'll be fun."

"I'll see what I can do." Catt began repacking the box with the discarded paper.

"What's that?" Em nodded toward the red ball and card lying on Catt's desk.

"I received them in a box from Pet Products today."

Em grabbed the card. "This is wild! Another case! Just like the one last year with the missing necklace.

Last year, Catt had discovered the body of her fashion-model client, Candice Berry. That had made Catt the chief suspect. The sisters had teamed up and conducted their own private investigation. Their association to the theft and murder had generated unwanted publicity for Catt, and that still haunted her.

Em placed the card on the desk. "Do you recognize the handwriting?"

"No." Catt shook her head.

"Do you know anyone at Pet Products?"

"I met the owner, John Carpenter, once through Candice Berry. They knew each other through animal causes. That's how I was introduced to their products."

"Do you think he sent it?"

"I don't know who sent it." Catt paused. "Although I recall Candice mentioning that John sent her several notes about animal events that ended with a rhyme."

"That's odd. Did you ever see any of them?"

"No."

Em pointed toward the organization's address on the back of the card. "Their warehouse is in OBX. I thought they were local?"

"They have a hub in Virginia Beach, but everything is shipped from the warehouse."

"Well, it's fate. You *have* to go with us now."

"What do you mean?"

"Hear me out. Since you don't recognize the writing and it was delivered in a blue box from Pet Products, it's reasonable to think John Carpenter or someone on his staff sent it."

"But why would they do that?"

"That's the little mystery we need to investigate. We can start with their warehouse since the note refers to OBX."

"Well, I am curious about them."

"Great. I'll get my detective gear ready. Black cap, top, and pants. I can't believe I get to work on another case." Em rubbed her hands together.

"Oh, brother. That's what I was afraid of."

CHAPTER TWO

On her way to her first dog-walking appointment for the day, Catt stopped by the corner pharmacy to pick up pain medicine for her client, Nora Page. Nora had been diagnosed with breast cancer and was unable to run daily errands. She had texted Catt to walk her dog Hudson.

The contemporary condominium building, The Loft, where Nora and Hudson lived, was two blocks away. Catt enjoyed her stroll along the boardwalk, even if she did have to dodge slow-moving tourists and fast-moving runners, many accompanied by leashed dogs. The Loft never failed to impress Catt when she first caught sight of the six-story, brick building. It overlooked the beach and boardwalk and was home to many wealthy residents and most of Catt's clients.

"Hi, Catt," Josh Hayden, a client of Catt's and resident in the building, greeted her as she entered the building. "Who are you walking today?"

"Hey, Josh. I'm heading up to Brock's to walk Grayson then Nora's to walk Hudson."

"Any chance you could walk Jersey Thursday morning?" Jersey was Josh's pup, a cute poodle/Bichon Frise mix.

"Do you have a show on Thursday?" Catt referred to the monthly show where The Loft allowed residents to sell their crafts. Josh sold beautiful handmade jewelry.

"Yep, but the set-up person bailed, so I have to fill in. It's gonna be an early morning and a long day for me."

"Early works perfect for me since I'm going to OBX with Em later that morning."

"What's happening at OBX?"

"Just a get-away."

"Sounds fun. Jersey will be waiting for you Thursday around eight."

Catt pulled out her phone and tapped the screen. "Just added it to my schedule."

"Great." Josh paused. "How about dinner next week?"

As Catt had learned during her investigation last year, Josh was a busybody who knew everything about everyone at The Loft. "Uh, I'll check my schedule since I'll just be coming back from my trip." Catt waved goodbye and took the luxury elevator up to the sixth floor to Brock's apartment.

She unlocked the door and was greeted by Grayson, a gray, miniature poodle. He stood on his hind legs, begging to be walked. "Hey, boy." Catt reached into her pocket and grabbed a treat. "Anyone home? It's Catt," she called out. No answer. Brock had mentioned he might be out running errands when she stopped by.

She made her way through the chic foyer, enriched with collages of beach scene paintings by local artists. She stepped into the kitchen and grabbed Grayson's leash from the wall rack. As she turned, her eye caught a blue box sitting on the table, one with a dog and cat graphic on the side. That was the same company she ordered her supplies from online and identical to the one delivered that morning with the mysterious note. It was a popular website for animal lovers, so it wasn't a huge coincidence. And yet . . .

While she wouldn't be so bold as to check and see if he had received a secret message, too, she made a mental note to talk to Brock about the red ball and message she had received. There could be a connection, since it had mentioned the theft of his necklace.

Catt leashed Grayson and headed out the door. "Let's go get Hudson." They walked down the deserted hallway to Nora's unit. Catt knocked on the door.

Nora's toy poodle Hudson barked as her client answered the door. Hudson huddled behind her. "Hi, Catt. As you can see, Hudson's waiting for his morning walk." Nora held the door open. Grayson and Hudson sniffed noses.

Catt reached into her pocket and pulled out a small bag she'd picked up at the pharmacy and handed it to Nora. "Here's the medicine you asked me to pick up. Are you feeling okay?"

"The chemo has been murder. But I'm hanging in there." Nora appeared worn and tired.

"Is there anything else you need?"

"No. You're too good to me, Catt."

The dogs barked.

"I think they're ready. Where's Hudson's leash?" Catt asked.

"In the living room. Follow me."

Catt followed Nora through the stylish apartment decorated with glass figurine tchotchkes from Nora's travels. Nora, a former flight attendant, had earned her money the old-fashioned way: she'd married it. Four times. But with Nora's recent illness, she had little energy to focus on simple tasks like walking Hudson, let alone the full-time job of pursing a new man.

Nora handed Catt the leash. "I'll take the medicine then lie down for a while."

"Good. Get some rest. I'll be quiet when I bring Hudson back."

Catt made her way out of the building and onto the boardwalk that stretched for three scenic miles along the oceanfront. The dogs enjoyed the ocean breeze on the warm June day, thanks to one of her clients who had petitioned the City Council to allow dogs during tourist season. Catt shook off the melancholic feeling when she remembered that Candice Berry and her dog didn't get to enjoy the ocean walks because she was murdered before it was enacted.

Catt approached Samantha "Sammy" Norris, her newest dog walker. Sammy had worked for an animal hospital part-time while going to school. During her interview with Catt, she mentioned needing more flexibility in a job. So far things were working out nicely.

"Hi Sammy. How are Chopper and Ollie behaving today?" The two beagle-terrier mixes belonged to new clients, James and Ava Cartwright, and were still in the trial phase as clients.

"They're good dogs."

Hudson and Grayson sniffed the two new friends.

Catt knelt down to pet Chopper. He extended his paw toward her. "Aww, what a good boy." Ollie remained fixated on Hudson and Grayson.

"How's it going?" She glanced up at Sammy.

"Good. I have two more from The Loft."

"Thank goodness the humidity is low so we don't overheat the dogs."

"And my hair." Sammy held the leashes in one hand while tightening her ponytail with her other hand.

Catt glanced at the schedule on her phone. Sammy had been the one to set up the app for her, enabling them to update the schedule and share information in real time. "I really appreciate you keeping the schedule up to date."

"Oh sure. It's easy and keeps us on track."

"By the way, I need a backup walker from Thursday to Sunday while I'm visiting OBX this weekend. Any chance you could help out? There's extra cash involved," Catt said.

"Can I work around my schedule?"

"That can be arranged. There's three scheduled Thursday and four on Friday. The two on Saturday and Sunday are flexible. I'll make sure no others get added. I appreciate it."

"My pleasure." The dogs tugged their leashes. "I think they're ready to go. See you later." Sammy waved her hand in the air and headed down the boardwalk.

Catt was thankful she had found Sammy, a loyal employee that she could trust. And someone who could walk the dogs while she enjoyed a much-needed vacation and a chance to poke around the OBX for information on the mystery box.

CHAPTER THREE

Catt opened Brock's door and unleashed Grayson.

"Did you enjoy your walk, boy?" Brock, a former Virginia Beach City Council member and trust-fund baby, approached from the hallway. He scooped Grayson up in his arms.

"Oh, I didn't realize you were here," Catt said.

"I just returned. How'd he do?"

"He met two new friends from The Loft. Chopper and Ollie. They belong to the Cartwrights on the fourth floor."

"That couple who retired early from all their boring investments and who let their dogs do anything they want?" Brock's tone showed his disdain for "new money."

"What do you mean?" Catt placed her hands on her hips.

"During our monthly meet-and-greet of new building residents, they brought their two terrors who peed on the floor and gnawed the wooden barstool legs. Their 'pet parents,' " Brock curved his fingers to make air quotes, "as they call themselves, did nothing to stop them. So, I kindly told the woman, Ava, to please restrain her dogs. That's when she told me her babies were still in potty-training and to mind my own business."

Catt had met the Cartwrights when she interviewed the dogs, as she does for all potential new clients. Although they were a bit obnoxious about retiring young from all of their wealth, Catt had found them to be warm and genuine toward their dogs. The Cartwright's never had children of their own, and Chopper and

Ollie served as substitute offspring.

"Plus, I don't understand why they don't walk their own dogs." Brock made a disgusted face. "Nothing against your service, but they are retired."

"They volunteer with several charities, which is why they hired my service." Brock was one to talk, since he did not walk his own dog, even though he had the time.

"Oh, I'm sure. With all their millions." Brock set Grayson on the floor. He darted to the kitchen, his nails scratching against the wood floor. "He's probably thirsty."

She followed him to the kitchen and placed Grayson's leash on the wall rack while Brock filled his water bowl. "I see you get supplies from the Pet Products company that I order from." Catt nodded toward the blue box on the table.

"Grayson loves their stuff."

"I did, up until now."

"What do you mean?" Brock asked.

Catt explained about the tampered box, red ball, and note.

"When did that happened?"

"Yesterday. Although I do order from them, I didn't order anything this week." Catt paused. "When did you get your delivery?"

"Yesterday."

"Was there anything different about your order?" Catt asked.

"No. Although, I had a new delivery man."

"Blonde, young driver named Shane?"

"I didn't get his name but that matches his description. Why?"

"Since he's a new driver, it made curious about him and the tampered box." Catt made a mental note to ask Shane the next time he delivered supplies if he'd noticed her box being open.

"Do you think he had something to do with the cryptic message?" Brock asked.

"I don't know."

"Obviously that's some sort of threat in the package."

"Well, yeah." Catt touched her finger to her lip.

"What's going on inside that brain of yours, Catt Ramsey?

You look lost in thought?"

"Since the message had OBX on it, I'm heading down there soon with my sister. I may have to check things out."

"You really think there's more to this?"

"Don't ask me why, but I do."

"I don't know how you keep getting mixed up in these scandals. But please be careful. This could be dangerous. Let me know if there's anything I can do."

CHAPTER FOUR

Thursday morning arrived, and Catt had forty-five minutes to walk Jersey and be back at her apartment for the nine o'clock meet up with Em and Jonathan Ray. If all went according to plan, they'd be enjoying lunch on the beach in OBX.

She entered The Loft lobby as the resident vendors set up their craft tables. She saw Josh at a back table and headed that way.

"Hi Catt. Jersey is ready for his walk," Josh said.

"Great."

"You still headed to OBX for the weekend?" Josh straightened a necklace on a stand on the table.

"Yeah."

"Well, enjoy your trip. And don't forget about dinner next week."

A customer approached the table asking about a necklace.

Whew. Saved by the strand. Catt nodded to Josh as she backed away and headed to the sixth floor to get Jersey. She entered Josh's apartment and was greeted by Jersey. "Ready to walk?"

He jumped up and down.

Catt grabbed his leash and headed to the boardwalk. It was a perfect June day with a slight breeze. She made her way to the oversized King Neptune statue at the entrance of Neptune Park on the boardwalk at 31st Street and Atlantic Avenue. Jersey looked up at the top of the bronze statue and breathed in the salt air.

The Cartwrights, accompanied by their dogs, approached.

"Hi, Catt," Ava Cartwright said. "I thought that was you. Who's the cutie with you?"

"Oh, hi. This is Jersey. He belongs to one of your neighbors."

"I certainly hope he doesn't belong to that God-awful Brock Randall." Ava smirked.

Catt frowned. "No. But I do walk Brock's dog Grayson. Do you know Brock?"

"We had the unfortunate pleasure of meeting him at the meet and greet. He scolded my babies for accidentally peeing on the floor. It was totally uncalled for."

Catt didn't want to take sides. "Oh, I'm sorry to hear that."

"I reported him to the building manager. That evil man scared my dogs, and we don't appreciate it," Ava said.

James stood silent next to Ava, his arms crossed.

Catt glanced at the time on her cellphone and changed the subject. "What brings you two out today?"

"Chopper and Ollie were chomping at the bits to go for a walk," Ava said.

Jersey sniffed Chopper and Ollie.

"Well, you have a gorgeous day for it. And I appreciate you hiring my service to walk them. They have been really good to work with."

"That's good to hear. They are very special to us." Ava smiled.

Jersey tugged at his leash. "I have to go. I'm headed to OBX with my sister."

"Oh. Is it a girls' weekend?" Ava asked.

"Yes. Should be fun. See you all soon." Catt scooted off and returned Jersey to The Loft, and made her way to the Woof-Pack Dog Walkers.

Catt had her suitcase packed and dog equipment bundled up by the door as she sat in her office waiting for Em and Jonathan Ray to arrive. She was thrilled that the cottage in Nags Head allowed animals.

The screen door opened and her travelling companions

entered.

"Hi, you two." Catt leaned back in her chair. "Where's your stuff?"

"Sitting next to your SUV," Em said.

"Great." Catt grabbed her bag and equipment, and they headed down the stairs, Cagney and Lacey in tow.

Once they were buckled in, with Em riding shotgun and Jonathan Ray in the backseat with the dogs, Catt asked, "Ready to roll?"

"Born ready," Em said.

Jonathan Ray gave a thumbs-up.

"*Woof*," Cagney barked.

Lacey stuck her head out the window.

"Settle back and enjoy the ride." OBX was an hour and a half away. Catt turned the nose of her GMC west to the highway, and their adventure officially began.

After crossing the North Carolina line into Moyock, a sleepy town straddling the Virginia/North Carolina line, Catt stopped at a popular convenience store for a quick break. Jonathan Ray and Em headed inside the store to pick up snacks and beverages while Catt took the dogs to the grassy area outside.

She pulled out her phone and checked the dog-walking schedule. Sammy had added a new slot to the weekend schedule. Catt texted Sammy. *I noticed a new slot on the schedule. You okay with that since I know your time is limited?*

Sammy texted back. *Yes. My schedule changed, so I can take on extra walks.*

Forty-five minutes later, Catt drove across the Wright Memorial Bridge.

They drove along in summer traffic, looking for milepost 10. Milepost markers help visitors locate restaurants, shopping, and in Catt's case, lodging. Catt turned into a driveway and parked next to the blue cottage on stilts, just yards from the Atlantic Ocean.

Catt and Em ooohed and ahhed at the house's open floor plan with a kitchen, dining room, and family room decorated in lighthouses theme.

"I love my bedroom," Catt shouted to Em and Jonathan Ray as she dropped her luggage and equipment on the floor. "I can see the beach from my room." Cagney and Lacey jumped on the window seat to observe the quaint neighborhood.

Em entered Catt's room. "Mmm . . . lots of people are in the water enjoying the waves. We need a beach day."

Catt nodded.

Jonathan Ray stood at the door. "Come check out the deck."

The three stepped onto a large outside deck that also faced the water.

"What's first on our to-do list?" Em asked.

"Wine?" Catt answered.

"Sounds good."

After unpacking the beverages and snacks, Catt poured the wine, a crisp pinot gris that paired well with fresh sea air and handed Em a glass. Jonathan Ray cradled a bottle of Yingling beer. The group settled into deck chairs and relaxed under the umbrellas.

Catt tipped her wine glass toward Em and Jonathan Ray then took a healthy sip. Catt asked, "So, when do you plan to do the metal detecting?"

"Right before sunset. Less people will be on the beach. Plus, it's still light out and we have a better chance of finding loose change, jewelry, and treasures from the day." Jonathan Ray grinned.

"Are you sure it's allowed?" Catt asked.

"Yes. On the northern beaches above Nags Head."

"Do you need a permit?" Catt sipped her wine.

"No." Jonathan Ray chugged his beer.

"Sorry. I'm worried. I'd hate to see you two get locked up."

"Not to change the subject, but when are you going to the Pet Products to try and solve the mysterious note?" Em asked.

"I plan to drive by there tomorrow morning and then go visit the warehouse on Saturday." Want to go with me?"

"I do. But why the drive by?"

"Well, I looked up their hours for tomorrow. They'll be closed for repairs."

"What kind of repairs?"
"Don't know."
"Hmm. That might be a good time for us to poke around."
"That's what I was thinking. You in?"
"Try to go without me. I'm curious now," Em said.
Catt rolled her eyes and took another sip.

CHAPTER FIVE

After breakfast the next morning, Catt and Em met on the back deck, ready for a day of investigating.

"Where's Jonathan Ray?" Catt asked.

"He's doing some research on his computer and said he'll catch up with us later."

Catt and Em got in the car. The GPS guided them to the warehouse.

"Well, here goes nothing," Em said as they pulled into the parking lot.

"I'm hoping it's something," Catt replied.

Catt eased the SUV past the company billboard with the blue box logo. She made her way toward the vintage, brick industrial building, renovated with modern fixtures, paneled doors, signs, and lights that were attractive and inviting. It was similar to buildings in downtown areas renovated into restaurants and breweries. As Catt drove toward the southside parking lot, a uniformed man stood waving his hand.

"Who is that?" Em inched closer toward the dashboard.

"I don't know but apparently he wants us to stop."

"Can I help you?" The young man had a quizzical look on his face.

"We were hoping to take a tour," Catt said.

The man frowned. "They're not open today."

"Will they be open tomorrow?"

"Uh, yeah. But it's limited on Saturday."

"Do you know why they're closed today?" Em faced the driver's window.

He shook his head. "Some type of dispute with the owner John Carpenter."

"Oh really?" Em said.

"You can head out the side exit." He pointed toward the street.

"Okay. We'll stop by tomorrow," Catt said.

Chapter Six

Later that morning, Catt and Em headed to the beach to relax. But Catt's thoughts kept returning to John Carpenter, the owner of Pet Products. What kind of dispute was he involved in? Catt pulled out her phone and accessed the Pet Products' website. In true corporate-branding fashion, it had the blue box logo and informational brochure. She scrolled past the product line of pet foods, treats, and toys she was already familiar with, and went straight to the About Us page. A picture of John Carpenter, a handsome, fiftyish, dark haired man holding the infamous blue box and a small poodle, filled the screen. The caption under the picture read John Carpenter, Owner, Pet Products and dog Fluffy. Catt enlarged the photo with her fingers for better viewing.

Em leaned closer. "Who the hell names their dog Fluffy?"

"Apparently, John Carpenter."

"Says he started the company ten years ago, and it's worth millions now."

"Their products *are* name brand and top of the line. And they have the best dog and dental treats." Catt continued to scroll the page.

"Interesting the security guard mentioned a dispute with the owner," Em said.

"He was a talkative fellow for someone that didn't know us."

"Maybe he's got his own dispute with him?"

"Maybe."

"What do you think it means?"

"I don't know." Catt swiped the web page with her finger.

"Is that his staff?" Em pointed toward several pictures on the page with bios.

"Yes."

"All beautiful women," Em pointed out.

"I noticed that, too," Catt said. "They open at eight tomorrow, but I'm thinking we go over around nine. We'll bring Cagney and Lacey and act like we're OBX tourists that have to see where their products come from." Catt closed the website and accessed Facebook.

"Do you think John will recognize you?" Em asked.

"Not sure."

As luck would have it, John Carpenter owner of Pet Products appeared on the page. Bingo! "I found him." Catt turned her phone toward Em.

A picture of a tanned, muscular John Carpenter sat behind the wheel of a pleasure boat. A big-haired blond in a teeny-weeny bikini sat in the seat next to him holding Fluffy.

"Wow," Em said.

"Double wow," Catt said.

"Looks like John is a ladies' man."

"Yep. And, according to his latest post, he and lady-friend Tina will be at the Sound and Creek restaurant this evening for a par-T," Catt said.

"Did he really post that?" Em asked.

"It's right there in living color." Catt pointed toward the post.

"So, he's a party animal who likes animals?"

"Looks that way."

"What's next?"

"Hear me out. I'm thinking we get all dolled up and head over to the restaurant tonight."

"For what?" Em asked.

"Hey, you said you were ready to do some sleuthing. Here's our opportunity."

"You think he wrote the note?"

"I don't have a clue who wrote that note. I'm just trying to get eyes on all the players. Plus, maybe we can uncover the dispute."

"Okay. I'll be ready. But first I'm catching a few rays." Em leaned back in her chair.

Against Jonathan Ray's wishes and better judgment, he, Catt, and Em headed to the Sound and Creek restaurant for their dinner reservation.

"Please follow me." A hostess grabbed three menus from the stand and made her way through the crab-themed, crowded restaurant. Catt was dressed in a strapless, soft blue jumpsuit that flattered her slim figure and blond hair, while Em wore a little black number that accentuated her curves.

Catt's nostrils absorbed the smell of the seafood delicacies, the freshest on the East Coast, as they walked toward their table. And according to Catt, the food was the best in the world.

"Here we are." The hostess stopped at an aisle table. She set the menus on the table's edge. "Your server will be with you shortly."

Catt sat down and grabbed the menu. She glanced around the restaurant and noticed a large group seated in an alcove. Further down the table sat John Carpenter in a stylish, pink shirt. The man they had come to meet. She nudged Em's arm.

Em raised her head up from the menu. "What?"

Catt nodded toward the large group.

"Is that him?"

"Yes."

A young waiter approached the table. "I'm Jonathan. I'll be your server this evening."

"That makes two Jonathans." Em pointed toward Jonathan Ray.

"Is that right? Well good name, my man." The waiter gave Jonathan Ray a bro nod.

Jonathan Ray bro-nodded in return.

"Can I start you off with something to drink?"

"Cabernet for me," Catt said.

"Same for me," Em said.

"Crown and ginger," Jonathan Ray said.

"Great choices. I'll bring some bread and butter with your drinks. Be back shortly."

"So, what's the plan?" Em leaned forward.

"I'm still trying to access the situation. It appears to be a fiftyish birthday party for one of John's college buddies."

"How do you know that?" Em asked.

"He posted it on Facebook."

"That's scary to know you can follow someone from their posts," Jonathan Ray added.

The waiter brought the drinks. Someone bumped into him, and he barely managed to prevent the drinks from tipping off the tray. "Sorry about that. It's busy tonight," he said.

"Yeah. I was looking at the large party to the right. The waitress appears to have her hands full with that group." Catt nodded toward several people in the party with their hands in the air apparently needing food or drink service.

"Oh yeah. That's John Carpenter and his group. He's a legend around here."

"Oh really?" Catt said.

"Yeah. He's known for throwing wild parties and having lots of girlfriends." The waiter placed the bread and butter on the table.

"Sounds like an interesting guy," Catt said.

"Yep. But he redeems himself by being an animal supporter and owner of a distributing company for animal products."

"It seems unusual that a distributing company is in OBX since the industry is tourism and seafood with one road in."

"Yeah. But that's his redeeming quality. He spent summers here as a kid and brought his company to OBX to add jobs and rebuild the economy after the last hurricane."

"So, he parties a lot but has a big heart?" Catt said.

"Yep. So, is anyone interested in the buffet? It has our famous crab-cakes, fish, crab-legs and much more."

"Sure. I'll do the buffet." Catt closed the menu.

"Me too." Em handed her menu to the waiter.

"Same here." Jonathan Ray remarked.

"Great." The waiter grabbed the menus. "Help yourself. Plates are available on the side of the bar."

After getting their dinners, the trio sat down to eat.

"The waiter was a chatty fellow," Jonathan Ray said as he cracked one of his crab-legs with a metal cracker.

"Sure was." Em stabbed her crab-cake with a fork.

As Catt picked through her fish, salad, and vegetables, she noticed John Carpenter get up from his table. He began making his way down the aisle toward them. "John," Catt blurted out.

He stopped dead in his tracks, giving her a once over.

Em sat straight up.

"Remember me, Catt Ramsey?"

"Uh, sure. We met through Candice Berry."

"Yes. I'm also one of your customers from Virginia Beach. The Woof-Pack Dog Walkers?"

"Of course."

"This is my sister Em. She's a dog walker with us and our friend Jonathan Ray." Catt waved her hand toward her dining companions.

John nodded and placed his hands in his pockets. "How's business?"

"It's great. I actually got a weekend off."

"Good. Balancing work and personal life is always a challenge. But most importantly, how is our service?"

"Great. My babies love your dental bones. As a matter of fact, I received a delivery the other day."

"That's good to hear. Well if there is anything you need, don't hesitate to let my staff know." He started to turn away.

"There is one thing." Catt held up her finger.

John frowned. "What's that?"

"We would love to see your warehouse."

"Especially the blue boxes. Brilliant marketing," Em added.

Catt smiled at Em's quick response, since flattery did work in most situations.

Jonathan Ray glared at Em. "That can be arranged. Tours are listed on our website. Or you can call our office, and we'll set something up next time you're here."

"I really appreciate it. But since there's no time like the present, I'm here now," Catt offered.

"We actually stopped by today and found out you were closed," Em added.

John's eyebrows knitted together. "Yeah. We closed for repairs."

"I see." Em kicked Catt's leg under the table.

"It's just that we order from your company a lot, and all the dogs that we walk love your toys and treats. They recognize the boxes and even jump up and down every time we get one, so it would be great to get a tour. I have my dogs Cagney and Lacey with me this weekend." Catt laid it on thick.

"Ah, named after one of my favorite classic TV shows. Well, since you put it like that. I'm a sucker for animals who love my products. What kind of dogs do you have?"

"Yorkshire Terriers."

"How long are you in OBX?"

"Until Sunday around lunch," Catt said.

"I could arrange a tour in the morning. But since it's Saturday, only half of my workers will be there, so you won't see the full production but will still get a good feel of what we do. We'll have some samples for you too."

Catt clapped her hands in excitement.

"Say around nine?"

"That's perfect," Catt said. "Thank you so much."

"Here's my card. Ring the front bell, and someone will buzz you in."

CHAPTER SEVEN

After their meeting with John Carpenter, Catt and Em headed back to the cottage, opened a bottle of wine, and sat on the deck playing with Cagney and Lacey. Jonathan Ray commandeered the kitchen table to prepare for a late-night beach combing excursion

"I can say one thing," Em said.

"What's that?" Catt asked.

"You are braver than I thought."

"What do you mean?"

"The look on John Carpenter's face when you asked him for a tour was priceless."

"It worked, didn't it?" Catt sipped her wine.

"What's next?"

"Here're my thoughts. We learned from the security guard that John Carpenter is involved in a dispute and that John lied to us about it. And from the waiter at the restaurant that he has a flamboyant lifestyle but brought his company to OBX to help the economy. And he sent rhyming notes to Candice."

"Yeah . . . so." Em sipped her wine.

"Well. Since that's pretty much all we have to go on, I'm most interested in seeing what we find at the warehouse. Plus, we take Cagney and Lacey with us."

"What do you think we'll find?" Em's voice was low and serious.

"I don't know. But we need to look for any clues."

"Great. I will put my detective cap on while we're there."

"Don't be too obvious."

"I won't. They'll never know that I am mentally taking in everything on the tour."

"That's what I'm afraid of."

Jonathan Ray stepped onto the deck.

"How's it going?" Em asked.

"Pretty good. All set for trying a late night of metal detecting?" He looked down at Em. "You still coming with me later?"

"Wouldn't miss it," Em said.

Jonathan Ray walked toward the rail and leaned against it. "What are you two plotting?"

"Tomorrow's tour," Em said.

"Listen. I've only heard bits and pieces of all of this, but it could be dangerous if he knows what you are up to. I get the feeling that even though John Carpenter likes to par-T," Jonathan Ray air quoted the word, "he's no one to be fooling around with."

"Agreed," Catt said. "But I have to find out who sent me the note. And then I need to find out what it means. I would think John Carpenter would want to know that since it came in a box from his company."

"Then tell him," Jonathan Ray said.

"Not now. I need to look into it this more since I don't know who's involved yet," Catt said.

"Are you thinking that John Carpenter is involved?" Jonathan Ray asked.

"I don't know."

"I hope I don't find you two dead on a backstreet. Or worse, murdered in the warehouse."

CHAPTER EIGHT

The next morning after Catt cooked breakfast, she and Em ate on the deck.

"Did y'all find anything last night?" Catt sipped her orange juice and ate her toast.

"We found two rare coins. Jonathan Ray is heading to the antique store to get them checked out."

"Really?"

"Yep. He started researching it last night and was up very late."

"I'll leave him a plate in the microwave for when he wakes up."

Em headed to her room to change clothes while Catt viewed the dog-walking schedule and checked in with Sammy.

Em walked into the living room.

"I thought you weren't dressing in your undercover clothes," Catt asked, eyeing the black outfit her sister wore.

"Since this is an undercover assignment, I'm dressing partially in them," Em replied.

"Partially?"

"Yeah. Sans the jacket. It's so hot out it would look out of place and give away my cover." Em smirked.

Catt rolled her eyes. "Okay. Remember our goal is to look for any clues to uncover who sent the note." Catt gathered the dogs by the door.

"Got it. Let's roll, partner."

After loading Cagney and Lacey into the SUV, Catt and Em slipped into the front seats. Catt drove to the warehouse and wheeled into the parking lot, driving past the Pet Products sign. She parked in a front parking space and opened the back door. "We're here."

The dogs jumped down from the SUV, their leashes dangling on the ground. They made their way toward the sign indicating it was the office. Catt pressed the outside buzzer.

John Carpenter appeared at the door. "Well, hello Catt and group."

"Good morning," Catt said. "This is Cagney and Lacey, and you remember Em?"

"Of course." John checked out the crew before him as Cagney and Lacey wagged their tails, and Em adjusted her black top. "Please come in. Normally, my assistant greets our guests but I made a special point to meet you." John waved them inside.

They entered the lobby. It was decorated with wrought iron fixtures and encased pearl-white globe lamps. Brightly colored banners hung from the ceiling with the Pet Products' image. Beneath them were blue boxes and pet supplies siting on large white columns.

"Wow. I love this building," Catt said.

"Very cool." Em smiled.

Cagney and Lacey pulled on their leashes to sniff around the columns and product displays. Catt didn't notice anything except the faint odor of bleach.

"Thank you," John said. "I had it renovated after I bought the building. But now the business has grown with online orders and the great brands we offer."

"That's why I order from you," Catt said.

"Good to hear from happy customers," John said.

An attractive, brunette woman dressed in stylish jeans, flat shoes, and a fitted blue blazer with the company logo on the breast pocket appeared from a side door in the lobby. The blazer hugged her slim frame and breasts. She held an electronic device in her hands.

"Let me introduce Anna Morozova," John said. "Anna is our operations manager. Anna, these are happy customers from Virginia Beach, Catt and Em Ramsey."

Catt nodded toward the woman.

"Very nice to meet you." Anna let the "r" roll off her tongue. Catt recognized a Russian accent.

Anna's eyes sparkled when she turned toward John. Catt noticed Anna softening when she looked at him. Could there be more to their relationship than boss/employee?

"Anna will be your tour guide this morning," John offered. "I'll be in my office taking care of a few things, should you need me." He turned and headed down the hall.

"Right this way ladies, and we'll begin the tour." Anna led them to a glass partitioned area. "Since the machines are running and you have dogs, we cannot go into this portion of the warehouse where we assemble the boxes. I thought this would be of particular interest since John said your dog's love our boxes."

"This is great. But there are only a few blue boxes." Catt pointed toward the packing area.

"We had slight issue with blue boxes so we are using substitute," Anna said.

"Won't your customers be disappointed since they like the blue boxes?"

"No. We are including insert in substitute boxes to let them know."

"I see," Catt said.

Em placed her hand against the glass. "The boxes are assembled quickly."

"Yes. It's very efficient." Anna's accent was strong. "And I believe the dogs think so, too." She pointed toward Cagney and Lacey who stood on their hind legs behind the glass window, tails wagging as if they recognized the boxes.

Catt smiled. The dogs played their role as happy customers.

"Follow me." Anna walked briskly down the long corridor, and Catt and Em had to pick up their pace to keep up. "This is where the products are placed into the boxes."

Catt recognized the plush toys, chew toys, dental treats, and dog bones.

"This way," Anna said. "And to your right is where the inserts are added, which tell the history of our company and, of course, how-to re-order. The last step is quality control, where the orders and the contents are reviewed for accuracy. Finally, the boxes are placed on the docks for shipping, including internationally and of course to our Virginia Beach hub that you are familiar with?"

Catt nodded.

"Can we actually go in and see this part?" Em asked.

"We usually do not allow anyone in the warehouse, but since you are good customers and have friendly dogs, I will make exception. Follow me." Anna swiped her badge and pushed open the metal door. The group entered behind her. "Ladies," she said to the two workers, "I'd like to introduce you to two of Mr. Carpenter's special guests, Catt and Em Ramsey from Virginia Beach. And their dogs Cagney and Lacey."

Catt turned her attention toward two middle-aged women checking the boxes and inserts. One woman frowned when Catt and Em walked up. The other one, with the name tag Norma Jeane Baker, walked toward Catt and Em and handed them each a blue tote bag with the Pet Products logo. "Here's some of our products. There's chew toys and treats."

Catt and Em thanked her.

"Well, I hope you enjoy the tour." Catt had to listen carefully to understand Anna's thick accent. "Please follow me to lobby."

After saying goodbye to Anna, Catt, Em, and the dogs remained in the lobby for a few minutes to thank John, but he never came back to meet them. The dogs started getting restless, so Catt and Em headed to the car.

"I have a thought. Circle around the back of the building," Em said.

"Why?"

"The warehouse doors were open when we took the tour. I want to drive back there."

"Why?

"To see the boxes on the docks. Plus, I'm just curious."

Catt turned and headed toward the back of the building. Several men were busy loading boxes onto the shipping docks for pickup. "There's Shane, our delivery driver," Catt pointed out.

"Why is he down here? Isn't his route in the Virginia Beach hub?" Em asked.

"I don't know. But I am curious about him since he delivered the box to me." Catt rubbed her forehead. "This is all so confusing."

"Speaking of the tour, I looked Anna up online. She started working as a production worker three years ago for Pet Products and quickly rose to Operations Manager."

"Really?"

"Yes. Plus, John and Anna have much more going on than a boss-employee relationship."

Catt's mouth flew open. "How do you know?"

"Anna posted a picture of her and John on Facebook that's cozier than what an employer, employee relationship should be." Em turned the phone toward Catt.

Catt stopped at a red light. "Let me see that." The picture showed Anna sitting close to John in a boat with her hand on his knee. Both of them were holding drinks. "But I thought John had a girlfriend. The blond on the boat?"

"I guess he's got several," Em said. "

The light turned green, and Catt made a U-turn.

"Where are you going?" Em asked.

Catt headed back toward Pet Products, but this time she pulled into a parking lot across from the company and parked. "I'm also curious about something."

Em turned toward Catt with a puzzled look.

"Remember the lady that gave us the totes before leaving the plant?"

"Norma Jeane?"

"Yeah. We're going to follow her. I've got a few questions for her."

CHAPTER NINE

"Are you crazy?" Em yelled.

"No. I just think Norma Jeane Baker knows something."

"And that's based on what? Giving us samples?"

"That and the way she glared at Anna," Catt said.

Em slapped her forehead. "You're going to get us in trouble."

The next thirty minutes passed slowly, with Em giving Catt her two-cents about following someone they didn't know.

"Look. There she is." Catt pointed to a sporty red Mustang barreling out of the parking. As the car zipped past them, Catt said, "Yup. That's Norma Jeane driving." Catt pulled out of the parking lot, careful not to be seen.

Norma Jeane cut a hard-fast right at the light and sped up.

Catt continued to tail her.

Em held on tightly. "Damn. She drives fast for an older broad."

Norma Jeane turned left at the next light just past the Wright Brothers' Memorial.

Catt followed her down a back road off of Highway 12 that led to the sound side of the Outer Banks, an area with less tourists.

Norma Jeane wheeled the Mustang into the driveway of a small, white cottage. She parked it and stepped out of the vehicle. She made her way to the large front porch. A sixtyish, man with gray-blond hair swung the screen door open. His head turned left, and then right before letting her inside.

"That man looks familiar," Catt said as she continued down the road then circled back toward the house. She pulled into a grassy area with no one around and parked.

"Now what?" Em asked.

"We do surveillance," Catt said.

"I love surveillance, but is this safe? I mean, in broad daylight?"

Catt locked the doors and let the windows down. She glanced back at Cagney and Lacey, who were asleep in the back seat.

"Jonathan Ray is not going to like this," Em protested.

"You've done stakeouts for me before."

"Yes. But something seems fishy about this. In fact, it's wrong. And scary. I'm on a back road in OBX, and no one but you, me, and the dogs know we are here."

Just as Em finished her sentence, a shadow appeared to the left of Catt's driver's door.

"Hold it right there, you two." A gun clicked near Catt's ear.

Catt looked into her rearview mirror, her body trembling with fear. The man from the white cottage was holding a gun, pointing it right at her heart. Norma Jeane stood behind him, hands on her hips and looking ready to spit nails.

"Get out, slowly. Both of you," he ordered.

Cagney and Lacey began barking.

"And shut those mutts up," he said.

Catt hushed Cagney and Lacey and exited the vehicle slowly.

"Now come over here with your hands up." He waved the gun in the air.

Catt and Em stood on the driver's side of the vehicle. Cagney and Lacey jumped on the window to see all the action.

Catt looked closer at the man. "Charlie? What are you doing in OBX?"

"After retirement, I moved here to rekindle my relationship with Norma Jeane. But the bigger question is what are you doing here?"

"You mean we're being held at gunpoint by our former delivery driver?" Em whispered from the side of her mouth.

Catt frowned toward Em.

"Oh, my lord," Norma Jeane said.

"You know these two?" Charlie asked.

"Sort of. They were at my work today pretending to be interested in what we do. I got curious since they were so eager about our boxes. And so did Anna, who marched straight up to John's office to tell him so."

"Spit it out. Why are you following my woman?" Charlie asked.

"Because of the note." Catt's hands shook as she explained about receiving the note in the box.

Norma Jeane instructed Charlie to put the gun down.

He lowered it slightly.

Catt and Em lowered their hands with caution.

"But why on earth would someone send you a note to come down here of all places?" Norma Jeane asked.

"I don't know," Catt said.

"That's the million-dollar question." Em added.

"I don't believe them," Charlie said.

"Oh, I believe them," Norma Jeane said. "If it's anything to do with John Carpenter, I believe it. That man chases women left and right, does shady business dealings, but still manages to fool the public with his blue box concept. Blue box my foot." Norma Jeane spit in the dirt and rubbed her shoe over it.

"What do you want from us?" Charlie asked.

"We want to know who had access to put the note in the box?" Catt asked.

"How should I know," Norma Jeane asked. "It could be anyone. As you saw today, we have a process to fill each box from the invoice then seal the box and ship it out. It's that simple."

"Could it be someone who works the production line with you? The woman on the line gave us quite the stares today," Catt said.

"Oh, heck no. She's a wimp. She might look rough and tumble, but she's scared of her own shadow."

"What about the workers who load the boxes on the docks?"

"The boxes are sealed by the time they load them."

"But what's to prevent them from tampering with the boxes?"

Norma Jeane and Charlie both shrugged their shoulders.

"Do you know the driver Shane who works out of the Virginia Beach hub? He was on the docks today."

Norma Jeane crossed her arms. "He's my nephew. He's filling in for someone. Why?"

"He delivered the tampered box to me."

"He would never mess around with the boxes if that's what you're suggesting. I got him the job. It means the world to him."

"I see," Catt said.

"Does Anna ever work the production line?" Em asked.

"Are you kidding me?" Norma Jeane said. "The only time that woman comes to the line is to give us the third degree about this, that, or the other. She could care less about us."

"Why was the plant closed for repairs yesterday?" Em asked.

"We were closed but it wasn't for repairs."

"What do you mean?" Em asked.

"We had a temporary shutdown due to a dispute."

"What type of dispute?"

Norma Jeane placed her hands on her hips. "Our blue box supplier cut us off."

"That explains the substitute boxes. But if that's the case, you should have enough supplies on hand to keep operating for a while, even with a supply reduction," Catt offered.

"Normally. But during the last three months, we've received fewer and fewer boxes."

"Interesting. I have a favor to ask."

"What is it?" Norma Jean quizzed.

"Can you let me know if you see or hear anything suspicious about the boxes? Here's my card with my local contact info."

"You bet."

CHAPTER TEN

Catt woke to another beautiful summer morning at the beach. She had no worries, until a knock sounded at the door. "Nags Head Police."

Catt went to the door and opened it. Cagney and Lacey stood behind her, barking. "Yes?" she asked the handsome blond-haired man. The navy-blue suit was designed to impress ... and intimidate. Which it did.

"Are you Catt Ramsey?"

"Yes." Catt's wavering voice mirrored her inner trembling. What could the police possibly want from her? Had Em and Jonathan Ray's metal detecting turned out to be illegal after all?

"I'm Detective Dexter Harrington with the Nags Head Police Department." He flashed his official badge. "I would like to talk to you about the murder of John Carpenter."

"Murder?" Catt's hand flew to her throat as she took a step back. Had he just said murder?

Em appeared behind Catt. "What's going on?"

"Nags Head Police, Ma'am." Detective Harrington flashed his badge again. "And you are?"

"Emma Ramsey, her sister."

"Miss Ramsey, I was just telling your sister that John Carpenter was found murdered in his office yesterday. I would like to ask you a few questions about your visit with him. May I come in?"

"Sure." Catt stepped away from the threshold and motioned for the detective to enter. "But I don't understand. You said that John was murdered? How? Why?"

"That's what I'm trying to find out." The detective entered and followed Catt to the living room.

Cagney and Lacey resumed their barking, sniffing the detective's heels as he walked. "Shhh . . ." Catt waved her hand toward the dogs. They obeyed the command and slunk into a corner where they could observe the action.

Em fell in line behind her sister.

Jonathan Ray entered the room. "What's going on?"

"Police have some questions," Catt said.

Jonathan Ray's gaze cut to the man in the suit. His expression reflected the confusion that Catt was feeling.

Detective Harrington turned and flashed his badge once more. "And you are?"

"Jonathan Ray. A family, friend."

"Have a seat," Catt said to the detective.

They all settled in the coastal seating group overlooking the ocean. Catt's hands trembled, and she tucked them under her legs to still them.

Detective Harrington looked directly at Catt, those brown eyes boring into her. "I understand you visited Mr. Carpenter yesterday and toured his business?"

"Yes. I'm a client of his and wanted to visit the distribution center."

"Why was that?"

If Catt lied, she could be in serious trouble. She glanced at Em then turned toward the detective. "If you must know, I received a note in a blue box from John's business."

"Note?"

"Yes. It referred to a theft and a murder I helped solve last year, and it said to come to OBX to find out what's next."

"What does it mean?"

"I don't know."

"And?"

"I came here as it suggested, and Em and I asked to tour the facility to see if I could figure out who might have sent it. My dogs Cagney and Lacey came along, too."

"Did you find out?"

"No."

"Did you see Mr. Carpenter during the tour?"

"Yes, he met us at the beginning and turned us over to Anna somebody. I don't recall her last name. She conducted the tour."

"Did you see Mr. Carpenter again after the tour?"

"No. I never saw him again."

The detective wrote some things down in a little notebook. "Do you have the note?"

"Yes."

"May I see it?"

Catt went to her room and grabbed the card from her suitcase. She read it one more time. *You Solved a model's murder and theft…Now come to Pet Products in OBX to solve the rest.* The message now seemed to carry a sinister undertone that she hadn't picked up on before. Could it be connected to John Carpenter's murder? She sure hoped not.

Catt walked back to the living room, her bare feet making soft swishing noises against the hardwood floor. The noise echoed in the silence that hung heavy between the detective and her traveling companions. "Here you go." She extended the card toward the detective. The note shook in her hands, but she couldn't help it.

Detective Harrington read the note. "Did you mention this to John?"

Catt frowned. "No."

"Since it's from his company, wouldn't it have been wise to review it with him?"

"I wasn't sure if he was involved in sending it," Catt said.

"Why do you think that?"

Catt explained about the notes to Candice Berry. "So, I didn't discount him sending me a note." She shrugged her shoulders.

"Were you having an affair with Mr. Carpenter?" Detective Harrington asked.

"What? No!" Catt sputtered her words. "And trust me, that man is not my type." Catt settled back in her chair. Her whole body shook now. It was not a comfortable feeling.

"Then why did Anna Morozova say you and he had a prior relationship? And that your jealousy of his current relationship could be a motive for murder?"

"That's ridiculous." Catt's fear turned to anger. "And frankly, I take offense, you barging in here and accusing me like that. How did you know where to find me anyway?"

"From an unidentified source." The detective paused. "Did you kill Mr. Carpenter?"

Catt stood on shaky legs and drew herself up to her full five-feet six-inch frame. "Detective Harrington. I must ask you to leave. If you have any more ridiculous questions for me, you can reach me through my lawyer. Please show yourself out."

Catt called Cagney and Lacey, and the three made a quick exit out the back door and down to the beach where Catt collapsed into the warm sand.

Chapter Eleven

On Monday morning, the sunrise was beautiful over Virginia Beach, but a distracted Catt didn't notice. She texted Sammy that she was back at work. After viewing the busy schedule, Catt took off down the boardwalk to fetch Grayson for her first walk of the day. She let herself into The Loft building, and then into Brock's apartment.

"Hello, Catt," Brock said.

Catt jumped. She'd been doing a lot of that since being accused of murder. "Hi Brock. I didn't realize you were here."

"What's this I hear about you being questioned in conjunction with John Carpenter's death?"

"How did you hear?"

"Front page of today's paper."

Catt sighed. "It's not true."

Brock frowned.

"I mean it's true I've been questioned, just not true about me murdering him. I only went down there to find out about the note."

"The news is reporting you and John had a relationship and that you went to seek revenge. They are even saying you created the note yourself," Brock said.

"No, I didn't. You've got to believe me," Catt pleaded.

"Calm down. Of course, I believe you. Do you have any idea who is behind this?"

Catt rubbed her forehead. "I'm not sure." But that wasn't entirely true. She suspected Anna Morozova was behind the smearing of Catt's reputation.

"Look. I'm sorry you're in this mess, but it will get cleared up." Brock moved closer toward Catt. "Let me know if I can help."

"Thanks." Catt grabbed Grayson's leash. "Let's go, buddy."

Catt and the dog made their way to James and Ava Cartwright's apartment to pick up Chopper and Ollie.

"Hi, there." Catt greeted the two dogs and headed to the kitchen to grab their leashes. "Ready to go for a walk?"

After leashing them, Catt and the dogs made their way toward the door. The excitable Chopper and Ollie jumped up and down, knocking mail off a small table. Catt knelt down and collected the scattered envelopes. One caught her eye, one with a familiar animal logo. A closer look revealed it was from John Carpenter. Catt set the leashes on the ground. "Just a minute and we'll walk," she said to the dogs. The postcard from John asked for a donation to an animal rescue in the Outer Banks. At the bottom of the letter, a handwritten note to Ava from John. *Looking forward to seeing you in OBX, our twenty-year friendship is the best. Yours truly, John.*

Although the handwritten note was a rhyme, it did not match the writing on the note that she had received.

Catt grabbed her phone and snapped a photo of the postcard. She carefully set it back on the table. What does this mean? Were John and Ava good friends? Past lovers? Or on again, off again lovers for twenty years?

"Let's go." She grabbed the dogs' leashes and led her canine entourage out of the building and down to the boardwalk. Catt was glad to be back on her own turf and thankful it was not humid outside. She walked the dogs extra time as she replayed in her mind all the things Anna had said in the newspaper. Maybe by saying those things, Anna hoped she could take over the company. Whatever the reason, Catt was going to find out who killed John Carpenter, who wrote the note, and why Anna was lying.

CHAPTER TWELVE

After a restless night, Catt showered, made a pot of coffee, and fed Cagney and Lacey. She sat at her desk, paid a few bills, and updated the schedule. After eating, Cagney and Lacey approached Catt with somber looks. It was as if they knew she was going through turmoil. "I can always count on you two."

A few minutes later, Sammy entered through the screen door. "Welcome back." She grabbed a cup of coffee.

"Thanks for taking care of everything while I was in OBX." Catt opened her desk drawer and pulled out an envelope. "Here's the extra cash for helping out." She handed it to Sammy.

"My pleasure. And speaking of OBX, I caught the news. You okay?"

"I've been better."

"Do the police have any leads on who did it?" Sammy leaned against the counter.

"Besides me?" Catt rubbed her forehead.

"I'm sorry, Catt. I hope they find out soon. If there is anything I can do, please let me know." Sammy rinsed her cup in the sink and set it on the counter to dry.

The door swung open and Shane, the delivery man from Pet Products entered. "Delivery. Where would you like it?" He held a blue box.

"I better get going. I'll check in with you later." Sammy exited the door and headed down the stairs.

Catt was surprised to see a delivery since according to the paper, the Pet Products had shut down after the murder. She also hoped it did not contain another note. "Is it heavy?"

"No ma'am."

"I'll take it."

He handed her the box.

"I see you're still doing the route?"

"Yes ma'am. Is there anything else?"

"There is one thing. Last week, when I received a delivery from you, the contents inside the box contained a mysterious note from your company."

"Yes, my aunt Norma Jeane told me."

"Do you know who tampered with the box?"

"No ma'am."

"Did you see anything suspicious with the boxes that day?"

Shane removed his cap and ran his hand through his curly, blonde hair. "No. But I deliver hundreds of boxes every day. If there is anything suspicious, we have a protocol that requires us to report it to our security team. Plus, I don't have anything to do with what's inside the box. I just load them on the truck from our hub and start my local deliveries."

"I understand. Just thought I'd ask." Catt paused. "I'm surprised to see the delivery today and especially in a blue box since Norma Jeane mentioned the supplier dispute."

"Yeah. We closed temporary, but business has to continue so we reopened under our operation manager's direction."

"That must be Anna. I met her on the tour."

Shane nodded.

"Look. I know you don't know me, but I didn't have anything to do with John's murder. I was only trying to find the truth."

"I know. Aunt Norma Jeane said she was keeping an eye out for anything suspicious about the boxes. She didn't trust John Carpenter. Plus, she asked me to keep my eyes and ears open for any tampering."

Catt realized she had allies in Norma Jeane and Shane.

"Thank you." Catt opened the box with a pair of scissors. She pulled the paper from the box and grabbed the insert. *Scandal, murder, and theft. Now it's time for your arrest.* She showed the card to Shane.

Em entered. "Morning. What's going on?"

"Em, this is Shane, a delivery driver for Pet Products, and Norma Jeane's nephew and co-worker. I received another note."

Em had a worried look on her face.

"It's okay. Shane knows about it all and that Norma Jeane is helping us."

Em turned her attention toward the card. "Is that it?"

"Yes." Shane handed her the card.

Em read the note. "Someone is trying to set you up."

Catt pulled the box toward her to view the mailing label. "It was scheduled for overnight delivery from Pet Products."

"We have daily deliveries," Shane said. "But no one was at the plant yesterday."

"Is that so?" Catt glanced around her desk. "So that means this must have hit the queue the day John was murdered and sat there until you reopened." Catt paused while she let her jumbled thoughts settle into a more linear line of thinking. "Em, did you happen to see the blue box that was delivered before we left for OBX?"

"It's on the counter." Em grabbed the box and walked it toward Catt.

Catt viewed the label. "It was mailed two days day to our leaving for OBX."

"Who knew we were going to OBX?" Em asked.

Catt tapped her finger against her lip. "I mentioned it to Brock, Ava, Josh, Nora, and Sammy."

"Then it had to be someone who knew our schedule," Em suggested.

"True." Catt turned toward Shane. "I know you are on a tight delivery schedule, but when you get back to the warehouse, can you ask Norma Jeane to check on Anna's whereabouts when John was murdered?"

"Sure. But do you think Anna had anything to do it?"

"I don't know, but I would like to find out."

"Will do. I have to go. Norma Jeane will be in touch." Shane made his way out the door.

Em turned toward Catt. "Do you trust him?"

"I have no other choice. But take a look at this." Catt showed Em the photo of the hand-written note from John to Ava."

"I guess that means John didn't write the notes," Em suggested.

"I guess not," Catt said.

CHAPTER THIRTEEN

Later that morning, Catt received a text from Brock. I NEED TO TALK TO YOU WHEN YOU STOP BY TO WALK GRAYSON. Catt texted back that she would be by soon. After finishing a few things, Catt grabbed Cagney's and Lacey's leashes. They would be making the rounds with her today. The three walked to The Loft and then made their way to Brock's apartment.

In the 6th floor hallway, she found Josh holding Nora's dog Hudson on a leash while talking to Ava Cartwright, who held Chopper and Ollie's leashes.

Josh's expression appeared serious.

Catt was surprised that Josh was with Hudson. She approached them.

"Catt. I have some news to share with you." Josh's tone was somber.

Catt glanced at Ava, then Josh.

"I'm sorry to tell you but Nora passed away from breast cancer this morning."

Catt mouthed the words "Nora," but nothing came out. She cleared her throat and tried again. "Nora. What happened?"

"The rescue squad just left. Apparently, she had called them and passed as they arrived."

Catt could not believe it. She'd seen Nora less than a week ago. Although she appeared tired and worn, Catt had little reason to believe she would pass away anytime soon.

"Are you okay, Catt?" Josh grabbed her arm.

"Yes. I mean no. I don't know what I mean. I didn't expect this."

"I'm awfully sorry, Catt," Josh said.

"Me, too," Ava said.

"Did anyone get in touch with Nora's family?" Catt asked.

"Yes. The police contacted them," Josh said.

"What about Hudson?" Catt knelt down to pet him.

"Since I have a key to Nora's apartment, I'll keep an eye on Hudson until they arrive tomorrow," Josh said. "Do you want to come in and talk?"

"Thanks, but I'm okay." She headed to Brock's and knocked on the door.

Tears streamed down her face when Brock opened the door.

"Oh, Catt. Come in." He put his arm around her shoulder as Cagney and Lacey darted inside to see Grayson.

"Follow me." Brock made his way into the stylish living room.

The dogs sniffed each other until satisfied and then trotted to join them.

"Looks like you heard?" Brock asked. "Sit here." He waved toward a blue couch that matched his steel-blue eyes.

Catt sat down. "I can't believe it. Nora was such a dear friend and special client."

"I know." He walked toward the mini-bar in the corner of the living room and poured a shot of whiskey. He handed it to Catt. "Drink this."

Catt grabbed the glass and chugged it. It burned going down her throat. "Is that what you wanted to talk to me about in your text?" she asked Brock.

"Yes. I'm sorry. I couldn't tell you over the phone or by text."

Catt let out a heavy breath and handed the glass to Brock. "I understand."

Brock sat in the matching chair adjacent to the couch.

Catt relaxed back in her seat. Cagney, Lacey, and Grayson approached her. She reached into her pocket and gave them treats.

"You are really good with animals. And I know how much

Nora loved you walking Hudson," Brock assured her.

"I wonder, what will happen to Hudson?" Catt asked.

"I'm hoping Nora's family will keep him."

"Me, too." Catt sniffed.

"Feel a little better?" Brock asked.

Catt nodded.

"Do you have any updates about OBX?"

"I received another note," Catt said.

"What did it say?"

"That they will arrest me soon. I don't know what to make of this, but I do have inside help from someone from Pet Products."

"And who is that?"

"Two of their workers. As soon as I find out additional information, I'll let you know."

Grayson began jumping up and down.

Catt smiled at the dog's antics. "I think he's ready to walk."

"Are you up to it?" Brock asked. "You don't have to walk him if you don't feel like it."

"I'm up to it. It will do me good to walk him."

CHAPTER FOURTEEN

After returning Grayson, Catt ran into Ava Cartwright in the lobby.

"How are you doing, Catt?" Ava asked.

"Better."

"I'm sorry to hear about Nora. I didn't know her, but I understand you were friends."

"Thank you."

"Well, again I'm sorry." Ava paused. "By the way, I'm glad I ran into you. I have to make a quick trip tomorrow and was hoping that you could board my babies for the day. I know it's last minute, but my husband and I need to go out of town. Plus, I trust you with them."

Catt checked her schedule. "I do have a busy day tomorrow."

"If this helps, I'll be back late tomorrow afternoon and can pick them up at your office. I wouldn't ask if it wasn't important."

"I'll take good care of them." Catt updated her schedule.

"You are the best. Well, thanks again." Ava headed toward the elevators.

Catt made her way back to the Woof-Pack Dog Walkers with Cagney and Lacey in tow. While sitting at her desk reviewing the schedule, her cell phone range.

"It's Norma Jeane. I checked out Anna's whereabouts the day John was murdered. She left the warehouse around one and John was murdered between noon and three according to the police."

"Well that proves she was there when he was murdered and that I didn't murder him since I was following you during that time. Are the police going to arrest her?"

"Nope. Said they can't prove it. Plus, no motive."

"And they think I had a motive?"

"According to Anna, you are a scorned, jealous lover."

"Can you check one more thing for me?"

"Sure. What is it?"

"Are you attending John's funeral?"

"Yes. But only because they are closing the plant, and we're all going."

"I need you to keep an eye out for a woman named Ava Cartwright at the funeral."

"Who is she?"

"She's a long-time friend of John's."

"What does she have to do with all of this?"

"I don't know, but I have a hunch she's attending the funeral tomorrow. I'll text you her photo." Catt kept a photo of all her clients and their dogs for insurance reasons.

"Okay. Then what?"

"Bump into her and chat her up about John. Let me know what you find out."

That afternoon, Catt ordered supplies and handled administrative tasks for the business. Three quick knocks sounded on her door. Detective Dexter Harrington entered. Cagney and Lacey barked at him.

"Hello, Ms. Ramsey," Detective Harrington said.

Catt's eyes widened. Was he here to arrest her? "What brings you to Virginia Beach? Isn't it out of your jurisdiction?"

"Since I have official business here, I decided to stop by for additional questions."

"Okay. Have a seat." Catt waved her hand toward a chair in front of her desk. The detective took a seat. "Would you like some water?" She grabbed a bottle out of the fridge.

"No thanks."

No longer interested in their guest, Cagney and Lacey headed to their water bowls.

Catt twisted the top off the water and sat back in her chair.

Detective Harrington pulled a small notebook and pen from his pocket. "To begin with, what time did you leave the Pet Products warehouse the day John Carpenter was murdered?"

"Around eleven."

"And where did you go from there?"

Catt hesitated to tell the detective that she had followed Norma Jeane. She didn't want to outright lie, so she framed her answer with an element of truth. "To the beach with my sister."

"According to Anna Morozova, you drove to the back of the warehouse after the tour and entered through the open delivery door. She claims you snuck back into the building and went upstairs to John's office to kill him."

Catt frowned. "But that's not true. I never went into the building again."

"Anna stated you saw John at the Sound and Creek restaurant the night before and asked him about taking the tour? Is that true?"

"Uh . . . yes."

"So, were you stalking John at the restaurant?"

"Technically, yes, but I only went there to solve the mystery surrounding the note. I didn't kill him."

The detective made several notes, closed his notepad and stood. "I'll be in touch." He exited out the door and pounded down the stairs.

Chapter Fifteen

After getting Chopper and Ollie from Ava's apartment and walking them on the boardwalk with Cagney and Lacey, Catt received a text from Nora's sister asking her to keep Hudson for the day since the family needed to make arrangements at the funeral home. Catt then made her way to Nora's to get Hudson.

She opened the door and entered the apartment. Hudson stood at the door barking as the dogs scurried toward him. Hudson sniffed the dogs then darted down the hall into Nora's bedroom. Catt and her dogs followed. Hudson jumped on Nora's bed. Catt sat beside him while the dogs sat on the floor. "I'm sorry, boy. I know you miss your mom." Catt glanced around the room. Her heart sank. Nora would not be coming back.

She reached out and fingered several get-well cards on the nightstand. She flipped through the cheerful images on the fronts of the cards, offering hope, healing and comfort. At the bottom of the stack were two letters from different attorneys. Catt opened the letter with the Outer Banks address. It was dated three months ago. It stated that Nora received a final payment of $850,000 from her divorce decree from John Carpenter, her former husband.

Catt's eyes widened. She knew that Nora had been married four times but didn't know the names of any of her ex-husbands.

Catt placed the letter back in the envelope and opened the second letter. It was Nora's last will and testament from an attorney in Virginia Beach. The will stated that Nora's assets and

Hudson would go to her sister. She placed the will back in the envelope and set both letters back on the stand. She petted Hudson. "Let's get your leash. You're spending the day with me."

After closing Nora's apartment door, Josh approached them. The dogs barked. "Hush, now," Catt said to them. They obeyed.

Josh stopped by Nora's door. "Hi Catt."

"Hi, Josh."

"What are you doing?"

"Hudson is spending the day with me while Nora's family makes funeral arrangements."

"I see." Josh moved closer. "I fed and walked him earlier this morning and was checking on him again."

"Thanks for doing that. I didn't realize you had a key."

"Yeah. Nora and I became close when she got sick. She gave me a key. But again, I just stopped by to check on Hudson."

"Well, he's fine. I'm taking him for a walk then back to my office for the day."

"Okay. If there is anything you need, please let me know."

As Catt headed down the hallway with the dogs, she noticed Josh still standing at Nora's door watching her. Something had been very off in that interaction with Josh, but Catt couldn't quite put her finger on it.

Later that morning, Catt sipped her bottled water as she sat by the bay window in her office looking down on the fenced yard. Em and Sammy played with Hudson, Chopper, Ollie, Cagney, and Lacey. The dogs ran around the yard catching balls. Catt looked closer. The balls were red and appeared similar to one she had received. So, where had they come from?

A few minutes later, the door swung open and Em entered. "Just came to grab some water."

"Tell me. The red balls that you are throwing in the yard, where did you get them?"

"Oh. From the bag that Ava left for the dogs. Why?"

"The balls match the same red ball that was in the mysterious blue box that I received."

"You're right. Do you think Ava had something to do with it?"

Catt thought about the note she'd read in Ava's apartment, indicating a history with John Carpenter. "Do you believe in coincidences?"

"No." Em crossed her arms.

"I don't either, but I don't want to jump to any conclusions. She'll be back later this afternoon. When she comes to pick up her dogs, I'll ask her about the balls."

"Good idea."

"I'll text Brock to stop by this afternoon, too. If Ava is the culprit, then I want Brock to be here when I confront her."

"Good thinking. I'll text Jonathan Ray, just in case we need him."

"One other thing."

"What's that?" Em asked.

"When I picked up Hudson from Nora's a little while ago, I happened to see two attorney letters on Nora's nightstand."

"You mean you happened to open them?"

"Something like that. Anyway, guess who was Nora's ex-husband?"

Em shrugged her shoulders.

"John Carpenter."

"Get out of here. No way!"

"Yes, way. She received a final divorce payment of eight hundred and fifty-thousand dollars from John about three months ago."

"You're kidding me?"

"Nope."

"What does this mean?"

"I don't know. But I'll contact Norma Jeane and ask her about John's ex-wife. And I'm still waiting to hear if Ava attended John's funeral."

As the dogs played in the back yard with Sammy, Catt texted Brock to stop by. She then texted Norma Jeane about Nora and

John's marriage.

Catt's phoned dinged with an incoming message. A glance indicated the text was from Norma Jeane. "That was fast." Catt turned toward Em and read the message. "Ava attended John's funeral and she was very distraught. And John and Nora were married for about eight years. John was her last husband who had cheated on her with Anna. Nora sued and won a big divorce settlement, and John hated Nora for it."

"Interesting. But do you think Nora hated John enough to kill him?"

"No way. Nora was a gentle soul."

Chapter Sixteen

As Catt sat at her desk that afternoon, she made a few notations on a notepad about what things may, or may not, have a bearing on John Carpenter's murder. Josh's behavior at Nora's had been out of the ordinary, but why? John Carpenter had been murdered on a Saturday afternoon, so who was in the building at that time? His marriage to Nora. Was there lingering animosity between the two? Did John begrudge Nora? The last divorce payment? Did he know Nora left the money to her sister? Was Nora jealous about her rival, Anna? The suppliers dispute? Ava's stash of red balls, which are popular in any animal store. But it was her connection to John that made that seem unusual. So many questions, so few answers.

Em and Sammy entered the office, grabbed a few treats, and then took the dogs outside for a potty break and to play in the backyard again. Catt stayed behind, wanting some time alone with her thoughts.

The door swung open and Josh entered. "How's it going, Catt?"

Startled, Catt turned toward Josh. "What are you doing here?" He held Jersey in his arms, who was panting from the heat.

"I was walking Jersey and thought that Hudson might need a playmate."

"Hudson is out back with the other dogs playing. He's doing great. Does Jersey need some water?"

"Sure." Josh sat Jersey on the floor.

Catt reached into the mini-fridge. "Shoot. I'm out of water. Be right back. I have to go to the supply closet."

Catt returned from grabbing water to find Josh standing near her desk. His hand rested on her notepad.

Catt frowned. "Here's some water for Jersey." She grabbed a bowl and filled it. Jersey walked to the bowl for a drink.

Catt set the bottle on her desk. "So. You're out with Jersey today?"

"Yeah. But my thoughts are about Nora."

"Oh. What about her?"

"Well. I was kicking around all the things I did for her when she was sick. Run errands. Pay bills. Pick up medicine. Handle her affairs."

"I'm sure she appreciated it."

"But not in the way she had promised."

"What do you mean?"

Jersey finished drinking the water and made his way to a doggy bed, where he curled up and settled down for a nap.

"After Nora died and I went to get Hudson from her apartment, I started tidying up her bedroom. You know before her family was to arrive. That's when I found her will by the nightstand and read it. But I see from your notepad you also read the will."

Catt's eyes widened from Josh's curious behavior.

Josh walked closer toward Catt. He ran his fingers around the corner of the desk. "See, she promised there would be something for me if I did something for her."

"What was that?"

"Nora was distraught that she had received her last check from John, especially since he'd been a womanizer during their entire marriage and had cheated on her with the Russian.

"What do you mean?"

"Nora said if I killed him, she would add me to her will. She knew she didn't have much longer to live. But she didn't want John to live either. So that's when I set you up with the notes in the boxes. I got empty boxes, added the notes and red balls for an extra touch then switched them when the delivery driver pulled up to deliver them."

"You did that?"

"Yes. I needed someone to take the rap. And since you were involved in the theft and murder investigation last year, I knew you would be the perfect person. Plus, you rejected my advances toward you."

"But how?" Catt asked, her eyes widening in shock.

"When I found out you were going to OBX, I knew it was the perfect time to sneak into the warehouse and kill John. And, I could set you up for the blame since you were down there. As luck would have it, you, Em and the dogs were there, and the police accused you of killing him. And now that you know the truth, I have to kill you, too."

Josh moved closer. He pulled a rope from his pocket and leaned forward. Before Catt could duck or run, he wrapped the rope around her neck and pulled it tight.

The pressure on her neck made it difficult to breathe. Catt grabbed the rope trying to free herself, but the rope tightened. She tried to scream, but no sounds came out. Her fingers fumbled against the hard fibers of the rope. She looked at Josh's face. The look of determination on his face bordered on maniacal.

She didn't want to die. Panic rose in her belly as her tongue swelled and her eyes starting bugging from their sockets.

Her gaze swept the room looking for a weapon. Something. Anything. A water bottle was her only choice. Reaching, stretching, her hand snaked toward the water bottle. She wrapped her fingers around its neck and then raised it high above her head. Adrenaline kicked in, and with every ounce of energy she possessed in her body, she swung the bottle and slammed it against Josh's face.

He fell back, dropping the rope.

Catt took a deep breath as she made her move toward the door.

Josh grabbed her foot and yanked her to the ground. She smacked her head against the wooden floor.

Jersey stood up in the bed and barked.

Josh sat on top of Catt and placed the rope around her neck again. She bit his hand, hanging on like a dog with a bone.

"Ouch. You bitch!"

She coughed and choked but was able to take advantage of his distraction to wrangle herself from under him.

The door swung open. Em and Sammy entered with Cagney, Lacey, Chopper, Ollie, and Hudson trailing behind them. Dogs to the rescue!

Josh rushed toward the door.

"Stop him," Catt yelled. "He admitted to killing John Carpenter, and he tried to kill me."

Em grabbed a leash and swung the metal part of it against Josh's head. He fell across the doorway. Cagney and Lacey got tangled around his ankles, and Josh fell hard to the landing.

Catt scrambled up and gave chase, not wanting the killer to get away.

Josh kicked the dogs away and scrambled to get to his feet.

Jonathan Ray stood at the bottom of the stairs. "What the hell?"

Em ran out the door and swung the leash at Josh again, but he ducked, and raced down the steps. "Stop him. He tried to kill Catt."

Josh leapt down the final steps and barreled into Jonathan Ray.

Jonathan Ray wrapped his arms around Josh's waist and dragged him to the ground. The two wrestled in the grass. Jonathan Ray managed to get the upper hand. With Josh face down on the ground, Jonathan Ray pushed his knee into Josh's back and held him down. It was poetic justice that Josh's nose was pressed into a pile of fresh dog poop.

"Call 9-1-1," Em yelled.

Sammy used her cellphone to report the emergency.

The six dogs gathered around Josh, barking at him.

Ava and James pulled into the driveway. They paused for a moment, taking the scene in, before jumping out of the car. James helped Jonathan Ray hold Josh. Ava walked over to Catt and placed a comforting arm around her.

Brock and Grayson walked into the backyard. "What in the world is going on?"

Detective Harrington rushed into the yard and stopped short.

"What are you doing here?" Catt asked the detective.

"I got the video back from the warehouse. Josh murdered John Carpenter."

"Tell us something we don't already know," Catt said.

They all laughed. All except Josh, that is.

Catt walked into the backyard, holding a tray of snacks, beer, and wine. "I think we need this." She tipped the tray toward Sammy who grabbed a glass of wine and sat with the others on the lawn chairs.

"I'll take wine," Em said.

"A cold one for me," Brock said.

"Wine please." Ava smiled.

"Beer," James said.

Detective Harrington grabbed a beer from the tray. "Off duty now." He smiled.

Catt set the tray on a table and poured herself a glass of wine. She sat next to Detective Harrington. "What will happen to Josh?"

"Now that we have his confession, he'll be extradited back to North Carolina to sit in jail until a hearing and sentencing are set." He paused as the dogs played in the yard. "Will you be fostering Jersey?"

"I hope so," Catt said.

"I hope Josh goes to prison for a long time," Ava said.

"Me too." Brock clinked glasses with Ava.

Catt was glad to see Brock and Ava joining together. She glanced down at an incoming message from Norma Jeane. "Good news," she yelled to the group. "Pet Products will be taken over by one of John's relatives, and Anna was fired."

The group raised their glasses.

Catt turned her phone toward Em with the rest of Norma

Jean's message. NEW OWNER RESOLVED PAYMENT DISPUTE WITH BOX DISTRIBUTOR. IT WAS CAUSED BY LARGE PAYMENT TO NORA. Catt titled her glass toward Em and smiled.

Jonathan Ray grabbed a beer and popped the top. "While we're sharing good news, the rare coins Em and I found in OBX turned out to be valuable. Here's to future metal detecting."

"Hear, hear!" the group said in unison.

Catt turned toward the detective. "By the way, I know you said you were here working on business, but why did you stay longer?"

"Two reasons. First, the murderer's trail led me here."

Catt sipped her wine. "And the other reason?"

He winked at Catt. "Let's just say I'm looking at it. Cheers."

The End

COMING SPRING 2021

The 3rd Installment in the Mutt Mysteries Series

TO FETCH A VILLAIN

FOUR FUN "TAILS" OF MISCREANTS AND MURDER

More info at www.MuttMysteries.com

Be sure to LIKE Mutt Mysteries on Facebook
Follow @MuttMysteries1 on Twitter

CPSIA information can be obtained
at www.ICGtesting.com
Printed in the USA
FSHW022214210220
67193FS